TABATHA'S CODE

TABATHA'S CODE

MATTHEW D'ANCONA

ALMA BOOKS

ALMA BOOKS LTD
London House
243–253 Lower Mortlake Road
Richmond
Surrey TW9 2LL
United Kingdom
www.almabooks.com

Tabatha's Code first published in May 2006 by Alma Books Limited
Reprinted June 2006
Copyright © Matthew d'Ancona, 2006

Matthew d'Ancona asserts his moral right to be identified as the author of this
work in accordance with the Copyright, Designs and Patents Act 1988

Although aspects of this book are inspired by real events, each character in it is
fictional, a composite drawn from imagination. No reference to any living or dead
person is intended or should be inferred.

Printed in Jordan by National Press

ISBN-13: 978-1-84688-012-4 (hardback)
ISBN-10: 1-84688-012-2 (hardback)
ISBN-13: 978-1-84688-004-9 (paperback)
ISBN-10: 1-84688-004-1 (paperback)

FOR ZAC

CONTENTS

TABATHA'S CODE

But even at the starting post, all sleek and new,
I saw the wildness in her and I thought
A vision of terror that it must live through
Had shattered her soul.

– W.B. Yeats, A Bronze Head

We had all the momentum; we were riding the crest of a high and beautiful wave…

So now, less than five years later, you can go up on a steep hill in Las Vegas and look West, and with the right kind of eyes you can almost see the high-water mark – that place where the wave finally broke and rolled back.

– Hunter S. Thomson, *Fear and Loathing in Las Vegas*

PROLOGUE

SANTA CRUZ, CA, 1989

She stumbled as she ran up the sand towards him, a spray of damp particles preceding her advance. Behind her, the long mile of water shimmered in the afternoon light, its surface caressed by the pebbles of a light breeze. The rolling dunes of the waves receded towards the horizon, until they looked no bigger than the ragged brushstrokes at the edge of an oil painting.

Even at her clumsiest, as her limbs moved in hapless syncopation to her laughter, he found her movement beguiling. Her tangled tresses – striking on this beach for not being blonde – fell over her face and down to the shoulders of her wetsuit. She had the figure of a woman who might have done everything with poise and polish, conscious of the impact it would have on men. But that was not her way.

He stood up to look at her properly, torn between the desire to watch her a little longer and the urgent need to touch her – to touch her, perhaps, for the last time. As she walked towards him, stretching her arms out in a gesture of childish need and mock exhaustion, he felt tall. She made him feel tall. (What had she said once? "Raise high the roof beam, carpenters." Poems, always poems.) She hopped up and wrapped her long legs around him, her heels digging into his back and grinding sand into his T-shirt. They kissed, and he felt himself stir as she pressed herself against him and ran a teasing finger through his hair. The orange zinc on her nose smeared a little on his cheeks.

"Feeling hot, huh?" she said, smiling broadly.

"What do you think?" he said. "Flesh and blood."

"Fine flesh and blood, too," she said, and stroked his forehead in a way that signalled, to his regret, that this was not foreplay. "A fine figure of a man. You coming out again?"

She smiled at him, conscious that, having got up on his board once, he was content to call it a day. She, meanwhile, had just completed her fifth moderately successful run. "Come on, don't be so English."

"No, you go," he said. "I'll watch you."

"You don't seem to grasp the essential point of surfing, Nicholas. Which is that once you get up, you go out again and keep trying to stay up."

"I do grasp that essential point. And can I just remind you, for the record, who stayed up more often when we last did this stuff? In Big Sur?"

She laughed and knelt down beside him. "That is such a technicality. I was sick as a dog from the party at Daniel's the night before. So I would say – I would *say* – that it was a miracle that I could get to the beach at all, let alone stand up on a surfboard once. Almost as much a miracle that you did the same thing twice. Once hungover beats twice clean. You know it."

She planted her board – no less ancient than their suits – and reached into her bag for a soda. He looked out to where two teenagers were awaiting the next wave. The ocean spoke to them, passing on rumours of the next surge. Sometimes it lied, the anticipated rush of power dispersing into ripples of grey-green disenchantment. But now, suddenly, the coral-eyed spirits beneath, to which the young men were listening so intently, were speaking the truth, and the mellow undulations of the water were transforming themselves into a curved wall of implacable force, the swirling foam metamorphosing into white, jagged teeth at its crest. As the wall rose, the two surfers paddled furiously to synchronize themselves with its approach, as if they could tame it by mimicking it. One, his suit a blaze of orange and yellow flames, rose onto his board and rode the wave dazzlingly to shore. The other failed no less spectacularly, his whole body pitched above the crest in a crazy contortion, and then swallowed in a brutal gulp by the ocean he had dared to challenge.

She touched his cheek. "Hey."

He turned and smiled. "Hey. What do you want to do? Shall we dump the stuff and go get coffee some-where?"

"Sure. I said we'd meet Cody and Tina at that place on Pacific around three. What time is it now?"

He dug out his watch from beneath the T-shirts and an old *Santa Cruz Sentinel*. "Just gone two-thirty."

"Okay. Shit, we could have gone again, you know. We have these boards for another ten minutes."

He smiled, shook his head. "You're incorrigible. Tab the Incorrigible. Christ, that sounds like a sword-and-sorcery movie. Or a new and exciting soft drink. Come on, let's make a move."

Using towels, they changed behind Tab's pick-up

in the parking lot. He admired the slenderness of her upper arm as she slipped on a La Jolla Beach Club top, and the down on her thigh, visible at the hem of her khaki shorts. She did not work out or run, as he did, but she never seemed less than lean and sinewy, as if health were a bequest which was hers as of right. Her face, flushed by the sun, was still calm, even as she swore in companionable counterpoint with him as they hopped into their fresh clothes. The deep brown eyes did not betray the merest inkling of despair. That was part of her gift, wasn't it? Her cheeks knew the colour of anger but not the paleness of defeat. She would move on, and prosper. And what would he do? Well, he would have to see. Now, definitely, he would have to see.

"It's just time." That was what she had said only two nights before, as they lay in their sleeping bags after a day's hike in Big Basin state park. They had trudged ten miles towards the coast, up and down the trails by the twinkling falls, catching the eye of startled mule deer and bobcats. The camp fire was fading into its late-night tranquillity, all the reds and oranges in the world clustering at its heart and blending in chromatic communion. They had cooked vegetarian patties on an open fire and then gorged themselves on toasted marshmallows. The empty beer bottles formed a colonnade by the dwindling flames, but she had bagged the remains of the food and hung it from a branch to keep the bears at bay. He read to her for a while from the Raymond Carver collection she had brought, and then he turned off the flashlight and looked up through the forest ceiling of redwoods at the stars, reaching out to hold her hand. The Plough, Cassiopeia, Orion: he was never able to detect these astral patterns. But their presence pleased him: he liked the fact that they were *detectable*. There was a distant screech – a raccoon, or a coyote. There would be a fine mist in the morning, he thought. The pulse of their love-making still surged like a pleasant echo through his body, the remembered rhythm of deep longing granted true completion. He waited for sleep to come and claim him, wrapping him in its narcotic emulsion.

"I think you should go back soon."

The words seemed so alien, so hostile to the moment, that at first he did not acknowledge them. Better to resume his soothing audit of the great green canopy and its contents. The Plough, the coyote, the thousand-year-old redwood… his mind clung to this natural anchor. He looked at the fire, which seemed to flicker in confused sympathy.

"Nick, are you awake?"

He wondered whether to answer her. Perhaps she had not really said what he thought she had said. Perhaps it was only the wind whisking an ancient curse into their little grove, but soon to be on its way, thwarted and in search of riper prey. Perhaps she had said it, but would regret it immediately and never say such a thing again, if only he pretended to be asleep now. Yes, that was it. Keep your eyes shut and listen only for the soft footfall of the hungry bear. Listen out for the cascading silver water of Berry Creek Falls whose crystal dance they had peered into in the full heat of the day, sharing oranges and bread and stories of friends.

"Nick. I know you're not sleeping. Cut it out."

He bristled. "No, I'm not. What are you talking

about, anyway? You're crazy. Go to sleep. You hiked ten miles this afternoon. Get some rest."

"I'm not tired. I meant what I just said."

He turned to face her. It was too dark to scrutinize her features, to see whether she meant to disfigure his universe as she now threatened.

"Go back? Where do you want me to go back *to*?"

"I want you to go back home, and get on with what you have to get on with."

"What's brought this on? Half an hour ago you were talking about why the best stand-up comedians are in Chico, and Wal-Mart panties, and why you hate your uncle because he's a Republican, and now suddenly you're telling me to get on a plane and get out of your life." He heard himself gabbling. "I think you had one brew too many, Tab. It's the beer talking. Go to sleep. If you feel the same way in the morning, I'll hike to the airport on my own."

Catastrophe came in the form of her breath on the back of his neck. She had shuffled over in her sleeping bag and was now trying nervously to embrace him and bury her head in his shoulder. This, he knew, was the tolling of the bell, whatever he or she now said, whatever reprieve might be granted, whatever desperate measures he took to make her change her mind. She would not change her mind. It was in surrender to her own inexplicable decision that she had come over to him now, to seek his bodily warmth and to bring him the terrible news of that decision with the treacherous softness of her skin. He listened for a trace of doubt or the suggestion of tears. But the small voice was clear enough. "It's just time," she said.

Time. Had they had enough time? A year. No, a little more. A year and a few months since they had met in a gallery in Palo Alto. He was travelling across America and curious to see how Stanford compared to Cambridge. She was working part-time to pay her way through college. He wandered into the gallery – the "War Hole" – to cool off, but also because he liked a vivid black-and-white photograph of a rust-belt main street in its window. It was cool and peaceful within, the minimalist furniture a declaration of hip affluence, the smell of freshly brewed espresso competing with the aroma of lilies.

She looked out of place sitting at reception, fidgeting and screwing up her nose in frustration at something she was looking at. She lacked the angular rigour of her surroundings. With her hair tied back carelessly, surf shorts and an old tie-dye T-shirt with a few badges, she seemed in mutiny against its Spartan code. And yet she was, he thought, with complete conviction, astonishingly beautiful: Mediterranean perhaps, Greek or Sicilian? He saw intimations of perfection in her, but no self-consciousness. The restlessness, the bobbing head and the chewing of an apple: that was charming, too. It was strange to him to feel so compelled by another human being so instantly. He was used to experiencing emotions at a slight distance, qualifying them as soon as they arose. He wondered if he should leave.

Instead, he asked her what she was reading. Without speaking, she looked up at him, holding up the cover of a volume of Yeats, and a half-finished crossword. He nodded, desperate to ignite a conversation, but stultified: finally, if only to puncture the silence, he asked how the crossword was going. She shrugged and said: "Eight across: 'Gegs'. Two words, nine and four." He looked at her blankly. His confusion inspired her: "Yeah, yeah, yeah! Scrambled eggs. 'Gegs' is 'eggs' scrambled. Thank you. That was bugging me." She threw her apple core into a basket beneath the desk. "So who are you? No way can you afford anything in this place, I'll tell you that for free."

"And you can?" He arched an eyebrow and returned her smile. She blushed.

"No, but I work here."

He looked around the deserted gallery. "When?" She laughed again.

They connected, somehow. She smiled more than he dared hope – ensnared, he was sure, by his carefully dropped mention of Cambridge, his laconic charm. Much later, he would learn that she had been smiling at his awkwardness, and the endearing transparency of his infatuation. She introduced herself as Tab – short for Tabatha, a name she hated – and asked why somebody who looked like a tramp was wandering round fancy galleries. When he could think of nothing to say, she had laughed again. He had never met anyone so blunt, or so dazzling.

They talked for two hours – nobody else ventured into the War Hole – and then they went for drinks and food. It seemed that they were resuming a conversation begun that morning, interrupted only by the working day, as though they had been a couple for a long time. This both disturbed and enraptured him. He did not understand how it was possible to be consumed by desire, and yet immediately comfortable with someone.

When she invited him back to her apartment, they held hands on the sidewalk, laughing so vigorously at some verbal game they were playing that the step they had taken towards entanglement did not feel like a step at all. They watched television and she laid her head on his lap. He stroked her hair, allowed his fingers to brush against her questing lips. They went to bed and she told him without preamble, and with an insistence that aroused him even further, that she "needed to come, now". Afterwards, she lay in his arms and wept because, she said, it was not right that such sudden happiness should be the consequence only of chance, only of one person's listless decision to wander into a gallery. It was too arbitrary, too frightening. He comforted her and almost spoke of love. She said his voice reminded her of the BBC World Service, which enabled both of them to laugh and relax.

He stayed at her apartment for three weeks. After that, he went to San Francisco, pretending that he still intended to keep to his Californian itinerary. She returned to her poetry and textual criticism. But he could not stay away long, and she could not concentrate on anything in his absence. When he called her, she cried uncontrollably down the phone, only able to whisper: "Come back, I need you."

He returned to Palo Alto after a week, and they spent the rest of the summer together. They talked all the time. She told him that she was trying to escape the grip of her parents, long-divorced. She reserved particular anger for her father, a corporate lawyer, who had moved to Orange County in search of young blonde girls, and personified – or so she said – everything that she despised. Nick went with her to the meetings of the radical groups to which she was committed, and listened to her spray venom at "the System" and the "American Nightmare". He watched her friends, high and giggling, burn their country's flag in a backyard (where nobody could see) and chant furious slogans about the President. From time to time, she would exclude him from these political activities, but not often. She paraded him with pardonable vanity as a trophy, good-looking, dry and exotically English. Her friends liked his manner, his humour and the fierce devotion he inspired in her. At first he felt self-consciously white-limbed: but that passed as his tan began, at last, to look native. He earned a little spending money by washing up and doing bar work at joints where the manager didn't ask too many questions about green cards. Summer turned into Fall. The leaves yellowed and Palo Alto cooled. As November approached he felt he should go home to see his mother, which he did. For six dead weeks, they were apart.

To make him laugh, she sent him messages every day, the little literary codes that she loved. Even the simple ones baffled him at first. "Bard, 57, 1–2" was meaningless, until she explained to him, giggling, that it was an *obvious* reference to the first two lines of Shakespeare's 57th sonnet: "Being your slave, what should I do but tend / Upon the hours and times of your desire?" As the messages continued, he got better at untangling her encryptions. "Mrs Hughes, in the air, tree, 28" baffled him before he grasped that it was a punning reference to Sylvia Plath's 'Ariel', and the 28th line of the poem 'Elm': "I am inhabited by a cry". Yes, he was beginning to realize, this was how Tab communicated when it suited her. Not in his own English hybrid of repression and garrulousness, but in riddles, clues and cryptograms. She was horribly lonely without him, but sometimes she needed Sylvia Plath to tell him so.

On her Christmas present to him was a tag which read simply: "When you are old and grey... Love Tx". It was, as he knew it would be, the collected poems of Yeats, the poet she loved above any other, whose visions and passions she admired to the point of veneration. She could quote long passages by her lyrical master: not only those of careworn cliché, but also the lesser works, the twilit Celtic mysteries, the Rosicrucian spells. She spoke to him of Maud Gonne, the poet's Helen, and the Golden Dawn, his brotherhood, and Cuchulain, and the mythology of an Irish mind that was the peat from which her ideas and her games sprang like imps. Above all, she loved his exhortation to a friend whose work had come to nothing: "Be secret and exult". Nick kept the book with him, like a handbook to the inner life of his lover.

And then, apologizing to his mother for his feck-lessness, but hoping she would understand the heart's impatient tug (she did), he had flown back to California. This time, he knew the immigration services would be suspicious and so, with Tab's connivance and with the help of a university clerk who had a crush on her, he had obtained the necessary falsified paperwork to prove that he was taking courses at Stanford.

He was twenty-one when they met, she two years older. He had performed solidly at Cambridge, she with a precocious brilliance at Stanford. As they walked through the North Portal of its Old Quad, past the palm trees, through the sharp air and into the wintry shade, the antique revels of his old college seemed a very distant memory: the punts and the balls and the Backs and the white tie. Every week an essay, every week the trudge to the faculty library for books, every week a football match, every week a party in someone's rooms until the necessary oblivion was achieved. He had succumbed to the rhythms of the ancient institution without thought or complaint. The three years had passed by him, and passed through him. He did not leave Cambridge changed, nor had he changed anything there. But, in the California dusk, hand-in-hand with Tab, he had walked with fresh feet. He loved her obsessions, her intensity. Her politics were not his own – did he really have any? – but they made him feel animated by proxy. Her love of literature outstripped his respectable bookishness, but it challenged him to think as he had not thought before. Her love was as miraculous as it was inexplicable to him. He knew vaguely that he was attractive to women – the lazy attachments of his university days were proof enough of that – but he was astonished by the strength of her emotion. They argued often, but always made up. He quickly found it impossible to imagine a life without her, though dread of the unthinkable grew within him as the months passed and she bored her way further and further into the marrow of his life.

These memories coursed through him as he contemplated what she had said to him as they lay in the forest. "When did you decide this?" he asked. He sat up and pushed a stick into the belly of the fire. Sparks and hissing wisps of smoke erupted into the air, engulfing the three criss-cross sticks on which they had nestled the cooking canteen.

She was still lying down. She sighed. "Just now. A while ago. I don't know."

"I had no idea."

"I know. I didn't want this to be a long, drawn-out thing."

"How do you expect me to react, Tab?"

"I don't expect anything. I'm not in charge of you. I'm not in charge of anyone. It's just my opinion."

"Do you still love me?" He felt wetness in his eyes, but fought back the impulse. The nasty sedative of wounded pride kept him still.

She sat up and put her arms round his neck. "Of course. Of *course*. More than I – you *know*."

"Then why? Don't you want to stay together?"

Her pause was inscrutable. "It's not that simple. I wish it were. I – we've been together a while. But what are you going to do here, Nicky? Wash dishes for ever?"

"You're dumping me because I'm a dishwasher? Would it help if I was writing a thesis on the later plays of Tennessee Williams?"

She laughed. "That, I'd like to read. Look, sooner or later you're going to go back. Right?"

He shrugged. "I'm in no hurry."

"And become a lawyer?"

"Yeah, I guess. I don't know. I don't give a damn about becoming a lawyer. There are millions of lawyers already. Is that what you want? Me to train up for the rat race and help all the big companies you say you hate so much to get off when they've done something wrong?"

She ignored the provocation, mussing his hair. "And I'm going to stay at school for ever and do postdoc and stuff. Right?"

He considered her train of thought. Her control and her appeal to logic irritated him intensely. "Right. So you're planning on doing all this as a single woman?"

She slumped back, revealing at last her exhaustion and what it had cost her to tell him. "I'm not planning anything. I just – I know it's going to end sooner or later, and I don't want you to waste your life."

"But I'm not." A whistling – the nocturnal cry of a bird or tiny mammal – pierced the hermetic misery of the clearing.

"Maybe not yet. But, you know Nicky, one day you'll wake up and you'll realize that the person you once were has gone. Because all you'll be is my boyfriend, or something. Don't you ever feel that? I do. I've never let anyone get closer than you. And it's great. It's the best. But you pay a price."

He turned on her in scorn. "What *price*?"

"I'm not sure. But you do. When people get together, it's not... I mean, yes, it augments them. But it reduces them, too. It reduces them."

"I reduce you?"

"I'm not saying you. I'm saying, people."

"How do I reduce you?"

"I'm not saying you do. But you'll be reduced if you stay here for ever. You won't be the man I met for long. If you go now, it'll be perfect. Perfect. We won't have that... I don't know, all that *decline*, all that decay masquerading as comfort, Nicky. It'll still be special and precious. We won't be together just because we're frightened of the alternative. You'll do your thing, and I'll do mine."

He felt sadness begin to saturate him, and peevishness seep from his pores. "So you don't love me any more. It's obvious. I don't know why you don't have the guts to admit it. I hate that."

"Just try and think about what I'm saying. Just think about it. I knew how upset you'd be. But just -"

"Back off, Tab." Unbidden, to his fury, the tears were flowing down his cheeks. He turned as far from her as he could, trying to stifle his misery. He wondered if she could see the rocking of his shoulders, up and down, as he battled against the stormy current of shock.

After a while, he could hear from her breathing that she was sleeping. He stayed up until the first woeful fingers of dawn probed their way through the branches, when the little camp – bottles, ashes and bedding – was revealed in all its bedraggled wretchedness.

That image, more even than her fateful phrase, was still clear in his mind the next day as they wandered down Pacific Avenue towards the coffee shop. He remembered one of her favourite poems: 'O Do Not Love Too Long'. Yes, maybe it was as simple as that. But two nights had passed and neither had broached the subject with the other. She was breezy – liberated, no doubt, by the act of unburdening. He felt the weight of the news she had given him, but would not say as much. Their banter was the same, but had become a tool of evasion rather than a mark of their intimacy.

They passed through the shade of the parasols on the sidewalk, past the arcades and surf shops and cafés. He overheard a couple arguing over milkshakes, their

Labrador cooling off under the table. The woman shook her red hair angrily and definitively, the bob oscillating across her eyes. "No, Steve, no. No *way*. I totally will *not* have her for Thanksgiving." The man, his hair in blond dreadlocks and a ponytail, quivered with disgust. "I cannot believe you. I cannot believe you would do that to her."

"Look," said Tab. "Isn't that great?" In the window of the shop was a hand-written sign: "WE BUY AND SELL TRANSCENDENTAL BOOKS." Nick smiled. Tab the Incorrigible.

"Tabster!" The voice came from across the asphalt. It was Cody, yelling theatrically through cupped hands even though they were only a few yards apart. Tab's housemate from Stanford was, Nick had always thought, ludicrously tall, and his juvenile clothing only drew attention to this physical eccentricity. His "Suicidal Tendencies" T-shirt was a vast creation of tasteless merchandising, stretching halfway down his thighs, towards the fringes of ancient denim shorts and battered baseball boots. His hair was recently buzzed. He looked and sounded like a fourteen-year-old who had experienced a supernatural growth spurt in recent months.

Tab handed Nick her beach bag without comment and skipped across the road.

"Machin," she said, reaching up on tiptoe to kiss his cheek. "How was your day?"

"Trippy. My dad came by for brunch, which was sort of weird. He doesn't normally do that. You know, that's not the kind of thing they do in Fresno, I thought. I mean, *brunch*? But he said he wanted to see me before next semester, so – whatever. I mean, he paid. Me and Tina have been skating since he left. Did you guys eat?"

"Uh-huh. On the beach. We went surfing again."

"Cool. Tina's inside getting coffees. Go tell her what you want."

Nick hovered closer to Cody. He liked him, but the knowledge of his own imminent expulsion made it harder for him to be civil to her friends. He mumbled something that even he could not quite understand, the normal greetings snagging in his mouth like stale bread.

"Hey, Nick," said Cody, clasping his hand with a surfer's greeting. "What's up?"

"Not much. Been at the beach and then we thought the Boardwalk but it's full of kids, you know, so…"

"Yeah, right. Have you seen this?" Cody kicked his board up into his hand. "Look, man. This is my all-time favourite board. *All-time*. It's old, but it still has tits. See – Alva board, Trucker tracks, green Kryptonic wheels. The best."

Nick looked dutifully at the battered old skateboard and wondered how Cody combined his adolescent enthusiasms with a philosophy major at one of the world's great universities. Perhaps, in fact, there was no contradiction. Perhaps the philosophers of the future would wear transfer T-shirts and skateboard to their lectures, cogitating deeply to the whir of urethane on asphalt. Perhaps if Aristotle or Spinoza were alive now they would listen to Suicidal Tendencies: Socrates certainly would.

Tina and Tab emerged from the shop with coffees and sat down.

"Hey, Nicky," said Tina. "How are you?" She was a year younger than Cody, a High School sweetheart now majoring in computer science at UCSC, in whose honour she wore a banana-slug T-shirt. She was blonde, benign and rangily limbed – not unlike Julia, the girl Cody was seeing at Stanford but about whom Tina knew nothing. Julia had rung Cody's house while they were staying, but Nick had answered the phone and played dumb. He felt sorry for Tina, with her perfect tan and lazy eye. He sat down beside her in the shade.

"Your dad came by?" said Tab, biting into an apple.

"Yeah," said Cody. "It freaked me. Maybe he had been drinking. I don't know. He was all guilty, or something. It's the first time in, like, six months, that he's made an effort."

"Six months *minimum*," said Tina in unquestioning solidarity.

"Did he care about the mess in the house?" said Tab. The night before they had drunk tequila slammers and watched movies till they passed out on beanbags.

"Hell, no." Cody shook his head. "Like he gives a fuck. He lives like a pig himself. It's if my mom comes by that I worry. She's with the new guy most of the time now, but she's still all: 'This is my house and you'll show it some respect, young man.' You'd know if she'd been by, because our knees would be red from scrubbing the damn floor."

"My knees are red," said Tina.

"Only cos you don't know how to ride a classic board. After all this time, I still haven't taught you the basics. Not even a three-sixty."

A yellow bus stopped at the end of the avenue to let someone off. It was full of kids on a day trip from camp, fresh from the Boardwalk, sunburnt in their green and blue T-shirts and wild on candy. Nick saw two teenage girls on the back row, their braces visible even from a distance, engaged in scandalized conversation. He wondered what they were talking about and whether it would affect anyone or anything very much. He wondered what he should be talking about with Tab's friends. A kid with a pink nose and ginger hair, pudgy and burnt, caught his eye and stared at him. Nick stared back. The kid raised his fist, blinked and unfurled a finger with exquisite nonchalance. The bus moved on.

"I tell you, I can't wait to get back to school," said Tab.

"Oh, man. You're nuts," said Cody. "I have, like, four term papers to worry about. I do not want to be thinking about that. I do not want to know about Heidegger. I doubt that Mrs Heidegger wanted to know about Heidegger."

"Mrs Heidegger probably wrote Heidegger's books, asshole."

"Yeah, right," said Tina.

"And I care?" he said. "I don't care who wrote them, I just don't want to have to read them. I want to hang out here and do nothing. That seems to me to be the final purpose of life – which, to be frank with you guys, we obscure with a lot of bullshit about diplomas and degrees and jobs." Cody played with a packet of smokes, and warmed to his theme. "You see, Nicky here is my hero. He's just hanging around with you, Tab. He's funny as hell and totally mellow."

"Oh, I wouldn't want to be your hero," said Nick, sipping on his mocha. "I might let you down."

"No way. You wouldn't. I can tell that about you. Tab is all *driven* by stuff – you know, she's *committed* and shit – but you're the cool one."

"Yeah, meaning what?" asked Tab.

Cody shifted in his seat. "Meaning that Nicky has cool karma, and yours is for shit. This is probably his final turn round the planet and he's going to make the most of it, look for love, stuff like that. Whereas you, Bradley, are going to make a name for yourself at school, and go on lots of demos and moan about Bush for four years. Wrong?"

"Moaning about Bush *is* a sign of good karma, Mr Political. He's worse than Reagan. It's hard to imagine anyone being worse than Bush." She considered this proposition. "The only thing, maybe, would be if he made the presidency *hereditary*. You know, if he just handed it over to one of his sons and said: 'There you go, Junior. I'm out of here. Invade as many countries as you like. And don't forget to lock up at night.' I swear."

They all laughed at the idea. "You are so majorly paranoid, Bradley," Cody said. "I am scared to live with you, you know? You are one big grassy knoll, man. You're the only person I know who could dream up the idea of Bush handing it all over to his *son*. You still read way too many newspapers, man, and don't eat enough ice cream, or waste enough time in record shops. Your head is full of slogans. I mean you've seen the goddam house in Stanford, Nicky."

"I haven't," said Tina.

"No, well, it's nothing," said Cody, anxious not to divert the conversation onto dangerous terrain. "But you know, Nick – I mean, tell Tina – all the posters and the fridge magnets. Central America, the frigging rain forest, even her 'Fuck Dukakis' sticker. I mean, *Fuck Dukakis*? As if that hadn't already been done pretty successfully by the other side. But no: Tab's not letting old Dukakis off the hook even now he's in the political grave. He's still a fascist. One of my professors came by one time and said: 'My, my, Cody, I never knew you were such a *radical*.' And I just didn't have the heart to say it was my psycho housemate, Ms Bradley. Now Dr Nathan thinks that the reason I skip class is because I'm out saving peasants. Whereas the truth is that I'm probably at home sleeping off the effects of an excellent bong." He smiled at the thought.

Nick could see his cue. "Yeah. Well, everyone has a hobby, I guess, Codes. You skate, she saves."

"It isn't a fucking hobby," hissed Tab. Tina flinched as a splinter of seriousness forced its way into the soft pulp of their conversation.

"It's a fucking religion is what it is, man," said Cody. "Meetings in the house, people with beards coming by to drop off stuff, guys called *Leonard*. I mean, please tell her, man. I just want to pretend to study, go to lots of parties and get off my face next semester. I don't want to go to the john to hurl, and find it full of leaflets again. It's distracting."

"I don't know, Cody," said Nick. "I guess I think all that stuff is coming to a bit of an end anyway."

Tab skewered him with her eyes. "What do you mean?"

He straightened up and felt himself draw a deep breath. "I mean, it's nostalgia for the Sixties rather than anything very new. To be honest, I think if all that *stuff* was going to change the world it would have by now, and it hasn't really. And the world seems to be changing in a pretty different kind of way, anyway."

"I don't see any change at all," she said. "Same shit, different people."

He was, he realized, punishing her at last for her decision to end it. No screaming or shouting, but something much more effective, much more visceral: an assault on her beliefs. He could call her cold-hearted or plead with her to change her mind. But this was a more effective punishment. "Maybe," he said. "But look at Gorbachev, look how people are saying all sorts of new things in Germany. Even Bush is talking a different language. Maybe he's a bastard, but he's a politician, he sees the way the wind is blowing. I just think that whole Cold War thing we grew up with is ending, and when that's over, the game will be pretty much over. I mean, one side will win and the other side will lose, and that'll be that." He drained his cup. "I'm not saying that's a good thing. I'm just saying that's the way the world is moving, Tab."

She was bleached white with anger. With a few sentences, he had insulted her to the core and, though she knew precisely what he was doing, she could not stop herself rising to the bait. When she replied it was in a ferocious whisper. "That is such *horseshit*. Total, utter, ignorant horseshit. Do you think that if America wins and Russia loses, that everything is going to be over? Is that what you think? You are *so* wrong." She shook her head with the passion of absolute certainty. "So wrong. It's not about East versus West. It's about justice and decency and stopping people with big bucks from treating everyone else like shit."

Now he was angry, too. Angry with her presumption of superiority, the speed with which she became furious when challenged. "Yeah, yeah. I just think everything might change, and you might find there's not much of an audience for your – your radical chic any more. I'm not proud of it, but most people are more like me. In the end, they want a quiet life. They don't see any point to all this… all this *struggle*. Christ, it's real sophomore stuff." He caught her eye, reaching his mean-spirited peroration. "Face it, Tab: people don't want your revolution."

"That's because your stupid fucking English education didn't take you beyond a bunch of ancient customs and…"

"Don't lecture me. You may be right, but you don't have a monopoly on being right."

"Woah. Hey, guys, be nice," said Cody, alarmed by this inexplicably vicious confrontation and in no mood to explore its origins. "Wow, I was only fooling around about the radical shit. Listen, you can have a Che poster on every wall. And we'll hang an effigy of Dan Quayle in the kitchen every morning. I don't care. As long as you're happy, sister." He put an arm round his housemate. Nick saw she was trembling beneath Cody's embrace. Tina, quite unequal to the moment, had somehow minimized the space she filled, like a hedgehog hoping to be left alone.

At once, Nick felt the icy pleasure of vengeance give way to guilt. He did not know how much he believed of what he had said. But he had known that it would hurt her. Part of him wanted to hurt her for the terrible injury she was about to inflict on him, and for the pain of separation he was already suffering. He wanted to leave her with a scar, to reach across the table with an indignant claw and etch his emotions into her cheek, so she would walk with it for the rest of her days as a mark of her shame. But a larger part wanted to retract it all, to tell her that he wished he had her strength of conviction, which was one of countless reasons why he adored her, and that his calm, collected viciousness was the product of despair rather than hatred. He wanted, above all, as always, to touch her.

He had hurt her once before, though not intentionally. During Spring break they had visited the Grand Canyon, and hiked up and down the trails all day, laughing and talking even as they gasped for air and poured water over each other's heads to stop the ringing in their ears of extreme heat. At the end of their excursion, she had begged him to drive the pick-up, an uncommon admission of defeat. He took the wheel and headed back to Flagstaff, where they were staying with one of her college friends. She fell asleep almost immediately, her head resting on the seat belt as Patsy Kline's voice rose soothingly in the car. He stopped for gas and bottles of water, and Tab did not stir.

He drove off down a slipway and headed towards Highway 64, where they would join the long snake of jeeps and station wagons speeding home. Accelerating up a hill on a deserted stretch of road, he heard a sickening thump, the sound of something being wrenched from its place in the world and slammed on the brakes.

His heart thumped chaotically within, as he grasped with as much rationality as he could muster that they had not crashed but that something unpleasant had certainly happened. He peered over the dashboard, and could see nothing. Tab woke up, and he told her to stay where she was. He pulled a flashlight from his bag on the back seat and got out.

It took him longer than he expected to find it. In the long, dry grass by the roadside, its chest heaving, its side caved in by the impact, was a dog. It was an ill-favoured mongrel with the stature of an Alsatian and the head of a hound. From its jaws – damaged too, Nick saw – came a low, stuttering growl, no more than the last fizz of life. Its brown fur was glossy with blood, and he saw that in the short time since the collision it had soiled itself. Occasionally, it panted desperately. Its eyes were glassy and full of the rage of the moribund. But the dog was still alive. He went back to the car. She was awake.

"What is it?" she said. The gridded imprint of the seat belt was visible on her cheek.

"A dog. We hit a dog. It's complete carnage. I don't think there's much we can do."

"Oh my God. That can't be. Is there some place we can take it or something?" He could see tears gleaming already in her eyes.

"I don't think it would survive being put in the car. It's pretty messed up. I don't know what it was doing on the road. I didn't even see it."

"Is there a wrench in the car?" she asked.

"What?"

"Is there a wrench? Something heavy."

"I don't – Why?"

"Just look, will you? Christ."

He opened the back of the car and found a basic tool kit. There was indeed a standard wrench, blunt-edged and heavy in the hand. He walked back to the passenger door.

"I'm going to put it out of its misery," she told him, grabbing the wrench. "We can't leave it to suffer by the road. We just can't."

He considered her declaration, and realized that she was right. But it was not fair that she should have to do the deed. He, after all, had been at the wheel when the car had hit the dog. He should finish the job. They walked with the light-headedness of a funerary procession to the spot where the creature lay. Its condition was unchanged, although the stain of blood on the soil was spreading like a rotting rose. Its breathing remained frantic and defiant.

"Shit," she said. "Shit. Shit. Shit."

"I'll do it."

She looked at him, appalled, somehow, by his offer. "No way. I said I'd do it and I'll do it." She saw his expression and became sharp. "Just get out of my way. I'm going to need a big swing."

Even as she raised her arm above her head, he knew the blow would not be sufficient to the task. It was not that she lacked the strength. But there was a failure of will evident in her clenched muscles, her shaking legs, her narrowed eyes. She breathed deeply and yelled as the wrench sliced through the air. It caught the dog on the side of the head and its body went into a pathetic spasm, jowls twitching and legs dancing crazily in response to this further, unbelievable affront.

Tab stepped back, her knuckles white on the wrench. "Oh God," she said. "Oh God."

"Shit, Tab," he said. "For God's sake, quickly. Just do it again!"

She gasped, her chest heaving. "What? What?"

His anger at her indecision mounted. He felt sick, but his nausea was pierced by a clear recognition that she was not up to the job, and that he would have to intervene

"Here, give it to me. Give me the wrench." The dog whimpered.

She backed away, clutching the weapon clumsily to her bosom, frozen by dreamy indecision. "What? No. I'll do it. I said I'd do it and I'll do it. Just let me – just let me. I need to think, how I can…"

The crest of the hill was suddenly bathed in light as a vehicle – a truck, he thought – approached them. Its horn blasted in warning. He could see more clearly now the paralysis in her features. Without further thought, he reached out to snatch the wrench. She retreated, turning from him. He grabbed her shoulder and pulled her back round roughly, grasping it with his free hand. She resisted angrily, and they tussled absurdly, floodlit by the passing eighteen-wheeler, their cursing drowned out by the roar of its engine. The smell of exhaust fumes was heady and overpowering, compounding the strangeness of their conflict. She was doubled over as a last resort, but he was too strong. He prised the wrench from her, looked at her in fury and then, before she could obstruct him, brought it crashing down on the dog's head. And then again. And then again.

He watched, aghast, as the beast shuddered quickly towards extinction. It was all over in a matter of seconds, but he found himself praying silently for its release. At last, its desecrated body was still, and he closed his eyes in a reflex of primordial relief, his heart still pounding as the moment of crisis passed. After a while, he turned to look for Tab. She was not there.

Nick wiped the wrench on a patch of grass, cleaning it as best he could. Slowly, he walked back to the car and saw she was already in her seat. He got in and looked over to see that she was slumped against the door.

"Tab," he said. "Tab. It's okay. It's all done." He reached out to stroke her arm. She recoiled from his touch. He withdrew. "I'm sorry about that. But we couldn't let it suffer any more. You were right. It's over now."

She would not speak to him. Not for two days. And when she did again, it was on the strict, if unspoken understanding that the incident was not to be discussed, ever. She never said as much. But when she finally asked him on their last day in Flagstaff if he wanted her to go out and get breakfast, he could tell that the roadside nightmare was something she would never talk to him about. The fiction that he had acted brutishly and that she had finally forgiven him hung in the air, and he was content for it to do so. But he knew that her long silence had expressed shame more than anger. In the cold night air, he had discovered the limits of her will, like the border of a country, and that had hurt her. She had revealed a part of herself that she could not bear to be exposed, least of all to her lover. She had known what had to be done, but had not been able to act upon her own convictions. He saw that the episode would have to be erased from their stock of shared memories if they were to stay together. This was non-negotiable. And so he had never again referred to the dog, the interrupted drive back to Flagstaff, or even their day at the Canyon.

Cody's house – or rather, his mother's – was ten minutes' drive from Pacific. It was set behind a whitewashed fence on which twinkled unseasonal decorative lights. Cody explained with a shrug of disgust that his mother believed that the "neighbourhood always needed brightening up" and that she had once left an inflatable Santa Claus by the porch of their little bungalow until the beginning of February. But such absurdities were a small price to pay for a home which neither of his parents visited very often and which he had transformed into a student house away from campus. His own room, which looked out onto a little patio with a hot tub, remained a shrine to his adolescence, the posters unchanged, his bed defiantly unmade as if a teenager had crawled reluctantly from it at noon that very day. Records, tapes and skateboard gear were strewn over the floor. But he and Tina were using his mother's room, with its beige walls, beige linen and antique digital alarm clock. Only the pack of loose tobacco on the bedside table and the lingering smell of early-morning weed hinted at youthful pleasures. A little black marble crucifix above the dresser admonished them for their sins. Just below the cross was a framed citation to "Nancy Ellen Jacqueline Machin" for outstanding service to the Santa Cruz Christian Family Charity Project, and a photograph of Cody, pimpled, sweating and embarrassed on the day of his High School graduation.

Tab and Nick shared the spare room at the front of the house beneath the modest portico. Though installed for less than two days, they had managed to conceal its drab cleanliness – beige again – beneath a layer of laundry, discarded paperbacks and other refuse from their bags. They lay in silence for an hour, pretending to rest before dinner, unable to cross the gulf which had opened between them. He looked across to the full-length mirror and thought how ludicrous they looked, the soles of two pairs of shoes side by side in frozen disregard for each other. He did not know how to reach out to her, was not even sure that he was ready to do so. Her face communicated only stubborn indifference to him as she leafed through a book, frowning at passages he was sure she could not be reading properly. She sniffed from time to time, as if he was not there. The halo of her black hair on the pillow filled him with a sense of imminent loss.

Cody cooked a big vegetable stew and opened a bottle of his mother's wine. Through the kitchen window, Nick saw Tina sitting on the lawn in the lotus position, apparently meditating. She was, at any rate, oblivious to the cars which cruised past the fence, families on wheels heading back to TV dinners and arguments. The Californian dusk settled on the little village of one-storey homes in the cul-de-sac, the perfect blue of the ocean sky dappled with the honey-pale strands of the setting sun. A gull swooped close to the street lamp outside the house and then ascended once more to the heavens. A pygmy owl perching in the cedar at the end of the front garden looked up, outraged by the intrusion. Its eyes irradiated the eerie redness of the hour.

"So what are your plans, Nicky?" said Cody, stirring his creation on the hob. He had changed into Stanford sweats and was smoking a Marlboro. "I mean, are you and Tab going to hang with us till school, or do you have *moves* planned?" He said the word "moves" with an emphasis of admiring anticipation, as if he wanted Nick to amaze him with the heady daring of his next projected adventure.

"Well," he said, taking a sip of the wine. "Well, I don't really know. I guess I'll have to head back soon. I'm supposed to go to law school, you know, sooner or later."

"No way." Cody shook his head. "That sucks. You're really going back to England? Man, she'll miss you." He stubbed out his cigarette in one of the breakfast bowls. "She'll really fucking miss you. Her handsome, suave Brit. She loved to show you off, you know. Hell, *I'll* miss you and I'm not even sleeping with you."

Nick wondered if Tab had confided in her housemate that she had her own moves planned and that they did not include him. The two of them had, he knew, moments of deep conspiracy in which they would behave like wicked siblings rather than friends of convenience. It was hard to tell from Cody's manner whether he was truly shocked or putting on a show of surprise to protect Tab.

"Well, I guess she'll be going to school soon, and then, you know, be busy – and so maybe it's time for me to head back. I haven't really decided."

Cody considered this. "I'm not sure you can just up and leave, you know? I think this place has kind of got to you. Like the song, man: 'You can check out any time you like, but you can never leave'."

Nick smiled. "Yeah. It's true." He began to sing, "Such a lovely place…" Cody joined in.

He heard her calling to him from their room and chose to ignore her at first. After the fidgety tension of their afternoon, he was finding Cody's drawling presence pleasantly anaesthetizing. He wanted to stay in the kitchen and avoid any demands on his emotions for a while.

"Nick! Get in here, why don't you?"

Cody snorted. "Sounds like you're not off the leash just yet. Hey, though, we're eating in half an hour. So all guests are respectfully requested to curtail their domestic arguments to the bare minimum." He dipped a wooden spoon into the bubbling stew, tasted it and registered disapproval. "Not right yet. Do you think this needs more oregano? Or maybe paprika?"

Nick grinned and wandered off down the corridor.

He pushed open the door expecting her to be sitting up and braced for sullen confrontation. But she was under the sheets, her clothes already flung over his side of the bed.

"Get in with me. Quickly," she said.

He hesitated for a second, and then realized that her instincts were correct: this was the only way to restore some semblance of normality to their remaining time together. He pulled off his T-shirt and shorts and kicked off his shoes, smiling at his undimmed susceptibility to her. He was weary, too, of fighting his emotions. He got into bed and kissed her deeply as her hands moved to cup his face. She stroked him with an urgency he found hard to reconcile with her icy determination that it should be over. He reached below and stroked her back, caressing her until her bottom was in his hands. Her need reminded him of their first night together. "Oh, yes," she whispered. "That's *better*." He pushed inside her and watched as she rocked back on her head. He closed his eyes, as the irrepressible ecstasy, his unfathomable feeling for this woman, and this woman alone, consumed him once again.

After dinner, the four of them took their drinks out to the hot tub and gazed up at the night sky. Tina lit a joint and talked effusively about astrology and its impact upon her life. She was, she confided, a classic Virgo, but she was unusually scared of Jupiter for reasons which remained obscure. Nick watched Cody's eyes rolling and realized, with absolute clarity, that he, too, could not wait to get back to school and the more sophisticated charms of Julia. He wondered what would become of Tina when Cody graduated and left home for good. He would put down his board once and for all, probably, and head for a big city and a big salary: business school, maybe. She would stay in Santa Cruz, he guessed, and wait tables until she got a job at a tourist agency or a museum. As the tub hissed and frothed, Nick imagined the cost to her of the coming heartbreak: years of low self-esteem and lowered standards, the aching sense of opportunities squandered as she drove to work every morning and dated men she did not like. He imagined, too, how quickly Cody would forget her and how appalled he would be if, a decade hence, he and Tina should run into one another at some reunion, or at the home of a mutual friend.

At midnight, Cody and Tina went inside to watch TV. Nick stood up and reached for a towel, but he felt

Tab's hand grab his and squeeze it with an intimacy that was both irresistible and agonizing.

"Stay," she said. He lacked the energy to protest, and settled down once more, the tips of his fingers puckered from the bubbling water. She clasped his hand tighter and looked at him with a doleful expression he had never seen before.

"Listen," he said, finally. "I'm going to check flights tomorrow and see if I can get back from San Francisco by the end of the week. My ticket's open but it doesn't let me onto all of the flights. But it shouldn't..."

"It's so sad, isn't it?"

"What?"

"Us. This. Circling around each other in someone else's house. It's been so *good*, our time together, Nick. I never want you to forget that."

The obsequies were being observed. The passion of early evening had turned into propriety. He felt a rolling surge of grief mounting within him, but was not yet ready to yield. "I won't... Of course I won't."

"Because I know what you're like. You will forget unless I tell you."

"Well, how do you expect to tell me when I'm on the other side of the world writing essays on the law of tort? And you're here dividing your time between sit-ins and Ezra Pound? Let's be practical."

"I'll stay in touch."

"No, you won't."

"I will." She fixed him with eyes in which, unbelievably, there was a glint of mischief. She paused. "But not the way you think."

"What do you mean? Either you phone or write, or you don't."

She shifted closer to him. "That's bullshit, though, isn't it? I mean, if we do that, how long will it last? Six months? A year? Then it'll peter out. Christmas cards, maybe birthdays. You'll meet some babe at law school – no, Nick, you will, you're a very cute guy, it'll happen, they'll come onto you. And I have no intention of living like a nun. At *Stanford*? Give me a break. Things will change and it'll get awkward. I don't want to do any of that conventional staying-in-touch, we're-still-friends crap. This is more special than that. It deserves better."

He was frustrated by the tone of theatricality in her voice, the hint of performance.

"So. You obviously have something planned."

She smiled and laid her head on his shoulder. Out of habit, he ran his fingers through her damp hair, stroking her scalp. "I do," she said. "I do indeed."

"Well, out with it. If we stay in here much longer, we'll shrivel up completely. And I want another beer."

She ignored his attempt to lighten the moment with a reference to mundane appetites and discomforts. "You know how you told me that you started reading the *California Literary Review* when you were back in London? Because you missed me?"

"Yeah. I quite like it. All those righteous polemics about Saul Bellow. So what?"

"Keep buying it. When you're back home."

"Why?"

She stroked his chest. "Check out the personal ads. I'll leave a message for you. I won't use my name, but you'll know it's from me."

"How? There are dozens of those ads."

"Because you know… you know my style. You know how I write, and how I like to do things."

"What? Codes? Riddles?"

"If you like. But you understand them, and nobody else does. No one will ever know. For years and years, maybe. For ever, perhaps. I can send you a message across the world which is for you and only you. And you'll read it and know I'm thinking of you. Much better than some stilted phone conversation, or bullshit postcard. I want something as special as we are."

In spite of himself, he laughed. "Tab – you are really crazy. You really are. Do you know how much it costs to put in a personal ad?"

"Doesn't interest me. I get more money than I can spend off my terrible father. It's up to me what I do with it. It's filthy lucre, anyway… And it's my choice."

He finished her beer, which had stood untouched on the marble tiles for some time. They fell silent for a moment. "Can't you just call me occasionally? Or I'll call, if you like."

She shook her head. "I won't take your calls. Believe me. And if you write, I won't answer. I won't have any of that… of that *mediocrity* between us. It's disrespectful to what we have – what we've had."

"So let me get this straight. I buy the *Review*, turn to the personals, and look for a well-turned literary reference just to reassure myself that you still care."

"That's one way of putting it."

He could not stop himself smiling. "Nothing is simple with you, is it? Nothing."

"Take it or leave it, Nicky. It's a good deal. It's right. Trust me."

He sighed, aware that the normal political arrangement of their relationship had reasserted itself. "I'm missing something here."

She turned and kissed him. "Of course you are. That's why I love you."

He embraced her and thought of saying something, but then decided against it. They wrapped themselves in towels and joined Cody and Tina in the TV room. Candles flickered on the coffee table and the mantelpiece. Cody was watching a zombie movie intently, his bare legs in a minor spasm of excitement as a rotting monster loomed over a hysterical woman crouched in what appeared to be a potting shed. Tina had fallen asleep with her head on his lap. He was smoking a reefer and did not register their arrival immediately. "Oh, hi guys. I didn't see you. Did you turn off the tub already? This is such a cool flick. I've seen it like a hundred times and it kills me every time." Nick and Tab sat on the beanbags and tried to pay attention to the movie. After a while, she grew restless and went to bed. When he joined her half an hour later, she was already sleeping.

In the morning, she had gone. There was no note or explanation, although Cody, when he finally stirred at midday, speculated weakly that she had gone to see her mother up in the hills, or had business in Palo Alto: "What with the new semester, and all." Either way, Cody said, he felt bad for Nick. Tina hugged him and asked what he wanted to do. It did not take long for him to decide that he should catch a Greyhound to San Francisco that afternoon and get on the next available flight to London. It was all fairly straightforward now, really. Tab had made the decision for him.

Cody drove him to the bus stop and helped him with his bags. Tina wept as they said goodbye – a little too easily, Nick thought – and Cody gave him an extravagant bear hug, releasing him only when he had promised to write often. Then they left. He bought a Coke and a burrito, and sat in the sun, waiting for the next bus. He realized that he had left his camera and sunglasses at the house but could not be bothered to go back and repeat the valedictory rituals. He pulled out his passport and leafed through its pages. The small number of stamps depressed him, and he put it back in his shoulder bag. A man with a Bible in his hand tried to strike up a conversation, and left only when Nick told him he was not interested. The sunlight fell on the tarmac before him, suddenly blank and uncertain.

In the seventeen years that would pass before Nick saw Tab Bradley again, Cody Machin would drop out of school, graduate to heroin, and die of an overdose in a Bronx crack den on New Year's Eve, 1999. Tina Ramirez would marry the wealthy son of a congressman and raise a family – three daughters – in the more prosperous quarter of Sacramento. Neither of these names would mean anything to Nick by the time he saw Tab's face again, seventeen years later, a pistol at his head, on a mountainside in Italy.

PART ONE

THE SEALS ARE
OPENED

I

There was no visible source of light, but the walls were uniformly, dazzlingly bleached. Freddy could see scuff marks on the floor beneath the legs of the chair and a few flecks of ash on the other side of the table. Beyond these blemishes, the eerie whiteness gave no quarter. It had consumed him for an unspeakable number of hours already.

Sleep was impossible. After the first fit of seething panic when he came round, his body had gradually reached a truce with its new surroundings, a negotiation which was the product of instinct rather than courage. A circuit-breaker deep within had closed down his struggle. It was not that he felt calm – more that the low animal cunning which lurked beneath the human calculation had instructed his system to curtail the screaming and the sobbing and the contortions until they were absolutely necessary. Freddy did not think he would have to wait long. But the whiteness warped time: its visual violence bled the room of all other sensory experiences. There was no smell, no noise, no ticking of a clock or booming of an aeroplane overhead. It was impossible to say how many hours had passed already, how many days. It was impossible to say where he was, or when.

Munroe had told him this might happen, and he had not believed it. Focus on what you know, Munroe said: don't float in a pool of nothingness, or they've got you, like a sprat on a line. Focus on the real, on what you know, on what you can cling to... Easier said than done when your wrists are bound behind your back, your ankles are lashed to the legs of an old canvas chair, and you're stuck in the whitest room in the world, hideous boredom competing with hideous dread. What was the last thing he could remember? The corner of Hartenstraat and Keizersgracht, and the lanterns outside the house and the old lady cycling across the canal towards Reestraat. The car pulling up, and the door opening, and then darkness. Not even a sense of how many and how they had got away with it in broad daylight.

And before that? He remembered lunch at the brasserie on Nieuwezijds Voorburgwal, where the bar staff recognized him and welcomed him like a lost sibling. He had a toasted sandwich and a coffee and looked out at the little alleyway with its wall carvings and iron gate. His flight did not leave until the following morning, so there was time to relax and browse in the bookshops that dappled the Western Canal Belt. And then there was Marianne. "Don't play too much," Munroe said. "Just enough, Freddy."

Just enough... it had been a mistake to get talking to the girl. He could see that now. With the job done, he had gone for a long walk down past the university, towards the Muziektheater, with its concrete quads, and out along the river. He crossed over to Rembrandtplein and headed towards the arts centre he liked, opposite the Rijksmuseum. The centre was a magnet for young and attractive women, swathed in black, brows furrowed with their reading, just waiting to be impressed by a handsome Berliner in a brand new suit. And even if the bar were empty save for a couple of bearded poets arguing about poverty in Malawi, he could have a smoke and feel at ease with the world.

As it was, his luck was in. The café was busy, the fragrance of newly drawn beer hanging in the air; there was only one seat free, next to a young woman listlessly reading *Het Parool* and consulting her watch more often than was natural.

"Is this taken?" He smiled, careful not to seem too interested.

"No. Please." She returned to the Classifieds section. She was, he guessed, twenty-five, blonde and anxious. She was wearing a black dress and too much make-up. Her cocked head and nail-chewing suggested a twist of eccentricity that he liked.

He offered her a Camel, which she took, and introduced himself. Her name was Marianne and she was a publishing assistant living with friends in the Pijp. He told her only that he was on business in the city, which was true, and hinted at an affluent bohemianism calculated to intrigue her. He bought her a glass of wine and let her tell him about the best plays and concerts to be seen in Amsterdam. He liked the rhythm of the conversation, the sense of relaxed inevitability to which they had both, apparently, succumbed. And – why pretend otherwise? – he was exhilarated at the completion of his task earlier that day and, to an extent he knew Munroe would find appalling, felt entitled to reward himself.

Now, immobilized and ashamed by the urine that soaked his trousers, he grasped at last why Munroe and the inner circle regarded this sort of thinking as decadent and dangerous. It was not that they were ascetic on principle: rather, they feared dropping their guard for a moment. Freddy was not capable of such rigour – the rigour his comrades had fine-tuned in the punishing desert training camps. His commitment was real enough, but of a lesser order. He could not extract himself from the ordinary processes of human life so thoroughly. He wondered if his reflexes would have been that crucial half second sharper, that saving heartbeat faster if he had not spent the night with Marianne. She was an endearing and generous lover, if a little too talkative afterwards, as they smoked and listened to the fizz of the city at 3 a.m. Where was she now? Where, for that matter, was he?

"Freddy."

The two syllables carried no edge of enquiry or command. If anything, they suggested parental dis-appointment, the sadness of the weary father called late at night to bail out his errant son. The voice was warm and soft, a baritone which filled the room without strain. It came from behind. Freddy struggled painfully to see who had joined him.

The man who walked round the table and sat op-posite him was indeed paternal in countenance. Tall and heavy-set, he moved slowly and with patrician ease, taking things at his own pace with the air of one who was accustomed to doing so. He straightened the creases in his suit trousers and ran his fingers through grey hair that was still thick. There was a fleshiness to his features that made Freddy wonder if he had recently shaved off a beard. The eyes that met his across the table were sharp and blue.

It was a while before the man spoke again. "Do you know where you are?"

Freddy shrugged. He wanted to cry. "I don't. I don't know where I am. How could I?" He could smell his piss, and felt ashamed. "Who are you?"

The man put a pack of cigarettes on the table and arched an eyebrow as if the question was mildly surprising. "Me? Oh, my name is Diether. You have been giving me the runaround, Freddy. I thought I'd lost you at one stage."

"When?"

"Your tradecraft on the way from Schiphol to Centraal Station was not bad. You pretended you were getting off at Sloterdijk, and that threw my people. There was a crowd of kids… well, you know how it is. You played it well."

Freddy felt his gorge rise as he realized how long the police had been on to him. From the very beginning. They had seen him arrive at the airport, seen him on the train, probably seen him finish the job a few hours later. And then? Well, then they had let him get comfortable with Marianne, and taken him out when they were good and ready. Oh yes, Munroe was going to love this.

"Do you mind if I smoke?" Diether said. "It helps me think."

"Go ahead."

"Thank you." The man lit up without offering one to his captive. "So. We should talk, I suppose."

Freddy shifted in the chair, his wrists chafing against the cord.

"I don't know what you want. I don't know who you are."

"You are such a small piece in the big picture, Freddy. I don't think you know what you're involved with, frankly."

"Listen, I really don't know what the fuck this is all about, but I want a lawyer. I'm a German citizen."

"So am I," Diether said.

"Talking English, though. Somebody's listening, I suppose. Well, speak whatever language you like. This is crazy. I'm on business from Berlin, I was going to fly back a few hours after you… arrested me. Christ! You can't just tie people up and leave them in a room for hours. There are laws, there are rules. Get me a lawyer."

Diether crossed his legs and attended to a kink in his sock. "Freddy. Let's not get carried away. A lawyer is no good at all to you. I need to know what you know. And then we can get you out, and cleaned up."

"I want to use the bathroom now."

Diether ignored him and blew a smoke ring which hovered between them balefully. "Tell me what was in the case."

The case. Well, if only he knew. Munroe had given him instructions to pick it up in Frankfurt. The location of the drop was not revealed to him until he got to Amsterdam. There was a message waiting for him at the Hotel Camus, telling him to call "Jacques" on a local number at 10 p.m. This he had done, and a female voice had said only "Nine". He added one to this figure, as instructed, and at ten the next morning stationed himself by the absurd phallic structure of the Nationaal Monument in Dam Square. It was raining furiously, and the tourists were huddled beneath the awnings of the cafés lining the great civic piazza. Freddy waited under his umbrella for five minutes before a woman approached and said to him: "Do you know the way to the Oude Kerk? I want to see the Baptistry. In an hour."

He arrived early. Best, then, to get inside and take a turn round the building: he wanted to keep moving even though the case was becoming steadily heavier in his hand. As a family bustled past him in the ticket office, he felt a spasm of panic that the venue for the drop was too public, that he was too conspicuous. But it was this that made it easier for him to blend in, to melt into the throng. It was easier, Munroe always said, to get lost somewhere public. It was in the streets where few people walked that you stuck out.

It was a while since he had visited this medieval church, with all the accretions of seven centuries cling-ing to it like molluscs. He liked the misericords in the choir stalls, warnings against sloth and drunkenness, and the great declaration of the 16th Century that "misuse of God's church" had finally come to an end. He liked the dimly visible vault painting of the Last Judgement, Christ with a sword and lily. Perhaps, most of all, he liked the curious, impenetrable signs and symbols etched into the floor, evidence of a forgotten masonry and its secret language, of conspiracies and caucuses which had left their mark. But his mind was not on their meaning on this occasion. Checking his watch, he walked into the Baptistry and waited.

It was a claustrophobic space, confining except in its soaring height. He looked back through the grille to the stained glass at the opposite end of the church. A baby cried in a pram, as its parents headed towards the Maria Kapel. A middle-aged couple in raincoats poked their head round the door of the Baptistry and retreated without comment.

"New here?" The man stood beside him, examining an inscription through his glasses. He took off his cap, adjusted the peak and replaced it.

"Oh, yes," said Freddy. He let the case down gently.

"Enjoy your stay," said the other man, picking it up.

"Of course," Freddy said. "I will." He turned round and left the church, remembering not to walk too hastily or to avoid the eye of anyone he encountered. As he was enveloped by the cool air outside, he realized that he was bathed in sweat. But the truth was that the job had been easy.

"So I'll ask you again, Freddy. What was in the case?" Diether's head rested in his hands, the stub of his cigarette snug between two knuckles.

"Here's the thing: you won't let me see a lawyer. Well, there's not much I can do about that, seeing as I'm tied to this chair. Then you ask me a bunch of bullshit questions about stuff I have no idea about. What am I supposed to say? Do you want me to make it up? Okay – it was full of diamonds. No, platinum. Any good? All right then: confidential documents. How's that?"

"How about money?"

"Sure. Whatever you like."

Diether sighed. He removed a notebook from his inside pocket, jotted something down and replaced it.

His brow, Freddy noticed, became even more imperious when he was writing.

"Freddy, Freddy. This is no good. No good at all. Do you think that sort of nonsense is going to get us anywhere? I know about the case, where you were staying, the girl. All of it. What I need to know is what was in the case, and who sent you."

They knew a lot, that much was clear. But there was no mention of the church, or the meeting in Dam Square, or the message to call Jacques. Maybe Diether's officers had stumbled more than once; maybe the slip on the train was only one of many errors they had made in pursuit of him. Where had the chase begun? In Berlin? In Frankfurt? Diether was sure to be bluffing about some of it. What did Munroe like to say? Remember: if you're stopped and you get away with it, you become twice as useful. Would he ever get a chance to laugh about this with Munroe? He thought of his mentor's face on the first night they had got drunk together, in Berlin. They had friends in common, and Munroe seemed to take to Freddy immediately. "You'll thank me one day, Fred," he would say. Thank him for what? For drawing him towards a terrible secret, implicating him, but never quite admitting him into the innermost circle? Munroe had never allowed him to meet the one person Freddy most wanted to meet, the person who ran the show. There were limits to Munroe's friendship, and thus to Freddy's gratitude. He did not feel much gratitude now.

In the silence, Diether reached down to his briefcase and pulled out a file. It was slim and featureless, except for a blue ribbon holding it together. He seemed to hesitate before opening it up.

"Do you recognize these pictures?"

The cord was beginning to rub again, and Freddy's bladder was desperate for relief once more. He strained over the table to look at the black-and-white photographs that Diether was spreading out on the surface.

"Striking, aren't they?" said Diether. "In case you can't tell, they are pictures of a person. Her name was Anna Schmidt. She was the wife of Oskar Schmidt. Yes, *that* Oskar Schmidt. As in the Schmidt Corporation. As in one of the richest businessmen in Europe. As in the clothes you're wearing, the fabric in your car, maybe your bedding. So far, so good?"

Freddy tried to take his eyes off the pictures. He wanted to be sick. He nodded feebly.

"Schmidt married late. He was in his late forties when she came to work in his office. You know the kind of thing. They had kids pretty quickly, Florian who's nine and Lisa who's a couple of years younger, I think. So, happy ever after? Absolutely. Until a week ago."

Freddy looked up and squinted. He saw red spots shifting to blue. He did not want to look Diether in the eye. There was a sing-song in his captor's voice which, for the first time, conveyed true menace.

"So, Oskar goes to South America on business, and the following day Frau Schmidt sets off for her daily trip to her analyst. The car drives out of the estate and then, on the sliproad outside, she's ambushed. The driver is dead before he can hit the phone, and she is dragged out and whisked away before she knows what's happening."

Freddy looked down at the pictures. It was just

about possible to look at them, if you pretended that they were abstract patterns, not images of reality, the Rorschach traces of a ghastly assault on Nature.

Diether stood up. He pulled an apple from his pocket and bit into it.

Freddy felt his mouth become horribly dry. Finally, he croaked: "What happened?"

Diether swung round. "What happened? Well, not much for the first few hours. It wasn't until lunchtime that one of the staff at the estate tried to get in touch with her, and called and called: nothing. About the same time, Oskar is woken up in his hotel in Rio by his mobile ringing. And a voice – disguised, of course – told him that his wife had been lifted. So Schmidt says, 'Listen, I'll do anything. *Anything.*' And you know what, Freddy? He meant it. He really did. Because that's the truth about these things. Terror is the last true outpost of equality. It makes us all equal. No amount of money or power can protect you at a moment like that. Schmidt? He'd have given up the whole empire, all the factories and the sweat shops and the armies of workers, all of it handed over in an instant just to see his lovely Anna back home safe and sound."

Diether sat down, as if suddenly tired. He seemed absorbed. After a while, Freddy broke the silence: "What did they want?"

"After ten hours and thirteen and a half minutes precisely, there was a call – an instruction to pick up a package at a barn about fifteen kilometres away. Inside the package…"

Diether held up the first of the photos.

"Christ. Christ."

"After that, every two hours there'd be a new photo, in a new location. All very well-organized. We had people all over the city, sweating our best informants. Nobody knew a thing."

"I don't understand. Didn't they ask for anything?"

"I calculated that if I could get the woman some medical attention immediately – and it would have to be *immediately* – then she had an even chance of surviving. With Schmidt's full authority, I was promising helicopters, untold sums of cash, you name it. They didn't want to know. The phone went dead, every time. They had one of the world's richest men willing to give up his fortune, and they didn't even come to the table. *There was no negotiation.*"

"And then?" asked Freddy. "Then what?"

"Then we got a map reference, telling us where to pick the body up, or what was left of it."

Diether stood and turned his back on Freddy. He seemed physically diminished by the story he had just told, as though its savagery and its cold, godless ending had feasted on his very heart. Freddy wondered how much time he had left.

"If I knew anything, I'd tell you. Anything. But I don't. I don't know anything about this."

Diether turned back, and Freddy saw from his black expression and the curl of his lip that his interrogator was on the brink of anger. The moment passed – what sort of self-control did this man have? – but it was a bleak warning. Freddy felt himself trembling in his cold, pee-soaked trousers.

Diether reached into his briefcase again and extracted a second file, this one heavier and untidier, the dog-eared edges of photocopies and old forms spilling out of it. This time, he did not sit down, but stood judgement over his captive.

"Let's see what we've got here. Frederick Christian Hengel, born – what? – just over thirty years ago, educated in Berlin, nice gymnasium, then university in your home city, some postgrad courses in Paris. Da-de-da. Presently owner of dotcom business, Hengel Enterprises, struggling a little I see. Unmarried. Financially okay, pleasant apartment."

"Well, then. Nothing much to know, is there?"

"Oh, that's just the pink form on top. I haven't got to the good stuff yet. Ah, here we go. 'Hengel: political activities'. That sounds more like it. Aha! Nothing very much in Berlin. But in Paris – well, that's a different story. Involved with the World Alliance from pretty much day one. Help with fund-raising, running the office, conference committees. Demos. Ah, this is from a bit later. Name listed on 'Stop the War' literature – this *is* back in Berlin – trips to London to liaise with groups there. More trips to Paris. Who's this?"

Diether held up a grainy black-and-white surveillance picture of Freddy, which he guessed from the longer hair and jeans was a year old. He was standing by an old Citroën talking to a shorter man, whose dark eyes and black curls were striking even in this snatched, low-quality photograph. He was a man who commanded attention.

"That's a friend of mine."

"His name?"

"Cut the crap. You know his name. Munroe Stacy."

"Mmmm." Diether sat down. "Munroe Stacy? Yes, Mr Stacy. So much we could say about *him*."

"I'm sorry, but what are you actually accusing me of? Opposing the war? Joining the World Alliance? Have you any idea how many members the WA has now? Millions. Most of them are middle-class professionals. I mean, do I look like some scruffy anarchist with a petrol bomb to you?"

"Not at all," said Diether, smiling. "I am merely exploring the political odyssey that led you to the dubious pleasure of Mr Stacy's company."

Freddy swallowed. No point in quarrelling with the evidence of the camera.

"Sure, Munroe's an old friend of mine. I'd bumped into him… He was pretty prominent in the WA when I was at the Sorbonne. We spent more time out drinking than we did talking politics."

"Was this the last time you saw him?"

"What does he know?" Freddy thought. That last meeting, just before Munroe shipped out… Munroe had been distracted, animated, testy. Freddy had listened to his orders and asked him where he was going. He would not say. What about the others – what about *her*? Silence. Munroe had sipped on a Pernod and told Freddy to do the job and wait for further instructions. They would come, in due course.

Freddy decided to gamble. "Oh, yes. We met up in Paris – when was it? – last Spring. Had some drinks, a good night out. He was addressing some kids at a seminar, I think, and then going to London." Freddy wondered whether he sounded remotely convincing. He was desperate for a smoke.

"Let me straighten you out about Mr Stacy's activities. He is, like you, a long-standing World Alliance member

– nothing wrong with that, as you say. So are many politicians in Europe these days, I imagine. Munroe was on the Central Committee for two years, Head of Campaigns, but never a spokesman, more a behind-the-scenes kind of guy. All perfectly legal, all pretty legitimate. Lots of literature attacking global business, the war, America, ecological degradation. Yes, he's a member of many groups. He gets around. One of these organizations, Students Against Globalization, or STAG, had its third annual convention in Copenhagen last year – don't worry, I know you weren't there. Shame you missed it. By day two, the whole group was in complete turmoil: fist fights, typical student shambles, it seems. But from all this chaos emerges a result. A radical caucus, the so-called 'New Weathermen', seized control of the whole student organization. The only person who survived this little coup was Mr Stacy. Which is – *intriguing*, to say the least. He didn't conduct himself like someone who was enormously surprised by what had happened."

"Well, I don't know about any of this."

"And then, about six months afterwards, this com-muniqué was released: 'This is the first communication from the New Weather Underground. All attempts at negotiated progress having failed, our central committee has agreed to proceed urgently to a new phase of the struggle against injustice and oppression. We send warning today that we shall bring about a series of actions to draw the attention of the world to the global catastrophe of imperialism, corporatism and militarized capitalism. We live in the most violent society the world has ever seen. In that context, the commitment of our predecessors to non-violence is not only meaningless but treacherous. A revolution is not a spectacle.' Etcetera, etcetera. You get the idea, I hope. To cut to the chase, these guys were seriously pissed off and threatening to do something about it."

Freddy chewed on his lip. Was it worth throwing Diether a scrap in the hope that he might back off? "Do you know about the Weathermen?"

"Not much. Tell me, Freddy."

"Well, I don't know a great deal myself. Only what I've read. They were a bunch of Americans in the late Sixties and Seventies who went underground and bombed some federal buildings. I think they sprung Timothy Leary from jail, too. They were pretty extreme, did armed robberies, gave the FBI a serious run for their money. Identified a lot with the Black Panthers, and George Jackson, when he died in prison. Vietnam was what brought them together in the first place, I guess, and when the war ended, they turned on each other. Some of them went to jail in the end, I think."

"A funny name – the Weathermen, I mean."

"Yeah. Bob Dylan – 'You don't need a weatherman to know which way the wind blows'."

"How poetic. So we had some New Weathermen. I suspect that our new friends have been brought together by war, too. But in the Middle East this time, not South-East Asia. And they obviously have some money. And there was something about this – it seemed more than the usual children's crusade gone crazy. It had the smell of a group serious about going underground. Being underground is all about information control, living in a parallel universe. You can't keep mobile phones for very long, you have to use computers very carefully. Same with credit cards. You need a cellular structure so that if one gets busted the whole thing doesn't collapse. Most hardened young men in Gaza or the Pakistani borderlands aren't up to this way of life, let alone a bunch of white kids with over-active imaginations. But it is theoretically possible. Once a group goes underground properly, it is hard to get them. You need a proper informant." Diether looked squarely at Freddy. "Properly debriefed."

Freddy looked at his lap. His shirt, he noticed for the first time since Diether's arrival, bore the brown tie-dye pattern of dried blood spilt in violence. The stain around the crotch of his trousers had spread like a flower, wrinkling the material. He wondered what his own chances were. Did Diether know what had been in the case? How much did they have on Munroe?

"Could I have some water?" Freddy asked.

"Sure," said Diether, and pressed something beneath the table. A woman, mysteriously dressed in a nurse's uniform, brought in a tray with a jug of water and two glasses. Her hair was clipped back severely, and she wore the flat shoes of the hospital functionary. She nodded almost imperceptibly to Diether and brushed past Freddy as though he was not there.

Diether poured the water and stepped round to Freddy. He cupped his head with surprising gentleness and guided him to the glass, tilting it precisely to match Freddy's thirst. He gulped down the first glass. "More," he rasped. Diether obliged. His compassion, however contrived, was disarming. Freddy felt himself deflated and enfeebled. Mercy was a form of torment.

"How long have I been here?"

"A while. Let's go back to our friends underground and Mr Stacy."

Freddy blinked and tried to focus. He felt dizzy. "I'll tell you all I know, but you will be disappointed. Munroe is radical, it's true. So am I, probably, by your definition. Oh sure, there are the anarchists – the Black Bloc, we call them – who turn up at the World Trade talks, or on May Day, and cause a bit of a riot. But they're just thugs looking for trouble. When I was working with the WA in Paris, we used to tell the cops what we knew about that crowd if they had plans to jump on a rally and cause havoc. The reason so many people signed up with us and the reason you see families on the demos – kids in our T-shirts, mums with prams, it's fantastic – is precisely that we don't have a revolutionary fringe. The whole Angry Brigade, Baader-Meinhof, Weathermen thing. Well, it's so *old-fashioned*. It didn't achieve anything. My generation is very different. Munroe is an idealist, of course, and a hothead sometimes, but he's much too committed to all the legitimate stuff to jeopardize it. And don't forget: I am businessman, not a subversive. I don't want to see society collapse, or terrorists causing mayhem. Things have moved on a lot."

Diether grinned. "You are a good talker, Freddy. I can see why Mr Stacy uses you from time to time. You're a perfect bagman. You look good, but you don't stick out. I bet you've never been stopped by a customs officer in your life."

"I keep my nose clean. Look, no matter how often you try to join up the dots, it just won't work. Yes, I'm involved with WA. But I spend most of my waking hours trying to keep my business afloat, which is more than enough of a struggle for me. I'm sorry about Frau Schmidt, but I didn't even know she existed until you told me."

This was true. And this, he realized, was his biggest problem. Diether did not believe him.

"Ah, yes, Frau Schmidt. You're right. We shouldn't forget about her. Here was a classic kidnapping. Whoever did it could have become fabulously wealthy in a day. Enough money for several lifetimes, complete freedom. And they turned it down. This was a force organized enough to pull off a lift like that, and strong enough to say no to the potential rewards. Imagine that. The message was twofold. First, that we have power over you. Second, that you cannot buy us off. Do you see? This was a *punishment* rather than a threat. It was redress for a grievance. It is impossible to negotiate with people using such methods. And this is only the start, I believe." He played with the box of cigarettes, its edges frayed and worried by his restless fingers. "I think you can help me…"

Even in the stuffy white cubicle, Freddy felt a chill enter the room. Diether's tone was changing subtly but significantly. He had the manner of someone concluding his remarks rather than an interrogator at the beginning of a lengthy session.

"But what can I tell you?" Freddy pleaded. "All the people I know in the WA are like me. Dreamers with credit cards."

Diether stood up, with a sharpness that suggested to Freddy that this would be the last time he made his smooth perambulation of the room. He walked to the wall, peered at a tiny mark, brushed it and turned back, his hands behind him in a posture that was almost military.

"Freddy, we know what was in the case. Of course we do. Five million dollars. Big notes, all out of sequence. No wonder you looked so tired. It must have been heavy. Freddy. Please. Five million dollars? That's not for posters and badges and magazines. Who was the money for?"

"I have no idea what you're talking about. I brought a leather hold-all with me to Amsterdam and it's in the Hotel Camus. Room 306."

Diether sighed. "I know this must be hard for you to believe, Freddy. But I am the best friend you have in the world right now. It's downhill all the way after me. I'm a patient man. Some of my associates, however, are not so patient. They have been listening."

"Oh, for God's sake, I don't *know* anything. I don't know about your mad kidnappers. I don't know about Schmidt. I am a victim here, too." He felt himself about to sob and drew back. "Haven't I suffered enough? What do you imagine it's like sitting here in your own piss and blood? Do you think I would hold anything back if I could just get out of this – of this *fucking* chair?"

"Aren't you hungry? I am. I know a place where we could have herring and beer. Let's forget about all this. Everybody knows you aren't to blame. I don't really think that you know about Frau Schmidt. I just want to know who asked you to make the drop, and what the money was for. Freddy…" Diether paused, knelt down and looked into Freddy's eyes. "Freddy… Just tell me this: what is Second Troy? What is it? Who is in charge of it? Tell me about Second Troy, Freddy. Second Troy."

Freddy looked at him with wretched submission. He hesitated, then spoke with deliberation. "Fuck you."

Diether shrugged, with the resignation of a man who has done his best and can do no more. He pressed the button under the table and sat down again. He began to read a newspaper that was folded in his coat. After a couple of minutes the door opened and a younger man walked in, carrying a battered old Samsonite briefcase. He wore a white linen jacket, black T-shirt and loafers, and his skin looked freshly tanned. Smoothing his pony tail, he smiled warmly at Diether, who lit up when he saw him.

"Hey, Hans. I hoped it would be you. Great to see you. How have you been?"

The man laughed lightly. "I've been good, thank you. And you?"

"Oh, you know. So busy. I don't know whether it's night or day."

"You should take it easy, Diether. Have some fun once in a while. I'll take you out again. If you've recovered from last time, that is."

Hans chuckled, and pulled out a plain work surface that was artfully concealed in the wall. He placed the case down carefully and opened it. Freddy watched him remove what looked like a pair of old headphones and a small black box with a dial. There were several leads neatly laid out, and test tubes. Hans was attending to a syringe, which he filled from a labelled bottle, his eyes screwed up in concentration as he did so.

"You know, I must get the titration exactly right this time. It's so easy to go a mil over, and then it's not so good."

"That's true," said Diether. "One has to be so precise. That's one thing I've learnt from you."

"Uh-huh. No, that's *exactly* right. Good. Excellent."

"Have you been here long?"

"About an hour."

"Been listening?"

"Oh, sure. I've been listening."

"What do you think?"

"Shouldn't take long is my guess," said Hans. "I might be wrong. You can't always predict these things. Remember Stockholm? That was a long night, and I was so sure we'd be done in an hour! Let me get set up and I'll be with you in a second. Oh, is that water? Yes, a glass would be lovely."

Hans began to unpack the remaining contents of the case, humming quietly as he did. There was something that looked like a child's dummy.

Freddy started to rock back and forth. "This is crazy. You are crazy, both of you. I'm just a normal guy. I don't know anything about Schmidt or five million dollars. Please, I'm begging you. Do you think I wouldn't tell you if I knew? Jesus, please. I can't tell you what I don't know. Can I? Don't… I mean, come on… Is this… Are you supposed to be the good cop and the bad cop?"

Hans laughed with raucous good nature, as if he had never heard such a splendid joke in his whole life. He shook his head as he continued with his preparations. He was attending to one of the leads which had got tangled. "What makes you think we're cops?"

Diether turned to face him. "So, Freddy. Tell me. Tell me all about Second Troy."

2

Nick awoke to a room clicking its tongue in disapproval. At the side of his bed lay his leather jacket, jeans and shirt in an asymmetric pyramid. Admonishing him on the chest of drawers stood an unopened bottle of wine, another that was uncorked and, mysteriously, some household bleach. He looked at his watch and waited for his eyes to defog. It was half-past seven. That meant he could lie beneath the quilt for ten minutes more, perhaps twelve, steeling himself for the melancholic slouch from bedroom to bathroom, and the reproachful greeting of the mirror. His head had not started to throb, but that was only a matter of time. A pillar of hazy light scorched the wall: he had not even drawn the curtains properly.

One day to go: that was always the consolation of Friday mornings. Only one day left of work before the brief remission from paralysing routine which the weekend provided. True, he never did very much with his weekend, except when it was his turn to look after Polly. But he derived a dim sense of freedom, however deluded, however swiftly it would be snatched away, from the prospect of two days' absence from the school. He could watch television, he could go to the pub, he could stare in the window of estate agents long enough to wonder why he was doing so. He would have the luxury of wasting time for his own reasons, rather than for reasons decided by others. He would sit in the park and cling to his right to do nothing in particular, growling inwardly.

It all depended, of course, what you meant by "the weekend". This was a point that his friend Topper had made to him on numerous occasions. "Nicko," he said, "the weekend is a relic of the totalitarian era. It persuades us to confine our pleasures to a time not of our choosing. It holds the party captive. It pens in our healthiest instincts. I won't have it." Topper's solution was to treat his life as one long weekend, a privilege that came with his wealth; Nick's was to start the weekend on Thursday night, defying the implacable logic that he would suffer on Friday for this feeble act of rebellion.

The night before, he had declined Aisha's invitation to see a film – pleading that he had a backlog of marking to clear – and instead met Topper at a club in Shaftesbury Avenue. He had little memory of the night-bus journey home, nor of what time he had gone to bed. Much too late, he assumed. He could still feel the alcohol warming his system and sending malevolent surges of adrenalin flooding through the inner maze of his body. He sagged a little as he realized that the full impact of the hangover – was it Margaritas this time? – would not make itself known in his bones until mid-morning, by which time he would be facing ordeals of a different kind.

The flat was still strange to him. On the first day, when Topper had helped him with his bags and boxes, he had thought it small, and had had premonitions of claustrophobia as he climbed the stairs past the kitchen and bathroom to the bedroom and lounge. The furniture had the forlorn quality common to all rented accommodation. Six weeks on, he had scarcely made the place his own. Two pictures of Polly – one of her as a jaundiced newborn, the other from her first day at school – stood in frames on the television. He had yet to unpack the portrait of Emily or the photograph of their wedding day, which he had discreetly brought with him on the day he finally closed the door behind him in Muswell Hill. There was no point, he felt, in draping the flat with a fake domesticity. He wanted it to match his sense of dislocation, to honour his decline.

He pulled on his towelling robe and shuddered as he stretched. The windows in the kitchen were smeared from his amateurish attempt to clean them the week before, and the lino floor was starting to get sticky underfoot. He made himself a cup of strong black coffee and stood by the fridge contemplating the various measures that were required in the next half-hour: he must shower, shave, dress, dare to step out of the flat, cycle to school and confront the horrors of the staffroom before the bell rang.

He stepped into the shower and waited for the boiler to splutter into life. Its paroxysms reminded him of a tragic car his father had held on to for twenty years – a fossilized Ford Escort – which had begged for euthanasia on many a cold morning, wheezing pathetically as the ignition was turned again and again. At last, the hot water gushed out, causing his skin to blotch in places as the steam rose around him. He shaved unsatisfactorily, lacking the motivation to get out and fetch a new disposable razor. White streaks of soapy water clung to his legs like chalky tendrils from below. After a while, he found himself humming one of Polly's favourite pop songs, and stopped at once, ashamed that he should enjoy the fruits of paternity while shirking its responsibilities. The nascent degradation of a full-blown hangover mocked his nakedness. Well, he still looked something like an athlete, or someone who had once been an athlete. He had kept a grip on his weight, he reflected with satisfaction: cycling every day, a regime of desperate sit-ups and teaching games two afternoons a week were keeping at bay the effects of lazy diet and nocturnal over-indulgence. But for how long? He did not want a belly like Topper's. The decay began within, forcing its way outwards. But he did not want to advertise to the world the crumbling of his life by letting himself go.

He towelled himself dry and changed. Now that he was no longer distracted by the morning chatter of a child, it was the work of a minute and a half to get himself into his classroom clothes, the camouflage of the half-hearted teacher: jacket, tie and timeless cords. Even his shoes – scuffed and workmanlike – communicated his lack of commitment, the shameful wink he gave to his pupils that he was only marginally more enthusiastic than they were.

Outside, he could hear the rumbling of the traffic on Archway. The house was described by Topper's leasing agents as being in Highgate, but it was no such thing. The main road was a brashly unambiguous boundary between the urban ordinariness in which he lived and the discreet greenery of the village. To cross it was to move from the world of bedsits and cramped family homes into a gated oasis of detached houses, delicatessens and fashionable brasseries. Trucks careered angrily down Archway. He pedalled across and up the tree-lined roads on the hill, suddenly plunged into the dimmer pools of light refracted through chlorophyll. He rode past the deserted church, towards the understated mansions and the driveways, with their sports cars and four-wheel drives.

The school was half a mile from the cemetery, perched behind a phalanx of oak trees. Its main building was Georgian, pillared and recently restored to something approaching stateliness, but it stood in aesthetic unease amid a jumble of modern extensions and outhouses: new classrooms, a sports hall and a music block. Boys and girls in their blue St Benedict's blazers made their way towards the portico, chattering and jostling. One of them, a fourteen-year-old in Nick's class called Sayeed, called out to him as he cruised past on his mountain bike. He remembered that Sayeed's essay on the role of Nature in *As You Like It* was sitting unread, along with sixteen others, on his coffee table at home. He smiled weakly and did his best to feel guilty. There was something unspeakably ludicrous in a bright teenager such as Sayeed believing that he, of all people, could guide him in the ways of life, let alone help him pass his GCSE in English. He chained his bike to the railings in the teachers' car park and followed the river of blue blazers into the crepuscular light of the school.

"Nick?" Aisha was pretending not to be waiting for him in the lobby as she leafed through a sheaf of spreadsheet timetables. She looked tired, he thought, her make-up a little more thickly applied than usual. She pulled at the hem of her long grey skirt, trying to keep her voice down as children swarmed past her towards assembly in the great hall via their classrooms. "I called you last night. Where were you?"

He sighed, the hangover kicking in viciously. "I went out in the end. Topper called. I wasn't going to… but… Well, you know…"

She looked even more alluring when she was sad, he thought, her cheekbones frozen by the recognition of petty betrayal. She nodded. "Okay. I was worried, that's all. I just wish you had told me."

They walked down the corridor and descended the stairs to the staffroom. He wondered if their pupils thought of them as a couple or mocked them behind their backs. Probably. What the headmaster, Mr Frobisher, called "inter-staff liaison" was frowned upon at St Benedict's, not least because it was seen to encourage what Mr Frobisher called "inter-pupil liaison". Nick had wanted to say that if Mr Frobisher had helped to organize the sixth-form disco then he would have realized that his charges needed little encouragement to engage in "inter-pupil liaison". And surely "inter-staff liaison" was better than the "inter-staff-pupil-liaison" favoured by his predecessor, Mr Garnett, who had taken early retirement with tearful gratitude after his intense interest in a fresh-faced fifth former called Barney had been called into question.

"Anyway, I'm sorry," he said. He stopped by the door marked *Strictly no admittance to pupils*. "You must think I'm a bastard. I *am* a bastard. Are you free tonight? No, that came out wrong."

Aisha shrugged. "We'll see." She leant towards him and avoided his eye. "I'm not sure this is going anywhere, Nick."

He looked up at the board above her head, on which past Captains of Rugby were listed in faded blue lettering: 1904 CB WARREN, 1905 DB AUBREY, 1906… He felt his gorge rise as his spirits headed in the opposite direction. He and Aisha had been seeing each other, if that was what it was, for less than two months. When she arrived as a junior French teacher, highly recommended by a Catholic girls' school in Dorset, the attraction had been more or less instant, and they had contrived meetings, first at school and then outside. The meetings soon became trysts, fuelled by white wine and thrilling intimations of the forbidden. Aisha knew he was married, and hesitated at first to respond to his advances. But when she discovered that he was moving out of his family home and was already sleeping in its spare room, she had relaxed a little. She was seven years his junior, and lonely in London. Having inherited her mother's olive complexion and her father's strawberry-blonde hair, she was stealthily exquisite, her English awkwardness mingled with a whispered exoticism that he found attractive.

"Well, anyway," he said. "Let's talk about this later."

She nodded. "What sort of day do you have?"

"Double fourth year, a free period. Then my own class after lunch, and the lower sixth. And then – oh Christ – I'm supposed to help Guy with the sets for the bloody play. 'Stagecraft', he calls it. I just want to go home and wrap myself in a hot towel."

She laughed, turned and disappeared into the

staffroom. After a few seconds, he followed her in and hung up his briefcase on one of the pegs.

The head of science bustled past, his ancestral tweed jacket apparently moulting around the leather elbow patches. He was carrying a small laboratory tripod and an ancient textbook.

"Good morning, Nicholas."

"Hello, Brian. How are you?"

The older man swivelled towards him with surprising daintiness. "You see this tripod?" Nick nodded. "Do you know where I found it?" Nick shook his head. "In the boys' toilets, jammed behind a cistern. Beneath, as it happens, a graffito which declared the carnal intentions of one of our sixth-form boys towards one of our fourth-form boys. Now why, do you suppose, would anyone in their right mind want to put a piece of lab equipment in there?"

Nick suppressed his smile. "It's a mystery to me. I'm the last person you should ask. I was meant to be a lawyer, you know, and then one morning I woke up and I was in front of twenty-five thirteen-year-olds trying to explain why Macbeth murders Duncan."

"When I was a teenager, we lived in fear of a thrashing…"

"Sorry, Brian. I'm afraid the days of thrashing are gone. We're at the mercy of the little bastards now."

It wasn't, in truth, such a mystery that Nick had found his humble niche in St Benedict's, in a job whose responsibilities he fulfilled with scrupulous mediocrity. The towering heights and heroic lows which he hoped would be his lot in life – the galvanic waves of triumph and disaster – had eluded him. He had gone to law school half-persuaded by those who had steered him towards this path that he might become a brilliant advocate. But, even as he attended lectures on contract, Roman Law and *mens rea*, he had grasped with dull certainty that he lacked the ambition even for this well-signposted path to success.

When a friend from Cambridge mentioned that his flatmate was looking for a young graduate to help him research a television programme, Nick immediately suggested someone: himself. Television had held no greater attraction for Nick than the law. But the work at Vision Thing Productions was easy, paid enough to cover the costs of renting a small flat, and gave him a get-out-of-jail card from law school. He traded his textbooks and moots for a tiny cubicle in an open-plan office in Clerkenwell, where he churned out treatments for programmes that would never be made on alien abductions, vampires, the Holy Grail and the Raj.

At Vision Thing Productions he had met a young assistant producer called Emily Michaels. She had graduated with a First from the University of Leeds, her home town, and then moved to London determined to find a job. After six weeks' sleeping on a friend's sofa, she had been accepted for a month's work experience at the company, and had never left.

It was Emily who asked Nick to research the Aztecs. She peered over his partition and walked straight in, a striking presence with her black polo neck, short black skirt and pale face framed with red hair. From the start, he could not imagine anyone more different from himself. She exuded anxiety and impatience. She was openly sarcastic rather than dry and laconic. He liked her at once.

"Are you the failed lawyer with nothing to do?" she asked.

"That's me," he replied, setting aside his *Times*. "Are you the thyroid case who's always telling people *what* to do?"

"I'm Emily. We're pitching for a new series in the States called *Stranger Civilizations*, and Keith wants a treatment by next Wednesday for a two-hour slot on the Aztecs. Montezuma. Sacrifices. Strange sun worship. Bollocks like that."

"Why's it called *Stranger Civilizations*?"

Her contemptuous expression suggested that this was the televisual equivalent of asking why the sky is blue. "Because it's the second series. The first was just called *Strange Civilizations*."

"And I suppose the third series will be called *Strangest Civilizations*? But what will they call the fourth one?"

Her eyes creased with mild irritation. He liked the crazy green of her mascara. She was vivid and vexed, a surprisingly pleasant jolt to his languor.

"Can you do it, or not?"

He paused and surveyed her. "How many words?"

"Start with two thousand, and we'll work from there."

Nick adopted a mask of mock seriousness. "Of course. I'll get on right away." He watched her walk away with detached amusement, barely noticing the elegance of her retreat and the smooth lines of her figure.

Three days later she asked him how he was getting on, and he had to confess that he had yet to put pen to paper. He had expected her face to blacken with fury, but instead it melted into something approaching fear.

"But you will do it, won't you?" she said softly.

"God, yes," he said as she turned to him. "I've been… you know, researching. Look at this little lot. Give me a day or two and I'll have two thousand finely turned words of purest Aztec bollocks." He pointed to a pile of books from the London Library on Montezuma, savage rituals and other related themes, and raised his eyebrows in sympathetic reassurance. She wilted in partial relaxation, her shoulders losing some of their stiffness.

"How boring is it?"

He considered this. "Extremely, as a matter of fact."

Emily giggled. "Really? Yeah, I supposed it would be. Even by the standards of this place, it's a brainless piece of junk." She sucked her pen with the venom of the thwarted chain-smoker. "Bloody juvenile, isn't it? I mean, is this what we got degrees for? To write execut-ive summaries of potboilers for programmes that'll never be made?" Her eyes were much more inviting than the severe gothic uniform she wore in the office.

"Yes," he said, putting his feet up on the desk. "That's exactly why. I mean, why write useless, derivative essays for free when you can get paid for it? It's irresistible. I have achieved my life's ambition already."

She joined in with a relish he had not expected. "Me too. It's what I dreamed of. It's so exciting to spend a fortnight on Churchill's dick – you know, the three-parter on great leaders and their sex lives? – and then be told by some Texan in a conference call that there's not enough shagging in the proposal. Keith made me rewrite it twice, told me to find some spice and, if I couldn't, to 'fucking make it up'. As in: make up the fucking."

An expectant, edgy silence fell between them. Emily broke it: "So – would you like to talk about the Aztecs over a sandwich? Or what?"

Churchill's dick… It was the precise moment when Nick had realized that Emily would form an important part of his life, and that this was an extremely good thing. She was unconventionally attractive, yes – this second encounter had awoken his hormones from their workplace torpor – but she was also disarmingly honest and smart. There was a kindness in her manner which he wanted to bathe in. Her nervousness flowed from an essential generosity of spirit: she knew that she lacked the native cunning of his own class and background, and the assumptions that went with it. For Emily, all success was contingent, all prosperity frangible. She did not believe that things would necessarily be all right, although she did more than most to ensure that they would be. As he got to know her, he was as humbled by this artless sincerity as he was increasingly drawn to her physically.

They went to bed for the first time after a night out at a wine bar with colleagues. By then, the foundations had been laid: they were bound by a spirit of tethered rebellion, by in-jokes and by a numinous camaraderie which had thus far enabled them to express warmth for one another without risk. The leaving drinks at Roget's Bar for an assistant producer called Nye gave them the opportunity, at last, to scout the next furlong of emotional terrain and see if it was secure.

Roget's was all that one expected and feared of a media watering hole off the Tottenham Court Road. Underground, overpriced and badly lit, it snared its clientele in a spider's web of wicker and pine: chatter about cinematic dreams and unmade television series hung in the air with the cigarette smoke. It was used by Vision Thing Productions for celebrations too important to be held in the pub, but not important enough to merit a bistro outing. Nye's farewell – a voluntary redundancy masquerading as a "change of pace" – was one such occasion.

Surrounded by workmates whom they spent their days mocking, Nick and Emily had enjoyed the frivolous eye contact and the eroticism of idiolect – the private language of references and shorthand that gave verbal expression to their emerging partnership and excluded all others. At one point, as the absurdly tearful Nye was "saying a few words", Nick whispered a malevolence into Emily's ear which made her laugh with embarrassing vigour – a sign of the coiled expectation within her, as well as the effect of six glasses of Chablis. As the others applauded Nye's speech, distracted and drunk, she allowed her fingers to brush against his. From that moment of contact, and of release, it was a small step to the pavement, to the taxi, to her flat in Wapping and the enveloping loveliness of her scatterbrain bedroom.

Fifteen years had passed since that sultry night of mutual discovery and exploration – of respite and un-conditionality. In truth, it seemed longer, longer ago than his childhood or his birth. It was a memory of hopeful warmth which had no place in his new life.

He felt a cold gust blow down the corridor past the

door of the staffroom where he stood, and his reverie
was broken by the bell – never less than half-deafening
– announcing the beginning of the day's first class. There
was no hiding place now. He bowed his head and made
his way to face the judgement of the fourth year.

"Sir?"

Nick turned to find one of his fourth-year class,
Robby Kavanagh, loping behind him in black shoes
and outlawed white socks. The boy was fifteen and
oppressed by the gangly, pimple-ridden ills of that
age. He seemed not to fit his skin, still less his clothes.
His hair – until recently the curled crop of a diligent
chorister – was now an explosion of tufted highlights.
Robby wanted to look like a rebel, but this was only
his latest act of conformity: he desired the approval of
the tough boys in his class with no less devotion or
surrender than he had previously sought the blessing in
all things of his parents and teachers.

"What is it, Robby?" said Nick. "You should be in
class already."

"I know, sir." Robby looked with mild disgust at his
feet, which were shuffling as if independently. "Only,
there was somebody looking for you."

"Oh, really?" he said. He wondered who was after
him: in the mild paranoia of his hangover, he wondered whether it was a lawyer, dispatched by Emily to
cause maximum embarrassment. "Who was looking
for me?"

"Don't know, sir. A tall guy. Well-dressed and that.
Asked for Mr Atkins." The boy became suddenly
swollen with pride. "I said I'd never heard of you. Told
him to eff off."

Nick sagged. It would do his prospects no good at all if one of his pupils had told Emily's lawyers to eff off. "Why did you do that, Robby? It might have been important."

"Don't know, sir. I just didn't think he should be roaming around asking questions. Thought I'd cover for you, sir." He smiled viciously, his incisors bared with the glee of youthful sadism seizing its opportunity. "Thought you might be in a spot of trouble, sir."

Christ, how embarrassing: to be told by one of your pupils that the law is after you. "Of course I'm not in trouble. Now… Robby." He nodded towards the door of the classroom, from which he could hear the sound of tribal ranting and vacuous chatter. "If you don't mind, I think we'll get on."

The boy loped into the room towards the frenzy of the tribe to which he so badly wanted to belong. As he followed, he heard a whoop of sarcastic delight as Robby's news was received and saluted by the pack. A fifteen-year-old with tertiary acne had already bested him, and it was not even ten o'clock.

* * *

The security system at Topper's gate had grown considerably more elaborate in the past month. Perched on the edge of Blackheath, the enormous white house with its palatial driveway was a magnet to burglars – and Topper was not having any of that. The last break-in had been foiled by Chris, his driver and live-in bodyguard, who had broken many bones – none of them his own – in the course of the encounter. Topper, who abhorred

such incidents for their tawdriness, had vowed that he
would never be placed in such a disagreeable situation
again, and spent more than £50,000 on the new system
with its lasers, closed-circuit screens and panic buttons.

To be admitted to the house it was necessary to
stand squarely in the pool of light triggered by a sensor,
press the button and wait to be cleared by whoever
was monitoring the CCTV inside. On either side of
the gates, Nick noticed, there were new potted shrubs,
questing towards the marbled ledge at the top of the
outside wall. The ironwork was newly painted, too: a
gleaming black that gave away the cheery novelty of
Topper's wealth. His more established neighbours allowed themselves a carefully constrained degree of
shabbiness, signalling that they were beyond worrying
about flaking paint or elderly curtains. Nick found
Topper's gaucheness endearing.

The gate clicked open automatically. He looked up
the paved drive to the door where a silhouetted figure
awaited him under a nightlight. It was Topper's wife,
Gwen.

"Nicko," she said. "You're late."

He walked past the four-wheel drive, the sporty
Mercedes and Topper's Roller. "I know. I'm sorry. I had
to go back and change. Bloody stagecraft. I was covered
in paint and crap." He kissed her on the cheek.

"Bloody stagecraft, eh?" she said, leading him into
the long hall with its spectacular chandelier and cool
tiles. "What's that when it's at home?"

Gwen was three years older than Topper, but could
pass for a much younger woman. Bottle-blonde, St-
Tropez-tanned and barefoot, she wore a cream cashmere

jumper, hipster jeans and a simple string of pearls. Every pore of her skin and sculpted line of her body attested to the expensive ministrations of West London spas: the treatments, pedicures, manicures, face masks, sunbeds, body wraps, algae, mud packs, and all the spells and potions that money could buy from the modern witches in white. Gwen had grown up in New Cross in a tower block, the youngest of five children. Her mother spotted her daughter's effect upon men at an early age and had made it her task to ensure that this talent did not go to waste, masterminding a marriage to a businessman who owned a successful chain of hardware stores and a gaudily extravagant home, fit for child-rearing, in Sundridge Park. The union had lasted five years, but had failed to produce offspring. This had not bothered Gwen unduly, but it had bothered her husband, who considered procreation to be as essential to a normal life as golf. When she discovered he was sleeping with his secretary, she had initiated divorce proceedings to the relief of all concerned.

Topper met her when he was still pursuing his first career, but had found her splendidly indifferent to how he made his living. She knew the score. Like Topper, she had already been round the block, and had the capacity to be truly loving – something which is granted to those who have had youthful romanticism scorched out of them by experience. There were no illusions with Gwen, and few disappointments. She and Topper had met at a nightclub in Beckenham through a mutual friend, and were married in three months. Nick was best man, and gave a speech that began in conventional badinage but quickly betrayed the admiration and affectionate envy he felt. The simplicity of what Topper and Gwen had was a rare and precious thing, and its resilience was no surprise to those who knew them.

"He's downstairs by the pool," she said, nodding towards the open door which led to the staircase. "Reading, I think. Alannah's off tonight, so you'll have to make do with my cooking. Don't you dare grimace, you cheeky sod. It's more than you deserve."

"You're right," Nick said. "I'm not worthy. I'm having one of those days where I expect to end up on a park bench. You know, where if you died and went to heaven, there'd be a cash bar and you'd be skint."

"If you're lucky." She pretended to punch him in the stomach. "Go on, piss off downstairs and get stuck in. I'll call you when the lamb is ready."

"You spoil me."

"I do. Both of you. God knows why." She turned on her heels and headed down the corridor towards the kitchen.

The basement was Topper's domain, his playground and his throne room. Here he relaxed, enjoyed his toys and his books. At one end of the room there was a cluster of sofas and armchair, gathered around an enormous plasma-screen television set into the wall. A kitchen bar and glass-doored fridge separated this area from a swimming pool and a permanently purring Jacuzzi. The far end was dominated by a photographic mural depicting the destruction of the Death Star in *Star Wars*, a film in which Topper invested almost scriptural significance and to whose deepest meanings he devoted many a small hour. The mural was a hallucinogenic disturbance in the sensual tranquility of the room: its lasers, sparks and pulverizing violence hinted at the rough-edged foundations on which the house was truly built.

Topper was not in the room, which meant he was busy in the annex that he had converted into a little cinema. The door to this inner sanctum – with its popcorn machine and four rows of velvet seats, complete with holders for drinks – was part of the mural, suggesting that it was possible to step from the steamy pleasures of the basement into the galactic chaos of X-wings and light sabres. This was not an impression which Topper did anything to discourage, though he was aware that his friends, and Nick especially, regarded the wall as a juvenile monstrosity.

"Nicko!" The door opened and the master of the house emerged in Hawaian shirt and long bathing shorts. He was unshaven, and his hair hung in an ill-disciplined fringe. But, like Gwen, he had the aura of purchased well-being, of subtle transactions shoring up and burnishing his health beyond's Nature's intention. "It's been too long."

Nick walked towards him, his heels clicking on the coping of the pool. "Actually, it hasn't been long enough. Considerably less than twenty hours by my watch."

The two men embraced, as they always did. Topper punched him in the stomach, as he always did, with considerably greater impact than Gwen.

Nick winced. "I *wish* you two would stop doing that. I don't have the solar plexus of a twenty-year-old, you know. And I don't have your girth to dull the pain. Bastard."

Topper patted his own belly as if it were the head of

a firstborn. "Ah, you just can't take it. Just like you can't take your beer. I had to pour you onto the night bus last night. Chris was wetting himself."

"Well, yes. I mean, not all of us have a kung-fu chauffeur to whisk us round town in a Roller, you know."

Topper slipped on his sandals and padded towards the bar. "That's not my point. My point is that, even if you'd got into a chauffeur-driven Roller last night you wouldn't have had a clue what was happening. One sniff of the barmaid's apron and you're a mess, you teachers." He reached into the fridge and took out two beers, flipped off the lids and handed one to Nick. "Here. You may as well get started again. Teacher."

"Don't call me a teacher."

"But you are a teacher, Nicko."

"Yes. But there's no need to rub it in."

"Ah, look. Here's the kung-fu chauffeur. How did it go, Chris?"

Chris was a small man, no more than five foot six, who personified quiet menace. He did so in a way that Nick could not quite define, but about which he was absolutely clear. Nick knew that Chris was indispensable to Topper as guardian and facilitator. He stayed in closed touch with his former special forces regiment – the "Hereford crew", as he called them – and occasionally brought home a dazzling piece of kit for his boss to admire. In Topper's garage was a lock-up that contained sophisticated surveillance equipment and other devices which he referred to only as "little gadgets".

"Oh, it was fine, Tops," Chris said. "Nothing unusual. Some verbals."

"Saw sense, did he?" Topper replied. "Good. Glad that's sorted. You made good time."

Chris shrugged. "Got lucky with the traffic. Anything else you need?"

"Not at all, mate. Get yourself some food and a beer – there's plenty of both in the kitchen. You're a fucking star."

"No worries." Chris turned and ambled off.

"Top bloke, that," said Topper. "No man of business should be without a Chris."

Nick shook his head and smiled. He wondered what form the "discussion" had taken, what the point at issue had been, and what shape Chris's interlocutor was in. It didn't bear thinking about.

Topper fiddled around with a remote control. The pleading vocals and mesmeric Celtic sound of early Waterboys filled the room with incongruous ex-hilaration. A row of fluorescent lights flashed in time to the rhythm of the music beneath the surface of the water, which still rippled from the lazy swim Nick imagined Topper had taken before his arrival. They sat on the loungers facing each other as if in deep con-spiracy.

"I thought you were seeing Aisha this evening," Topper said, swinging his feet onto the footrest. "Was she pissed off about last night?"

"Just a bit." Nick took off his leather jacket and threw it over the back of the lounger. He frowned. "It's hard. We have these snatched conversations at school, which are halfway between a row and making up. There's no time to be a proper couple. But then, I'm not sure either of us wants to be a proper couple."

His friend took a long slug of beer and belched appreciatively.

"Thanks for the listening ear, Tops. You're a real pal."

"Cheers. I try. I really do."

He turned towards the floodlit gigaton carnage of the Death Star and smiled.

Topper's real name was George Healey, but Nick had never called him George to his face, or when describing him to others. They had met when Nick was in the last throes of his unconsummated relationship with the law and drifting by night around London parties and pubs in search of distraction. He was introduced to Topper at a friend's house, and it was only after a lengthy conversation – about the competing merits of the different *Alien* films, the thorny question of Selina Scott's whereabouts and the rising price of season tickets – that Nick had realized that his new acquaintance was a dealer. George Healey was known by friends and enemies as Top Gear – and therefore, in observance of the male law that one nickname must spawn another – as Topper. His boys handled the gear and – in most cases – he himself picked up the money. His clients were all, in his own categorization, "gents": he would not trade with "kids" or "dopes".

He was rarely foxed or bemused by the demands of his perilous occupation. Overweight or not, he could, if need be, move with remarkable speed and more than a hint of physical menace. And Nick had never met a man with a clearer direction and sense of strategy. Though a star pupil at his Kent grammar school, a boy of origins no less humble than Gwen's who seemed destined for academic glory, he had known with a clarity that dismayed his teachers and broke his proud parents' hearts (until he bought them a flat in Tenerife) that university and the honourable grind of a profession were not for him. On one of their earliest nights out, Topper revealed that he would get out of the business as soon as he had enough saved to go into property. It was his dream to own real estate across London and to wallow in semi-retirement in a well-appointed home with a well-appointed woman. He provided a legitimate service, he insisted, met a demand which would never go away, and traded only in substances of the highest quality. It appalled Topper that he had to take measures to keep the police at bay – including, he said with a curled lip, substantial pay-offs to at least one very senior Met officer. He could not understand why the guardians of law and order should bother with an entrepreneur such as himself who would have been more than happy to pay taxes if his earnings had been declarable. Where was the harm? As it was, he was forced unwillingly into the twilight of the criminal milieu. From time to time, he would sport a bruise or a new scar and – very occasionally – something worse. On one occasion, he was hospitalized with two broken ribs; on another, he went missing for a week and returned bloodied, dishevelled and furiously testy. Such misfortunes, Nick rapidly grasped, were not to be explored, investigated or even mentioned if he were to remain Topper's friend. That was part of their unspoken contract. There was a gun in Topper's glove compartment: Nick knew this because he had found it, rummaging for CDs while Topper was paying for petrol. He had felt his stomach turn as he caught a glimpse of the violent netherworld in which his friend did business.

Finally, Topper declared that he would be leaving dealing behind entirely and would sink his considerable savings in bricks and mortar. As his new business flourished, he realized that it had some similarities with the old one. The instincts required, he discovered, were the same, not least because the fashions in postcodes were as fickle and as potentially lucrative as the fashions in proscribed chemicals. The trick was not only to have an intuition as to what was moving up and what was moving down – essential as that was – but to know the limits of that intuition. Five years after he set up shop as a legitimate businessman, Topper was a millionaire many times over.

"What I want to know is why you have to get divorced at all," Topper said. "I mean, can't Emily give it a while, with the trial separation? It's not been that long. Why rush it?"

Nick was stretched out on the lounger nursing his second beer. The first had been only moderately enjoyable, but its successor was banishing his horrendous day and the last symptoms of his hangover. "It's not that she wants to rush it. I think her view is that I have already had my chance and that… well, that it's been over for quite a while. Me and Em, I mean…"

"And what do you think?"

"I think I'll have to have another beer before answering that. Several possibly."

"Evasive, Atkins, evasive. You can't run from me, you know. I understand your circuitry."

"No doubt. It is so pleasant to have a multi-millionaire

drug dealer claiming moral authority over me. My pupils would love it."

"*Retired* dealer, if you don't mind. I'm a respectable property tycoon now, and have been for some time." He clicked the remote control again to skip over an unwanted track. "Which is why you are living rent-free but a stone's throw from your place of work. As I recall."

"Yes, yes. What a philanthropist. You only do it so you can wield even more power over me."

"Of course. It is good for my soul but also good for my ego to have the power to evict you." He drained his bottle. "Most agreeable."

"Yeah, well. Meanwhile, I've got Polly this weekend. Some of it, anyway."

"You know what your problem is, Nick?"

He sat up on his elbows and sighed. "No. What is my problem?"

"You're an emotional bungee-jumper."

"What the fuck are you talking about?"

"You can't help hurling yourself off the precipice even though you know it's going to be terrifying. You've got form on that, to say the least. California dreaming, and all that. And now – I mean, look at you. Half divorced, half in a new relationship, in bits about your daughter. In bits about other stuff, too. I'm amazed you have time to hold down a job."

The light from the pool danced on the ceiling like luminous strands of cotton. Nick savoured this benign assault – the verbal equivalent of the stomach punches favoured by Topper and Gwen – and contemplated an indignant response. "Other stuff, too" – that was below

the belt, and infuriatingly acute. But he did not have
the heart for a quarrel he would surely lose, one that
would certainly exhaust him. "You can talk. When did
you last work nine to five?"

"When did *you*? Everyone knows that teachers
knock off at 3.30 and then go to the pub. And, in any
case, I have earned the right to work a couple of hours
a day at my laptop and spend the rest indulging my
missus, or pottering about in my really rather unique
cinema." Again, the dreamy look of contented early
middle age crept across Topper's features. "I watched
The Empire Strikes Back this afternoon on my own. It
was perfect. Perfect."

"How very intellectual, Tops. No wonder you look
so tired. Whatever next: a seminar on the cinematic
genius of Jean Vigo?"

"Say what you like. I'd rather spend the afternoon
doing that than what you absurdly call 'stagecraft'. You
may ask: what's a grown man doing watching a *Star
Wars* movie on a Friday afternoon? I reply: what's the
point of life if he doesn't? I mean, look at you and
look at me. I have all the trinkets and toys that a man
of our vintage could desire. The handbags and the glad
rags, if you will. A beautiful and devoted wife. A home
of stunning elegance. A black-belt bodyguard who, in
spite of his undoubted fondness for you, would happily
come in here and break both your legs if I told him to.
I work little, and play often. Even if I continue to drink
and smoke, as I fully intend to, my actuarial chances
of a few more decades of this splendour are high. You,
meanwhile…"

Nick's minor torment was curtailed by the arrival of

Gwen, suddenly puncturing the masculine bubble of the den with a look of tolerant disdain.

"You two pissed already?" she called across the pool.

Topper acquired a fresh glow in her presence. "Not yet, my love. But we're working on it. Wouldn't want to disappoint you."

"Your liver, if you still have one, must be like a bloody colander. Don't think I'll nurse you through a transplant."

Her husband chuckled, as he made his way to the door. "Course not. By then you'll have drained Coutts of my hard-earned pennies and moved to Barbados with one of your personal trainers, I hope."

She kissed him. "Count on it. I'm not hanging around to watch you pay the price for your shitty lifestyle. Come on, Nicko. Grub's up."

Over dinner, Nick watched his friends across the varnished mahogany of the dining-room table, which spectrally reflected the shape of their faces in the candle-light. There was room for fifteen settings but the three of them were accustomed to sitting, at the end near the hallway, overlooked by a garish oil painting of Topper and Gwen with their adored collie, Cheese.

So this is where I find domestic bliss, Nick reflected. Not at my own hearth, with my wife and daughter, but here in a retired criminal's ludicrous mansion.

Nick kept up the pretence that he would get a minicab home to Archway, but he knew that they would insist he stay the night. The large bedroom on the second floor – originally called the "Blue Suite" by Gwen – had now become known as "Nicko's Room".

He had a change of clothes in the dresser, a washbag and an adapter for his mobile phone. The last detail, Topper said, proved that he had, to all intents and purposes, moved in. Nick never quite acknowledged this, but he was grateful for the hospitality his friends offered to him so readily. Full of beer, Burgundy and brandy, he did not want to move any further than was absolutely necessary until it was absolutely necessary to do so.

After dinner, Topper went up with Gwen to tuck her in, and Nick walked through the drawing room and into the garden. A cobbled path snaked through the flowerbeds and the lawn to the bungalow, where the upstairs lights showed that Chris was in and still awake. Japanese wisteria clung to a trellis on the back of the house, overlooking a bubbling pond with an Eros fountainhead. At the end of the garden Nick could just make out the gate to the tennis court which Topper had built a year after moving in and never used himself. To construct this sporting white elephant, he had bought a patch of land from a neighbour, at immense cost but without hesitation. The result was a space which had pretensions to the rural. Only the cat's eyes of the windows of nearby houses gave the game away.

The temperature was milder than Nick expected, and he walked out onto the lawn. The moon was almost full, and the same tarnished silver as the schoolboy football trophies on Topper's mantelpiece. He felt a million miles away from the petty indignities of the school now, pleasantly cleansed of its inane rites and hysterical ethos. Even Emily's behaviour, and the demented prospect of litigation between the two of them, could not get to him as he swirled the smoky cognac in its glass. But a deeper sadness leapt from within, grabbing at him.

"What's up?"

He turned to see Topper, glass in hand, standing on the steps down to the grass.

"Oh, nothing. Just taking the air. It's a nice night. And this brandy is especially…"

"No, I actually mean it, Nick."

"Mean what?"

"Something's bugging you. Not the obvious, I think. Not all the Emily stuff, bad as that is. You're… well, you're distracted. Less offensive than usual, for a start. Which is unsettling."

"Is it so obvious?"

"Just a bit."

Nick laughed. "You'd have to get up pretty early in the morning to catch you out, Mr Healey."

"True. I didn't get where I am today by being caught out." He drew imperiously on his cigar, the tip briefly glowing like a firefly with a lifecycle of seconds. "So. What is it?"

Nick turned away again. He suddenly wished he were in bed already, enjoying the lush effect of the alcohol as sleep washed across him in a sunlit tide. Was there any real purpose in dredging it all up, of revisiting poisoned territory they had mapped together a hundred times? "Other stuff, too" – damn his friend for his knowledge and wisdom. There was no escape sometimes.

Topper billowed out a pensive spiral of smoke. "Fuck. Ah, it's *her*. Isn't it? It's her again. Still."

The silence between them was punctuated only by the distant hum of a car on the heath. "Come on."

Nick looked over his shoulder. He contemplated silence, and realized it was no longer an option. "All right. Yes. It's her."

"Why?"

"Do we have to do this?"

"Yeah, I think we do. I think we do."

"It never gets us anywhere".

"Not the point. Just tell me."

He paused and then yielded. "No messages."

"How long this time?"

"Six months. Nothing for six months."

"So? It's been months before."

"So?" Nick growled. "So, you *asked*, all right? For God's sake. Good night." He swept past his host in a flurry of fury and embarrassment.

He was almost in the dining room when he heard Topper mutter to himself in the ruined voice he rarely used. "Christ. That bloody girl. That bloody American."

3

She waited on the bench and looked across the river at St Thomas's and Lambeth Palace. The fiery orb of the sun hung in the east and set the Thames ablaze. It was colder than the day before, unseasonally so, and for once she regretted ignoring her mother's advice to wear a winter coat. Her tweed suit and scarf had been warm enough as she walked from the Tube past the Members' entrance, St Stephen's and the drive leading to Black Rod's Garden. But now, in Victoria Tower Gardens, beneath the trembling trees, the insolent Spring wind was harrying her into a state of goose-bumped irritation. Only the Six Burghers of Calais – Rodin's black bronze cast – kept her company, a tableau of severe introspection on a weathered plinth. She rubbed her hands together and checked her watch. Simmonds would arrive in the next forty-five seconds. Their business would not take long.

"You wanted to see me." He sat down beside her on the raised bench without catching her eye, far enough on the bench from her to maintain the pretence that they were not keeping a rendez-vous.

"Yes. And?…"

"And… he's a mess. Completely unsuitable."

"We knew that. Tell me something I don't know."

Simmonds frowned. She admired his professional caution, while being quite certain that it was one of the characteristics that made him fundamentally different from her and that explained his lack of promotion. Simmonds was one of life's senior NCOs, brilliant at what he did, but constitutionally incapable of even aspiring to the officer class that she had joined so effortlessly. He wore a khaki gabardine, discreet pinstripe suit and well-polished brogues. But it was his body language that signalled the kind of person he was: clenched to the point of immobility, straining with every fibre to avoid the unseemly and to forestall the undesirable. She imagined that his toes were permanently curled in anticipation of some distasteful development or other. Before meeting Simmonds, she had thought the expression "lantern-jawed" a cliché, but it fitted him with uncanny precision. Even as he considered her instruction, his teeth ground together with a ferocity that involved complete cranial commitment. As his nostrils flared, she caught an unwelcome glimpse of stray nasal hair, a hint of the primal chaos that lurked within the fastidious casing that was Simmonds.

"You don't know the extent of his unsuitability. Lives in a world of his own. I can't see how he can possibly do this. It could seriously jeopardize…"

"What does Khayyam say?"

He shrugged as if in partial concession. "Khayyam says that he may be stronger than he looks. Keeps in shape, apparently. Determined when he wants to be."

"And what do you think?"

"Khayyam isn't always right."

"No. Usually, though."

Simmonds did not rise to her bait. "You know my position. I can't see it working."

"We've been through all this before. If there was any other way… But every other way has failed." She thought about lighting a cigarette, and then decided against it. "Does Khayyam say anything else about him?" she asked.

"That he's not ready."

She snorted in frustration. "That's all?"

Simmonds's whole frame dropped a few centimetres in a hydraulic manoeuvre of resignation. "No. Also that he is as ready as he'll ever be. Now or never."

"Right then. Today."

"Today? But…"

"If Khayyam says now or never, then it has to be now. Obviously." She watched a pleasure boat glide by, heading towards Chelsea. "We've delayed long enough as it is. We have to keep in mind the competition."

"You're sure?"

"No. But we don't have a choice." She pulled a tissue out of her handbag and blew her nose. "Do we?"

This time Simmonds did not reply.

* * *

For the second time in twenty-four hours a woman stood in a doorway and told him he was late. But Emily, unlike Gwen, was angry.

"More than an hour. Polly thought you weren't coming. I was beginning to wonder myself."

He smiled and shuffled haplessly. His shoes pinched.

"I'm sorry. I slept in a bit. At Topper's. I got here as fast as I could. In a minicab." The staccato of his apology, he thought, sounded pathetic.

She surveyed him with an expression that suggested anxiety masquerading as disdain. "Well, never mind now. Come in. She's waiting for you, and I want to get to the gym this morning."

She led him into the dark hallway, past the stairs and into the kitchen. After the tiled prairies of Topper's mansion it all seemed woefully cramped. When they had bought the house in Muswell Hill three months into Emily's pregnancy, its sheer scale had exhilarated them. After so many years in flats, wearily habituated to the noise from neighbours, to the sound of footsteps and music from above and below, the prospect of a life on more than one storey had seemed luxurious beyond measure. They decorated a room at a time, Emily stripping the old paper during the day until she grew too big to stand on a stepladder. It was a season of contentment, as they nested and waited for the baby. Her copywriting was earning some extra money and Nick had been promoted at St Benedict's, not yet disenchanted with his third career. For a while, the house had been a shrine to their new rootedness and their hope. The frost had not yet fallen.

Emily wore sweatpants and an old Adidas T-shirt. Her hair was up and she had yet to apply her make-up: without it, she looked vulnerable and burdened. For all that had passed between them, he still admired the shabby splendour of her defiance, the vigour with which she was trying to hold her life together, and him to account. But, as she watched the coffee machine bubble and hiss, and leafed absently through the morning's catch of brown envelopes and flyers, there was no disguising the price she was paying for her public stoicism. It pained him to think how easily he had once been able to console her at such moments. A touch on the back of her hand, a foolish joke, a good omelette. This, as much as the insomniac prowl at two in the morning, was the essence of estrangement. To see the puzzled shadow of past intimacy in the space that has grown between you.

"Is she all right?"

Emily handed him a mug of coffee. He nodded in thanks and waited for her to reply.

She sat down at the table, knocking a section of the *Guardian* onto the floor.

"Shit. Sorry. Yeah, she's okay." She rested her chin on her cupped hands, her fingers playing with her earrings. "Under the circumstances… She asks about it a lot, especially at bedtime."

"What do you say?"

She stiffened. "I say what we agreed. What do you think? That I'll take it out on our daughter? Come on. It's not her fault."

"No, no. I'm sorry. I just – it's not pleasant for me to have to ask. She's my daughter too."

"I think she's just getting her head round the idea that you don't live here any more. All I say is that you're staying in the flat for a while, and try to persuade her that it's exciting because she can stay there too whenever she likes." Emily sipped her black coffee. "At first she thought it was a game, I suppose. Now she's absorbing your absence a bit more. Her friends from school ask

her where you are when they come round, and I think
that hit her quite hard. Before you say anything, I'm not
making a point or winding you up. I'm just answering
your question. Okay?"

The kitchen was as he remembered it, neither aug-
mented nor diminished by his withdrawal from the
house. On the fridge was Emily's list of telephone
numbers, a painted Mother's Day card, and a PTA
letter announcing an Easter school fair. Polly's satchel
hung from the peg behind the door, beside Emily's
denim jacket and an old trench coat he had stopped
wearing but could not quite bring himself to throw
away. On the kitchen surface, among the jars of jam
and peanut butter, the bottles of wine and squash, the
old newspapers and school books, were the detritus of a
child's life and the tracks of a mother a few paces behind,
trying to bring some order to it. A single mother. Two
had become three; and now, without logic or mercy,
three had become two again.

In this, Emily had been the only constant, as wife
and parent: the maypole around which her husband
and child had danced. Polly had arrived, and then, six
years later, her father had left. He had not planned to
do so, and it was only a few weeks after he had moved
out that he had been able to look back and identify for
sure the moment of decision. It was not the night that
he had, quite naturally, followed Emily up to bed and
turned right into the spare room, as if he had been a
guest who had missed the last train after a very pleasant
dinner and had agreed, after a ritual shaking of the head,
to stay with his host. Nor was it the day that he had
woken up and, with no less confidence, packed enough

of his belongings to move out – that had merely been the hour of execution, the sombre completion of a plan hatched long before.

He remembered the moment when that plan had first taken seed: a moment of vile, unsolicited clarity in which a mute sense of decay had suddenly become outspoken and declaratory; a moment when emotional aphasia had become, with sudden horror, articulate. It was a decay that he found impossible to describe to others. He and Emily had not stopped loving each other, he supposed. But the daily supply of simple affection that irrigates the soil of love had somehow drained away over the years, leaving a brittle dust incapable of sustaining life. For months, they had behaved as normally as they could, awkwardly conscious that their relationship was expressing itself in the observation of familiar procedures rather than in anything that resembled honesty. There had been a drift: that was all. They were working harder, or a little harder, and they were sometimes too preoccupied with parenthood to attend to one another. But their jobs and their child were not to blame, convenient as such an explanation might have seemed in subsequent, furious audits. The force pushing them apart was like a barely perceptible current below the feet of a swimmer who turns to shore and realizes he has been carried sideways without knowing it. There was no angry disruption, no lurid outrage or adultery around which their grievance could coalesce, and about which they could complain to their friends over midnight glasses of wine. The decline was visible only in the length of time it took him now to answer her questions; in her occasional stammering on

the phone and his sudden abrasiveness in the morning;
in the sad relief with which each learnt that the other
would be out for the evening; in the unfamiliar tension
which entered the silence between them; in the way
they stopped sharing books and playing music to one
another; in the transformation of the television from
an entertaining source of babble to a welcome means
of defusing their embarrassment. From time to time,
they would stroll arm and arm through the museum
of their relationship, pointing warmly to one exhibit
or another, laughing at a fresh recollection or an an-
ecdote not yet worn through by repetition. But, like
all museums, this was ultimately a place of melancholy,
of badly painted drabness, where the incompatibility
of past and present was made vivid and unambiguous.
The search for reasons was pointless. There were no
reasons. Indeed, that was the problem. The rich pattern
of cause and effect which had once underpinned their
relationship – the knowledge that this led to that, and
that one thing led to another – had faded. Neither
was sure any longer what the other would do next.
The best-known had become strange. The familiar had
become indecipherable. They were frightened of one
another.

Love, rather than loyalty, postponed the moment of
declaration. Love, in this case, was a suburban creature:
closing the curtain on failure, refusing to acknowledge
the tribal emergency in its midst for the rebellion that
it was. Love was slow to recognize the failure of its
authority. Nothing was said until the moment when
Nick knew he must one day leave: and even then almost
nothing. On another evening of halting conversation

and trivial misunderstanding, he had withdrawn to the spare room, which doubled as a study, and pretended to hunch over his marking. He sat in darkness apart from the disc of light cast by the reading lamp on the neglected pages of his pupils' exercise books. Out of the window he could see their neighbours' garden, its deck and the deserted climbing frame, bejewelled in the rain. A burly ginger cat, appalled by every droplet, ran as if on grey, hot coals along the fence towards the door. Nick put his red pen down and wondered if this vista marked the terminus of his journey, a point of shuffling disembarkation and silent defeat. The thought bore down on him like the stone reserved by a village for the gravest sinners against the gods. It consumed him with lassitude and a grief that lacked any prospect of expression. It crowded out all other emotions and made communication of any sort seem quite unthinkable, at least until he had recovered some poise and could resume the mechanistic hypocrisies of his life.

There could not have been a worse moment, then, for the door to edge tentatively open and the light from the landing to flood in on his misery. He turned suddenly in his chair and snapped at her: "What is it *now*?" In a single syllable of emphasis, he gave voice to every gratuitous moment of petty conflict in the months before, every microscopic savagery, every cool frustration felt by either of them. But his sincerity was monstrous. In that moment, he was a stranger not only to his wife, but to himself. And for the first time since he had met her, Emily was truly lost for words. If only she would shout back at him, in love and fury, and heal the wound with righteous anger... If only she would reel them both back to the riverbank, wrenching them from this terrible speechless place… He wanted to hear her cleansing rage, a cry that would throw all the pieces up into the air and bring them back to their rightful place. But she was defeated too. This time, she could muster none of the lusty heroism he had relied upon so often. He watched as the silhouette in the doorway retreated without word or gesture, and the portal onto the outside world from his lair closed once again. He wondered how he had managed to reduce the vivid, angular woman he had met at Vision Thing to the subdued creature who now crept away from him so readily. A long while afterwards, he heard her pad up the stairs once more, the sound of taps from the bathroom, and the shutting of their bedroom door. The familiar creak, which sounded like a noise from another age, made him weep.

"Daddy!" He and Emily turned round as Polly skipped into the kitchen to join them. "Daddy! You're late, Daddy." She hopped onto his knee.

"I know. I'm really sorry, Polly-Wolly." He kissed her forehead. "I slept in like a silly old sleepy-head".

She nodded gravely. "Silly sleepy-head. It's naughty to be late. Miss Williams says if Crispin's late once more, then he and his mummy have got to see the head-mistress."

"Really?" said Nick. "Do you think I should see the headmistress?"

"No!" She giggled. "You're too old to see her. Too old, Daddy."

He pulled her close. The warmth of her small frame made him feel icy and damaged. "That's right, darling.

I am too old for that. Daddy's an old man." Her hair, he noticed, was more like Emily's with each passing week, and had acquired a few plaits: the first sign of sophistication on the innocent canvas of Polly's life. "So. What would you like to do?"

Polly swung from side to side on his knee, her pink socks visible between her jeans and trainers. "Um… Um… I want to stay here with Mummy and show you my new book."

Emily shifted uneasily. "No, Poll. I've got to go out. Do the shopping and stuff. You and Daddy go and get some fresh air and have some fun. If there's time, you can go to his flat and build a tent. That'll be exciting, won't it?" These were not easy words for her to say, he could tell. She was inviting her own child to conspire in the dismantling of their marriage, to accept and even celebrate the new partition in her life. A great tract of no man's land separated Nick and Emily now, barren and dusty, and Polly was its sole inhabitant, playing the distracted hopscotch of the child that has not quite awoken to the horrors of the world. It was not his daughter's sadness that made Nick most guilty, although that was bad enough: it was her desire to remain happy, her dogged resistance to the heretical notion that her parents might cause her real pain.

"Mummy's right," he said. "We can go and see my flat together. Or do you want to go and get pizza? And then we can go and see Grandma." He caught Emily's eye. She smiled with uneasy politeness as if acknowledging an acquaintance on the crowded platform of the underground, eyes meeting across newspapers, across time.

* * *

They emerged from Chalk Farm Tube onto Haverstock Hill, the station spilling out its haul of families, couples in sunglasses and lost tourists puzzling over their guidebooks. In the shade sat a tramp clutching a piece of brown cardboard on which was written: "NO HOME, NO MONEY, NO LOVE". His face was a leathery brown, the sun and the drink having baked and pickled their respective colours into his complexion. His grey strands of hair were ropey with sweat and his eyes blazed with confusion. But the abject tone of supplication on his cardboard was misleading. For some unfathomable reason, the sight of Nick and Polly roused the tramp from his glassy torpor into a fit of apocalyptic rage.

"You!" he bellowed, rising a little on his haunches. "You! Yes, you!"

Nick tried not to flinch, and squeezed Polly's hand in warning when she chuckled.

The human wreckage before them stirred into action. "Do you know who I am? Do you *know* this face? Speak, for the love of God. Course you do."

"That man is funny," said Polly. "He has a suntan. Has he been on holiday?"

"Come on," Nick said. "Just ignore him. Let's go to Grandma's now. We don't want to be late."

"Does he know you, Daddy?"

"No, darling." He leant over and lowered his voice. "He's sick. It's sad."

The tramp's whole upper body shook as though he were invoking mighty scriptural truths. "I am John of Leyden reborn! I am weary of the journey down the crooked path of Mount Tabor. I have come back for the Last Days. Remember this: 'And the stars of heaven fell unto the earth, even as a fig tree casteth her untimely figs, when she is shaken of a mighty wind.' You know those words, don't you? *Don't* you? You know that all is to be laid waste. And you, of *all* people, do nothing. And…"

"Look, here's two quid." Nick said, careful that Polly was out of earshot, handing the man the first coin he could find in his pocket. "Now shut up, all right? I'm with my kid."

"You and I shall meet again in Hell, sir." The tramp smiled, revealing a desecrated cemetery of broken teeth and stumps. "You are burdened with the knowledge, too. I can see. A terrible burden it is. But a worse sin to keep that knowledge to yourself."

Nick sighed deeply. Why was he listening to this psychotic nonsense? "Oh, for Christ's sake. Here's another quid. Try and keep the noise down, eh?"

The old man took the coin with a trembling paw. But his tremor did not diminish his confidence that he was in command of the exchange. "Who is worthy to open the book and to loose the seals thereof? Are *you* worthy?" He laughed dismissively.

Nick took Polly's hand again and marched her onto the pavement, past a down-at-heel hairdressing salon and a newsagent's.

"Why was that man so cross?" she said.

"I don't know, darling. Sometimes people get in muddle, you know? They say things they don't really mean."

Polly was silent for a few moments, her face moving

in and out of the shade. "Daddy. Do you and Mummy say things to each other you don't really mean?"

Without warning – though inevitably, he supposed – the sluice-gate had opened. "Um, I suppose so, yes, Poll. Yes. Everyone says things to each other sometimes which, you know, they wish they hadn't. Even grown-ups and mummies and daddies. They get sad when they do. But it doesn't mean they don't love each other."

Polly licked her fingers, still sticky from the glutinous pizza topping. She considered this argument. "But if they love each other, then why do they say those things in… in the first place?"

"Don't you ever say things to Crispin and then say sorry later?"

"Yes. I said that he was stupid once, so he cried and then I had to say sorry during rest period."

"Well, there you go. You still like Crispin, but you were mean to him by mistake. And then you said sorry."

"Are you going to say sorry to Mummy?"

Nick looked up at the cloudless sky for help. Its un-blemished azure seemed quite godless. There was no help to be had. "Well, darling. It's not really a question of saying sorry to Mummy." He felt his heart crashing insanely against his ribcage. "I love Mummy very much. But sometimes grown-ups disagree about something and they talk about it and they decide, you know, that the best thing is to live in different places and see how that works out. But they still get on and they see each other lots. Just like me and Mummy."

Polly jammed her hands into her hooded sweatshirt. Her voice was barely audible now, and it was only chance that a gap in the sweating traffic allowed Nick to hear her. "Sometimes Mummy cries at night. She thinks I don't know she does, but I do. She waits till very late, and she shuts her door, and then she has a cry. I think she's sad about something." She looked up at Nick. "Maybe you could help Mummy not to be sad, Daddy."

"I am the last person in the world who can help Mummy," he wanted to say. But he could not say those words to his daughter. He turned to her and smiled. "I'll always help Mummy if I can, Poll. Always. I tell you what: I'll ask her why she's sad and then she and I can talk about it together. And then maybe she won't…" He felt a rafter within him cave in, plunging into the pit of his belly, threatening the whole structure with collapse. "Maybe she won't cry so much. What do you think?"

Polly sniffed. She was evidently not impressed. "Did you know what that man was talking about? He said funny things to you."

Yes, he thought, I did know what that man was talking about. I wish I didn't. All those lines from 'Revelation', the book that Tab had favoured for a while as the template of her messages in the *California Literary Review*. Her book of the month. In the first years, she had stuck to Yeats and, occasionally, for the sake of variety, Walt Whitman or Emily Dickinson. The apparently salacious clue, "Emily's Ample, 1, 4", suggested the measurements of an overweight maiden aunt, but, as Nick eventually worked out, it referred to the fourth line of the first verse of Dickinson's 1864 poem 'Ample make this bed': "Excellent and fair."

This followed Tab's coded disclosure that she had been praised rapturously for the quality of her thesis. The combination of self-congratulation and shameless game-playing infuriated him, and he had resolved not to buy the paper again. It would make no difference anyway, he reflected, since the encrypted traffic was defiantly one way. He had stopped writing to her and leaving messages, first at her apartment, then, when she moved, at her parents' homes and, finally, desperately, with the Stanford Alumni Association. She was true to her word, as ever: she did not respond to him, at least not directly. His decision not to indulge her again was firm and angry. He would flush the memory of her from his system and avenge the power she had continued to exercise over him by ignoring the messages she would doubtless continue to send. But his resolve did not last. As the next appointed day approached – there were twenty issues a year – he could feel his will failing, as if her grip on him tightened as the moment approached. It was a strange lunar cycle of the heart, which took him through a punishing spectrum of emotions: hope that there would be a message, despair if there was not, exhilaration when he found her latest communiqué amid the sad, schmaltzy or supposedly steamy personal ads, relief that the thread had not yet broken, the wish sometimes that it would. Nearly every fortnight this lonely rite by the news-stand; nearly every fortnight, the rustle of newsprint, the darting eyes, the quarrelling sensations of captivity and release. From time to time, he felt absurd. But he did not – could not – stop. The craving was as enduring as it was vicious.

Tab's use of 'Revelation' did not last long, but

it confused him deeply. She had never shown the slightest interest in the Bible before, as literature or scripture. Indeed, he could remember her sitting in a San Francisco café on a balmy summer night, angrily denouncing the Episcopalianism of her father's family and the earthier Baptist faith to which her mother still had occasional recourse. In Tab's eyes, all religions, and especially American Christianity, were nothing more than corporate anti-depressants peddled by the powerful to subdue the billions they exploited. Churches, she said, were simply licensed drug dens, fleecing their customers financially and spiritually. Accustomed by now to her political stance, and the bouts of fury that came free with the pitcher of beer, he would have been surprised if she had thought otherwise, and he merely smiled as she announced these views. So the sudden introduction of 'Revelation' to her canon of texts three years after they parted in Santa Cruz caught him off guard. It took him several days of baffled frustration to work out what "Last Book" referred to. But when he did, the code unravelled quickly and straightforwardly: in most cases, each clue was a simple tripartite reference of chapter, verse and word number. Thus, "LB, 21, 1, 6" was the sixth word of the first verse of the twenty-first chapter: "heaven". "LB, 21, 10, 10–14" led him to "a great and high mountain" – a reference, he deduced, to Mount Whitney, which she had showed him in their first months together and which he had loved. What puzzled him about this phase – Tab's "Biblical period" as he later described it to Topper – was that she should be reading this book at all. This, he was sure, said much more about her state of mind than the scraps of information that she communicated in her riddles. The message was unexceptional. But the medium? Well, that was something else. Maybe that was the real message. How would Tab have put it? He was confusing signified and signifier. Through the dark glass of their contact, he strained to see whether she was poring over the ancient ravings of a God-besotted madman out of fear, or out of mischief. He wondered whether her choice was impious or earnest. He wanted to know if she was teasing him, or warning him of horrors to come. Perhaps neither. Perhaps both.

The use of 'Revelation' stopped as abruptly as it had started, like a faddish conversion unpicked in a moment of secular embarrassment. There was no May message at all. And then June came, and with it a communiqué about a week spent in Phoenix. This time Tab used Yeats's 'The Tower' and 'Lapis Lazuli'. Never again had she returned to the Bible. Whatever had drawn her to this text – to the language of Apocalypse, Judgement and the punishment of sin – had either passed or had been submerged once more in her soul. The scriptural interlude was not repeated. The day of reckoning was postponed.

Topper had never met Tab, but he hated her. When Nick showed him a photograph, he acknowledged her beauty as politely as he could – "Yes. Very nice. French?" – and drew on his pint with frosty indifference, to make clear that he had no more to say. Topper approved of Emily, even if the feeling was only weakly reciprocated. He saw in her what Nick had seen in her in their first weeks together at Vision Thing: an honesty and an intelligence that were singular. Emily could not reconcile herself to Topper's line of work, and feared that his influence over Nick would lead him into danger. But she recognized in him a core of wisdom, and a love for Nick to which she could not reasonably object: somehow, and absurdly, the scarred drug dealer in the two-sizes-too-small leather jacket brought out the best in her wayward lover. She rarely intruded on the two men's evenings together and, when she did, her conversations with Topper were stiff and unyielding. But Topper did not mind. He did all that he could to steer Nick towards marriage and domesticity with Emily. As a corollary, he did his best to purge his friend of his old obsession, ashamed on his behalf for his furtive subjugation, embarrassed to see Nick in thrall to a ghostly memory preserved in ridiculous classified ads. He understood the strength of feeling that had passed between Nick and Tab. He also grasped how cunningly chosen was her method of communication; how seductive Nick found the literary game, how select it made him feel. But Topper thought the consequences of this seductiveness were lethal, as well as silly. It preserved imbalance in a life where there was now at least a chance of harmony. Which, in Topper's book, was fucking stupid.

The night before Nick married Emily, Topper took him out for a meal and pleaded with him to cut the cord. Years had passed, he said, and it was time to forget about Tab. He owed it to his wife-to-be to consign his Californian past to the attic of his memory, and abandon the pretence that it could be kept alive in the pages of the *California Literary Review*. It was all part of growing up – wasn't it? Nick had looked at him with an expression of affliction and powerlessness which Topper found astonishing. He shook his head.

"No, Tops," he said quietly.

"Why not? It's time for a clean break, isn't it? On this night, of all nights."

Nick shrugged. "I know what you're saying. You're generally right, and you were certainly right about Emily, and getting my act together."

"Well, then."

"You see, it's hard to explain. I know it's juvenile and all that. It's not something I tell people. Ashamed, I suppose. A bit, anyway. But it reminds me of something I don't want to lose."

"What does it remind you of? Some golden age when you were a lovestruck prat, with no money, spouting poetry? Great. I'll have some of that."

"I don't have any money now. And no: it's more to do with… I don't know. It's to do with things being… it's about looking forward to things. You know, *possibilities*. Being in conspiracy with somebody. Stuff like that. I don't really want to let go of it, to be honest."

"Yeah, yeah. But, in case you hadn't noticed, you are now of voting age, Nicko. You can go to an 18 film *all on your own*, you know? You don't have to do things like this any more."

"What can I say? You've skewered me. I… this is part of me."

"No, it isn't. It's part of someone else. Someone else who is, frankly, crazy."

"Crazy? Why…"

"It's *crazy* to be spending hundreds of bucks on ads in a paper years after you had a fling with someone on the other side of the world. What does she hope to achieve? How does she know you read them?"

"I left phone messages for a while."

"Yeah, yeah. Back then. You were pining. Fair dos. But now? For all she knows, you're dead, moved away. Turned gay. Had five children. Who knows? The woman's a menace. She's psychotic."

"I wouldn't go that far."

"No, because you're almost as bad. *Co-dependent* is the word, I believe. I tell you…" He lowered his voice. "Some of my clients are pretty needy, if you know what I mean. They *need* what I supply, so to speak. But you? You're worse than the lot of them. This is beyond chemical. It's mental. This is worse than any habit I've ever catered for. You're getting *married* tomorrow, Nick. For fuck's sake."

"I love Emily."

"Glad to hear it. What does she think about all this?"

"Oh, Christ, she doesn't know a thing."

"What, none of it?"

"No. Well, she knows one of my ex-girlfriends was American. But that's it."

"What? She has no idea about all the *California Literary Review* rubbish? The mad codes and Yeats, and all that garbage?"

"No. Of course not."

"You really are mad."

"Probably. But I'm staying that way. So, get used to it." He raised his glass. "Cheers."

After that night, Topper had resigned himself to the intractability of Nick's position, but remained determined to manage his friend's obsession, to contain it and to restrain him from doing anything that would jeopardize the fledgling marriage. He agreed that he would no longer criticize Nick for his monthly pilgrimage to the nearest newsagent that stocked the *California Literary Review*, or mock his frowning preoccupation with the latest riddle. Nick, in his turn, promised not to speak to anyone else about Tab and her messages, and never again to try to contact her directly himself. The spectral presence of Tab Bradley was the only point of contention between the two men.

Polly skipped along the pavement, her feet plotting an intricately choreographed pattern, with rules for cracks, tufts of grass, litter and every kind of concrete junction. His mother's house was ten minutes from the station, five of them on Haverstock Hill. It was a walk he had completed on thousands of occasions, most of them when his father was still alive. He knew every detail of the route, every stained brick, every broken pane of glass, every asymmetry in the street signs and church notice board. He knew who had moved out of each house, and who had moved in. Whose dog had died, whose cat had been run over. Which record shop had become a convenience store, which post office had closed. He knew few names, but he was finely acquainted with the latticework of fortune, feeling and incident that made up the neighbourhood in which he had grown up. He could hear the listless stone beneath him muttering to itself, repeating the sepia mantras of an earlier generation. In the glare of the sun and with his child at his side, he felt that he was going back into the central cortex of his existence, the place where the fundamental decisions had been taken by himself and by others. In each street, around each corner, there was a little depth-charge of memory, the shock waves coursing through his legs and into his soul.

The house was absurdly large for a widow, four sprawling floors of cavernous rooms, and an attic which still housed his father's library: 4,000 volumes arranged by subject and alphabetically as if for public use. Nick's mother almost never ventured up there, although her cleaner, Mary, dusted down the shelves once a week as though a new librarian were expected any day to install himself at the small wooden table in the corner, with its electric fan and old Remington typewriter, and resume accessions. There were five bedrooms, one of which was kept for Nick, who had not stayed overnight with his mother for several years. Another, on the second floor, was known as the Spare Room – as if all the others were occupied – and had an en-suite bathroom, with clean towels and an excessive selection of colognes. Nick had often tried to persuade his mother to sell up and move into a smaller property, or to rent out the old family home. But she enjoyed its scale, as well as its familiarity. She and her husband had bought it with the intention of having at least four children, wondering if it would be large enough. But Nick had been an only child, the phantom siblings refusing with curled lips and silent tantrums to come into the world and fill the space allotted to them. Now, four decades later, his mother relished the empty spaces and steep stairwells, loving the fact that she could get lost, even from herself, in rooms with no purpose. There had been a time when every alcove had a function or a prospective function, when every square foot had been assigned a role, either in the present or in a fecund future. Having raised a child, but only one, and buried her husband, she could luxuriate in the purposelessness of the house, its irrationality and tumbledown indifference to the strategies and frenzies of the outside world.

She was waiting for them at the top of the steps, her arms stretched out in anticipation of Polly's jubilant embrace. Each time Nick saw his mother, he felt the same surge of deep love for her, and bottomless shame for his shortcomings. She knew him like the back of her hand, and read his moods without effort or compunction. Although she had never imposed ambitions upon him, her devotion humbled him and made him feel that his achievements, whether disappointing to her or not, were a mismatch in the cosmic scheme: that his performance in life had not rewarded his parents for the love they'd granted him. But did it really work that way? Was parental neglect punished and attentiveness given its due? Would his betrayal of Polly spawn cruel failure or undaunted success?

His mother and her granddaughter were kissing each other competitively and laughing at the contest. Polly hung from her neck, her legs curled round her waist with the trainers digging into her grandmother's navy-blue cardigan. He paused at the gate to let them enjoy this moment of uncontaminated excitement. Polly turned to him in glee.

"Daddy! Look!" She pointed theatrically at her grandmother's head. He squinted to make sure he was right, and made his way up the stairs.

"Is that dye in your hair, Mum?" He leant down and

kissed her on the cheek. There was indeed a purple streak in the respectable and otherwise uniform grey. She flushed a little, pleased that they were intrigued, but not quite sure of herself.

"Well, yes," she said, looking at him with an expression that reminded him of childhood arguments he could never win. "And what of it? Am I supposed to do my knitting and play bingo quietly while your generation wrecks the world?"

"Oh Christ, Mum, save it. We're not even inside yet."

"Grandma," Polly said, pulling on her collar. "I have a new book. It's about a witch who makes trees come to life with her wand. And then she meets a girl called Lola and they blow up a house. Can we read it?"

"Of course we can, darling. We can read it while your Daddy is doing some chores for me. Come in and I'll get you some juice."

"I want Coke."

"Polly, be polite," said Nick.

"Well, let's see what we have in the fridge, shall we?"

His mother led them through the hall, which was gloomy after the bright mid-afternoon sunshine. Though it was twenty years since his death, Nick still felt his father's presence keenly as he entered the house: he remembered the sound of his key in the door, his masculine aroma, his weariness after a long day at the office. For a man who had hoped to spend his best years as a concert cellist, a career in administration – even in the world of music – was trying, and Nick was sure that the dissatisfactions of work had contributed to his

father's early death. But he had always found time at the
end of the day for his son, time to listen to his breathless
stories of the day, the triumphs and ordeals. The David
Roberts prints – of Luxor, Cairo and Baalbec – still
hung in the hall as they had three decades ago, when he
had delivered these earnest monologues to his father.
Only the rug – worn through by the traipsing of a
son – had been replaced. Nick wondered what that
kneeling child would have made of the man he had
grown up to be, and the half-parent he was becoming.
He wondered what his younger self would say to Polly,
what foreknowledge of the failures to come he might
whisper to her in a moment of sad comradeship. Would
she nod and smile, or look in broken incomprehension
at the fresh-eyed simulacrum of her father as a child?

They followed his mother down two short flights of
stairs to the basement kitchen and den, where she spent
most of her time. It was a bright, airy room, leading to
the long, overgrown garden. Nick could smell the cakes
that she liked to bake for Polly, and freshly brewed tea.
Their visits were something his mother treasured, and
her delight in her granddaughter was limitless. She
had hoped for more grandchildren, but was growing
reconciled to the fact that Polly was going to be, like
Nick before her, the only one. And that, in the end, was
enough. It was enough for Maggie Atkins to see that
something radiant and undamaged would long survive
her, and that her errors in bringing up her son, such as
they were, had not disrupted the forward passage of life.
She would die, decay into dust and be forgotten, or so
she said. But Polly and her children would inherit the
world, and save it from the terrible damage inflicted by

its present custodians. When her husband had died alone on an empty train, to be found late at night by a guard turfing out drunks, Maggie had felt hope flee from her. It was not right that William Atkins, her sad, loping lion of a husband, should die in this way. It was wrong that she had not been at his side to comfort him and thank him, and caress his cheek as his soul flexed, sighed and departed. It made a mockery of all that preceded it, and left her panic-stricken by an enveloping emptiness whose coming she had not remotely expected. But Polly – pulled into the world with forceps as rudely as her grandfather had been ejected from it – had filled the long-suffered void.

"So, you two, sit down and I'll get the tea." She walked over to the oven, which was warming the cakes. "Look, Polly. I made you flapjacks."

"Yum," she said, settling down at the table. "Thanks, Granny. Did you make them today?"

"Just now, love. Are you hungry?"

"We had pizza. But I'm *still* hungry."

She turned to Nick. "What about you?"

"Maybe later, Mum. I want to hear about your hair. Are you courting or something?"

This made her laugh. She poured two mugs of tea, and opened a can of Coke for Polly. "Actually, no. Funnily enough. But I… well, I was just thinking how *boring* I was getting. I mean, I looked in the mirror and I thought, 'For God's sake, I look about a *hundred*!' I mean, I accept that, for some reason I'm not quite sure about, you have to start wearing cardies when you're over sixty and take lots of pills, and your ankles hurt. Oh, and we're meant to discuss educational cruises."

"And read books with plastic covers."

"Well, yes. But I'm not exactly on my last legs, am I?"

"No, Mum. Who said you were?"

"The mirror, frankly. I took one look at myself and thought it was time I ordered one of those environmentally friendly cardboard coffins and just put it here in the kitchen ready for me to fall into at the appropriate moment. Which rather pissed me off – close your ears, Polly. So I went down to the chemist's and got myself a bagful of hair stuff. Amazing what you can get now. And this was the first thing I used."

"And the last, I hope."

She regarded him with shrivelling contempt. "That is *so* typical of you and your appalling generation."

"Here we go. How can one innocent remark about a hair product possibly be a symptom of generational decline, Mum?"

"Well, isn't it? You can't even cope with a streak of funny hair. It's hilarious how repressed you are. I mean, you're not even *Thatcherites*." She said the word with the same italicized recoil with which she would have said *paedophiles*. "No, don't interrupt. At least the Wicked Witch and her lot did something, evil and destructive as it was. You could *respect* them. But your lot... well, where to start? I mean, you're all so conservative it isn't true. You agonize about your pensions, and your cars, and your holidays, and school league tables, and you have *targets* for everything. Completely mysterious. And the politicians you vote for are all the same and, frankly, the whole planet is falling to pieces all around you, and none of you is doing a bloody thing about it. Sorry, Polly."

"Finished?"

"Just getting started." She sipped her tea in exultant satisfaction. Polly blew bubbles in her Coke, gleefully conscious that her father was trapped between two generations in cahoots.

"So would you respect me if I dyed my hair?"

"I would probably keel over and die from shock. The most rebellious thing you've ever done is to climb over your college wall after curfew."

"Harsh, but fair. You see what a hard time Grandma gives me, Poll?"

Polly shook her head. "Grandma is right, Daddy. You should dye your hair too."

"Trouble is, I'm a teacher. I don't think Mr Frobisher would employ me if I tried to teach English at a fee-paying school with a purple streak in my hair."

"No," his mother said. "But look: the whole point of that con shop masquerading as a seat of learning is to sell a 1950s morality at 21st-century prices. Your father and I sent you to a comp, and you still got into Cambridge. These days, every sucker round here wastes half his salary on sending his kids to a place where they can wear a boater and a blazer. Not exactly progress, is it?"

"Not sure about the boater, Mum. And anyway, the reason I got into Cambridge was that you and Dad were completely middle class, and taught me loads of stuff on the sly at home. I seem to remember someone in this room promising me five pounds if I could read *War and Peace* in a week. And taking me to see *Twelfth Night* at the Barbican because you thought my English teacher was useless. Or is that a *Thatcherite* memory?"

She waved away this argument. "Oh, shush. When you get to my age, it is truly astonishing to see that the world is not only not getting better, but actually moving *backwards*."

"Grandma," said Polly, suddenly restless. "Can I go and see the frogs?"

"Course you can, love. There's some spawn, too, if you look carefully. Don't fall in, will you? I don't want to have to dive in. My purple will run."

Polly shook her head and dashed out, grabbing a flapjack on the way.

Maggie Atkins enjoyed these occasional outbursts very much. It was true that she regarded Nick's generation as pitiful in every way that counted, and her theory that progress had ground to a halt under its auspices was one she had aired in the past with no less relish. But her objective was as much to remind herself of a time when she was more vigorous as to tease her son. As Maggie Dixon, before she had stopped work and started to use her married name, she had enjoyed a brief moment of minor celebrity in the journalistic world for her reporting skills – and even more for the splendour of her legs and obliging readiness to show them off. Although her marriage to a mild young cellist was the occasion of some surprise and much sadness in the pubs of Fleet Street, William Atkins had soon been accepted by her circle as an affable and undoubtedly intelligent young man, whose high seriousness concealed a wry sense of humour and a considerable reserve of charm. He knew about all sorts of music, too, and impressed her colleagues by announcing the precocious talent of a new band called The Beatles. The couple's supper parties became legendary: Maggie would cook a great stew and invite twenty people to sit at the table and on the floor, drinking wine and smoking until it was light and she made them all morning coffee. As the decade passed and grew ripe, the guests started to bring joints and other substances, but never persuaded Maggie and William to join in. Their pleasure was to set the stage, to put the props in place and to stand back a little and watch the hacks and the musicians mingle, feast, couple and disperse. Maggie always said that she remembered that time as somehow paisley, a rich and messy blend of colours and shapes.

It was not, in her memory, a time of political revolution, but of something much stranger. And this was how she explained it to her son when he was old enough to ask: it was a moment when, for the first and perhaps only time in history, it seemed that the purpose of life was not necessarily to worry, not exclusively to fret and fend off fear. This was odd, when you thought about it, because she and her friends had lived in the shadow of the mushroom cloud, and in the knowledge that everything might be destroyed utterly by the caprice of two men on opposite sides of the world. But somehow that was not the central fact of Maggie's life, or of anyone else's that she knew. Anxieties and crises came, but they came as impostors. In those days, it seemed to her that, when the final brush stroke was applied, the unsuspected image might, after all, be that of a sunrise. That was all.

Nick filled their mugs, and they sat in silence for a while. A fly buzzed around the uncovered cakes, pursuing crazed circles before settling by the sink.

"You're looking tired," she said, finally.

"Well, I suppose I am."

"Living alone *is* tiring. I still find that, anyway, after all these years. I was definitely less exhausted when Dad was alive."

He nodded. "It's no liberation, that's for sure. I wish it hadn't turned out this way. The flat is fine, you know? Topper and Gwen keep an eye on me. I have a lot to do at school."

"Yes, but that's not enough, is it? I mean, it's no way to live."

He clasped his hands on the table. "I don't know yet, Mum. I did what I felt I had to do. Leaving, I mean. It didn't feel right any more, for some reason. We'll just have to see where things are heading."

"And Emily?"

"No change, really. I reckon she means to go through with it, though. I think there was a lawyer looking for me at school yesterday, would you believe? I imagine he was going to serve me with divorce papers."

"At school? That's a bit much. Is she that angry?"

"I didn't ask her about it this morning. She's pretty cross. I mean… I'm no saint, without going into the details."

His mother rubbed her finger across her forehead and winced. "Yes. Well. I don't really want to know the details, to be honest. I just want you all to be okay. I worry about Polly a lot."

He sighed. "Me too. How do you think I feel? It's terrible for her. But we are where we are. She is going to have to get used to the way things are now, I think. And Em and I are going to have to get used to it too. If only for Poll's sake."

The phone rang, and his mother got up to answer it. She whooped in delight – "Nora! My darling!" – when she discovered that it was her oldest friend, now living in Boston and, it quickly became clear, planning one of her occasional visits to London. This pleased Nick. Nora would stay in the Spare Room for a week. She and his mother would go to a play or two, perhaps the opera, and have pub lunches together, drinking halves of shandy and reading sections of the newspaper to one another. On the last day, they would intend to go to the Royal Academy and end up having a very long, very boozy lunch at a bistro in Mayfair, at which Nora would reveal, through stagy tears, the details of her latest infidelity, and her latest plan to leave her third husband, universally known as A.J. Maggie knew that Nora would not leave A.J. and, in recent years, she had even come to doubt the authenticity of Nora's claims to adultery. But she adored the intrigue and her friend's zestful wickedness. The advent of Nora's arrival was good news.

Maggie replaced the phone, sighed happily and busied herself with something by the sink. She began to hum, a tune which he quickly recognized but could not place.

"What is that?"

"What is what?"

"That."

She turned to him. "It's a dishwashing brush, darling. They give one to every woman when she gets married. And, I imagine, every male divorcee. Yours is probably in the post. Or maybe the lawyer was going to deliver it to you by hand at school."

"Try not to talk bollocks, Mum. I mean that tune. The one you were humming."

"Oh, that. It was… well, it was 'Little Boxes', I think. Yes. Do you remember that? Dad liked that one. Although it was me who got him into Pete Seeger in the first place, funnily enough. Usually it was the other way round. I don't think I even have it any more. I gave away most of those records. Even the Bob Dylan."

"What are the words?"

"The words? To that song? Oh, God. I'm embarrassed now. I never could remember lyrics that well. How does it start?" She half-sang: " 'Little boxes, on the hillside, little boxes made of ticky-tacky, little boxes, little boxes, little boxes all the same.' Something like that, I think."

"I remember," he said. "What's that line? 'And the children go to high school, and then to university, and they all have little boxes, little boxes all the same.' That's it. God, it's years since I sang that."

She sat down and patted his hand. "You used to sing it with Dad."

"I did. I did. Funny that it should come into your head now." He smiled weakly.

"Yes," Maggie said. "Odd. I don't know why these things sneak up on you. I found myself singing 'Feelin' Groovy' in its entirety in the post office the other day. Came as a bit of a shock to Mr Singh, I can tell you. All that stuff about kicking down the cobblestones and saying hello to lamp posts… I don't think Mr Singh knows very much Simon and Garfunkel. And what with my new hair…"

"I remember wondering what that song meant when I was small," Nick said. "The Pete Seeger, I mean. I couldn't figure it out. I just thought it was a nursery rhyme, really. Just nonsense. And now you spell it out… well, it was a warning, wasn't it?" He ran his fingers through his hair in a gesture that his mother knew indicated agitation. "It's the world of compulsory suburbia you lot – I mean you and Dad and your friends – well, you assumed you were leaving behind, when in fact it was the world ahead. Yours was the last gasp. I mean, let's be brutally honest. Look at me: I ended up in a little box, didn't I? Just went with the flow, did what everyone else does. Before you know it, you're thirty, with a mortgage and a kid. Even saying that makes me sound such a cliché. And the truth is: it didn't do me any good, or anyone else. I wasn't very good at all that. Was I?"

For once, his mother had no ready reply. It was a while before she answered, and her voice was different: quieter and gentler. "I wasn't thinking of you, love. It was… it's just a song."

Outside, Polly shouted to them that she had, at last, spotted a frog.

* * *

It was almost eight o'clock by the time he got back to Archway Road. On this occasion, his notional weekend with Polly was going to be no such thing: only a few hours, in fact. In the morning, she was going for a day on the river with Crispin and his parents, and Emily wanted her home for bed that night. So his crazy traversing of north London – the itineration of a life in disrepair – concluded with a final shuttle from Chalk

Farm to Muswell Hill, and now back to the fringes of
Highgate Village, and the final melancholic quarter of
an hour which took him from Archway Tube to his
flat. An evening dust had settled on the road, which
opened up before him, a deformed grey limb stretching
down towards the pit of London. The expensive glades
of the village, through which he rode every working
day, seemed to be closed to him now. The tallest trees
stood sentry, reserving the right to deny access to those
who impertinently strayed into the grove. As he walked
down the hill, past the hardware stores and bus stops, he
remembered Polly's pavement tap dance, his mother's
hair and Emily's glacial smile. The smile of his betrayed
wife, the smile he deserved.

He reached the end of his road. It was not too late
to go for a run on the path by the old railway cutting,
to the tunnel and back, enough to make him sweat
off some of the indulgences of the previous forty-eight
hours and to soak up the tension of his encounters
with Emily. No, it was not too late. But, by the same
token, it was not too early to go to the pub.

The Wykehamist was a barn of a place, a Victorian
palace which had been essentially unaltered by two
world wars, a cold one, and the passing of the mil-
lennium. These pulverizing forces had barely scratched
this awesome temple consecrated to man's desire for
intoxication. And what, in truth, had changed in a
century and half? True, the beer had become more
gaseous and more expensive. The pub's ugly panelled
walls were obscured now by vast video screens, on
which the punters watched racing, American football,
table tennis from Taiwan – anything, really. Pulsating

music boomed from speakers high above the bobbing heads of lone drinkers. But the chandeliers were the same as the day the Wykehamist had opened. So too was the odour of loose tobacco and white spirit. The oil portrait of Bishop William of Wykeham, the obscure inspiration for the pub's foundation, still hung behind the bar, now nestling amid the glowing optics of what Topper called "horror liqueurs". And, as on the day it first threw its doors open to the thirsty men of north London, drinkers could still hide in its many corners and nooks and sit, slack-jawed, leaning against the walls, whispering to themselves as the light from outside faded once more. Nick liked to hide here.

The barman was a grizzled Irishman of indeterminate age − anything between twenty-five and forty, it was hard to tell − who had already reached nodding terms with his new patron. Nick knew instinctively that this was an honour to be taken seriously and squandered at his peril. He would not make the mistake of abusing it by being over-familiar: the usual error of the middle class when admitted to a place governed by proletarian rules. He guessed that the Wykehamist was a place where it took many years to achieve the status of a regular, where it was wise not to make idle conversation, where it was a good idea not to ask questions about the old man from Cork who brought round a black hat at closing time, soliciting loose change.

Nick ordered a pint of Guinness, paid and went to sit next to the empty fireplace. As he sipped the dark liquid, welcoming its warm consolations in his belly, he wondered whether he was equal to an inventory of his day. No, probably not. What was the point of tracing the arc from a moderate hangover in Blackheath to a solitary drink in an Irish pub on the fringes of Highgate? He had criss-crossed London, bouncing from the safety of Topper's mansion to the thick emotion of the deserted marital home, to the gallery of memories that was his mother's house, and now back to his own little refuge. The Guinness slipped down. He ordered another.

An hour passed before he left the pub. He was pleasantly restored to a state of fragile equilibrium, and he did not want to risk it by drinking even more and heading towards the unpredictable swampland of euphoria and despair. It was reassuring, too, to select restraint occasionally, to go to bed knowing what the morning would bring, and not dreading it. He would not spend this Sunday with Polly. But perhaps he might redeem himself a little with Aisha? Yes, that was it. He would cook himself some pasta and maybe have a glass of wine. Then, he would call Aisha.

The clasp of the hand on his shoulder was as shocking as a blow, with the difference that the impact was not over in an instant. He felt himself start, and then resist, and then yield, his body reflexively recognizing a force it was wise not to fight. He stifled a cry for help. There was no further violence, only the sensation of an unbreakable lock on his shoulder. Then a voice – of quiet, sympathetic authority, menacing only in the sense that it presumed total compliance.

"Sorry about that," it said. "Now, please, get into the car."

As dislocated as this oddly polite command was, it at least made clear to Nick that he was not about to be mugged. He felt a surge of indignation wrestle with the nausea and consuming fear. He fought against the grip, with negligible success.

"For *Christ's* sake," Nick hissed. "What is this? Take your hands off me. Who are you?"

"If you'll just come with me to the vehicle, sir," the voice continued, "we can explain everything to you. And we can keep the fuss to a minimum."

Fuss: it seemed a risibly inadequate word for what was happening. The grip loosened sufficiently to allow Nick to spin round. The man was tall and military in bearing, his suit definitely a camouflage for some darker purpose. He smiled, utterly at ease with the impunity with which he evidently conducted his affairs. There was no weapon, no baying accomplice. As he walked towards the vehicle, Nick realized that his shoulder would bear an ugly bruise. The man knew how to apply pressure and how to leave his mark.

Suddenly, a demented thought dawned on him. Good God, no. Could she really be so angry with him?

"You were at school yesterday, weren't you?"

"No, sir, I wasn't."

"Yes, you were. Listen, I know you're employed by my wife. This really isn't necessary." He was embarrassed as he heard his terrified babble. "I told Emily that I'm willing to talk about everything. I'm not trying to evade my responsibilities. For Christ's sake. You can see where I live. I've left her the house. I just spent the day with our daughter. She doesn't *need* to do this. It's senseless."

The man sighed, as if some gloomy suspicion had just been justified. "I don't work for your wife, sir. Now – *please* – step into the car."

As vile as Nick's deduction had been, it was at least

logical. Now logic had deserted him, too. There was nothing left to cling to: this was not a mugging, nor the terrible vengeance of a wife maddened with rage. Only seconds before, he had been finishing a quiet pint in his local. Now the car door opened, and he felt a small but insistent shove at his elbow as the man made his expectations clear. Nick could see no means of escape now, nobody to shout to for help. The trap had snapped shut. He clambered in awkwardly, his face bathed in sweat.

On the back seat sat a small, elegantly dressed woman. She smiled at him, and nodded to the man to shut the door.

"Good evening, Mr Atkins. I am sorry about all this but you'll understand what's going on very shortly. You are in no danger from us. Please be as calm as you can so that we don't have to restrain you." She looked out of the side window. A young couple in matching shell suits walked past hand in hand, a strange reminder of the world as it had been a minute before. The man was in the driver's seat now, and turned the engine on. He caught the woman's eye in the rear-view mirror.

"All right," she said. "Let's go, Simmonds."

4

The panic, when it came, was all-encompassing. For a few seconds – seconds in which his instincts were dulled by the terrifying strangeness of his predicament, the stillness within the car – he did nothing. But then the adrenal glands began to do their work, and his body burst into violent life, every cell straining madly towards flight, the sap of fear coursing hectically through him. He began to kick the back of the driver's seat with the viciousness of a thwarted child, swearing mindlessly and pulling at every handle and switch on his door. He thought his tendons would snap, his bones splinter, the veins on his forehead burst. Only when the car screeched to a halt did he remember his earlier recognition that all this was pointless, that he was, for no clear reason, absolutely at the mercy of these people.

The astonishing blast of Simmonds's fist in his face – the terrific precision of the blow – and the vista of red spots which exploded before his eyes was as brutal a demonstration of this fact as he could imagine. He slumped against the window, his cheek numb from the awesome blow. He felt his shirt being rolled up and the scratch of a needle. Then, a foetal warmth filled him, his skeleton melted within him, and he slipped under.

When he awoke, he was surprised to find that he was not restrained, except by a seat belt. He blinked, wondering how long he had been unconscious. He began to speak, but the woman put her finger to her lips.

"Don't try just yet," she said. "It takes a while to wear off. You were only out for a quarter of an hour, but you'll find that your words are a bit slurred for a little while. A bit unsteady on your feet for an hour or so, probably. I imagine your cheek will hurt a bit, too. We can give you something for that in due course."

She was bird-like, an avine creature perched decorously on the back seat. Not in a way that could honestly be called attractive, but compelling to behold. Her hair was a non-descript colour – mousy, his mother would have said, with a sniff – and her clothes were beyond smart in their desexualized plainness. She wore plenty of make-up, but the effect was to keep male interest at bay rather than to draw it close. It was a mask of deterrence, not a soft-lipped whisper of promise. And she was small. That was what struck him most powerfully. As she looked directly ahead, as though she were alone on the seat, he could see that she was not only short, but slight, bonily framed. Her size might have made her timid, but he could see instantly that it had done precisely the opposite.

It was clear that there was no point trying to work out where they were heading, if anywhere. Simmonds did not drive in a way that Nick found recognizable. He was neither cautious nor reckless; and yet the route that they were following could not possibly be described as normal. They would drive round a block in a residential area twice, Simmonds checking his mirrors – there were three inside the car alone – with the intensity of a learner. His vigilance was epic, all-consuming: it defined him, Nick realized. The car whirled and turned balletically. Its prime purpose was not motion, but evasion. Simmonds did not want to travel from A to B. He wanted to avoid them both, and every other letter of the alphabet.

"All right, now listen," the woman said. "There are things which I need to discuss with you, Mr Atkins. I fully understand that you are alarmed, and disoriented. But I really need to know from the up that you're not going to try to do what you did when you got into the car. Do you understand?"

Nick pondered this gambit and wondered whether it was wise to say anything. "Are you arresting me?"

She turned to him, genuinely amused. "Arresting you? God, no. You've obviously never been arrested if you think this is what it is like."

His lips felt rusty from what he assumed must be bleeding from the punch. The roots of his front teeth still hummed painfully. "I have, actually. Long time ago."

"Ah, yes. When you were at Cambridge. What did you do?"

This throwaway display of knowledge was evidently calculated to unnerve him. Fear curled through the ligaments and discs of his back. "I don't... Look," he said, "who the hell are you?" His cheek was beginning to hurt badly. There was swelling, too. "If you're not arresting me, what are you doing?"

"There is a technical legal term for this, but to be

honest I won't insult you by using it. It prevents your lawyers – if you have any – from suing us, or from compelling anything like a court appearance should you subsequently file a complaint. I hope you won't, to be honest, but we have to have these safeguards in place, even in a case such as this where we're actually protecting the individual."

Nick had felt many emotions and unanswered needs in the long day since he had left Topper's house. But he had not suspected that he was in need of protection. Not, that is, until an implacable hand had ruptured the pleasant, peaty reverie into which the Guinness had so lovingly and reliably ushered him. Then, and only then, had he felt the need for help.

He turned to face her, leaning his shoulder against the headrest. His body was still chemically becalmed, out of step with his brain, which was slowly recalibrating itself to this altered world. "Protect me from whom? Your driver?"

"I'll get to that in due course. But, as you'll see, it's important that we take things in the correct order. Simmonds, have you seen it?"

Simmonds caught her eye in the central rear-view mirror. "Two cars back, red BMW. Yes, it's been with us a while now. Since Hampstead, actually. Can't see how many – I think two, but the windscreen is tinted."

"Well, let's lose it fast. I don't want any mishaps now."

Nick saw Simmonds nod quickly and then felt the car surge phenomenally ahead. He grasped the door in sudden alarm, the lingering paralysis slowing his terrified reaction. The shops and greenery visible through the passenger window suddenly became a drunken blur, the noises from the street a compressed and decompressed Doppler whine. As the car turned a corner, Nick was thrown sharply against the door, a helpless deadweight.

"Still on us," Simmonds said. "He's a persistent bastard, this one."

The road hugged the fringes of a housing estate into a sharp pin-bend, leading to a roundabout and dual carriageway. As the car climbed to sixty, it slithered centrifugally around the turn. The red BMW, now directly behind them, mimicked their every move. They drove in convoy twice around the roundabout, Nick amazed that either driver could maintain the traction of his tires on the road. Then Simmonds stepped on the accelerator and sent the car hurtling crazily down the dual carriageway. Raw bursts of power seemed to pass through its frame and its passengers: the wind roared through them and over them. But the red BMW bared its teeth and persisted with its mimickry, pulling ever closer to their bumper. The provocation was intense. The driver was counting on Simmonds losing his cool and making a mistake.

"Okay," said the woman, looking round, "I've had enough of this. Do whatever you have to do to lose him. I don't care."

Simmonds took them – and the red car – off the carriageway and down towards a much narrower road. Nick guessed they were still doing seventy as they careered into its winding, hedge-lined path. He listened for the doom of an approaching car's horn, his body braced for an impact that now seemed inevitable. The BMW, meanwhile, was gaining on them.

"Still with us," she said with more irritation than alarm. "You're right. This one *is* cocky."

"Hold on. I am going to try a bit of a – *manoeuvre* in a moment…"

This time, Nick held on to the door grip with both hands. Out of the window he could see all the colours of straw and metal racing past him. Nothing was distinct or defined any more; everything merged into a great blur of organic mesh, leaves and grass, sweeping past them to and from oblivion. He realized that he was crouching now, waiting for Simmonds's "manoeuvre". But he did not realize that the turn would be quite as sharp as it was, or that the car would groan as angrily as it did, like an enraged horse taking a fence only under the most severe duress. The metal tendons proclaimed their agony; veins throbbed on the vehicle's brow. Simmonds battled with wheel, brake and pedals, barely keeping control of the snorting beast as it skidded and screamed.

Nick had not yet absorbed what had happened. But when he turned around the car had gone, as if vaporized by Simmonds's brutality and cunning. The driver had not been able to match this final turn, shaken off at last and speeding away in the wrong direction.

Nick realized, with what little detachment he could muster, that the symptoms he was suddenly experiencing – a teetering giddiness, unstoppable tremor and an inability to speak – were the first waves of clinical shock. He wondered if his captors and self-appointed guardians would know what to do with him if his body now shut down and said: enough. Would they administer first aid and take him to a hospital? Or would a cyclist find him in the morning, discarded on the roadside with a bullet in his brain?

"Right," she said. "Let's start again. Simmonds, do you know of a good place where we could stop? I'd like a coffee, and to give Mr Atkins a break from all this excitement."

A few minutes later, Simmonds pulled the car over into the gravelled car park of a quiet hotel and drew to a halt by a picnic table on which an empty crisp packet rustled. It was dark now, but the driveway was served by a row of ground-level floodlights.

"How do you feel?" It took Nick a while to realize she was talking to him.

"For God's sake." He felt himself retch, a dry and painful sign that his body was awakening. "Are you serious?"

"Of course," she said. "Why wouldn't I be?"

"It's just – well, that's not what I expected you to say."

"I'm surprised you *expected* anything. I ask the question because it sometimes helps people who've been through something as shocking and no doubt unpleasant as that. Perhaps not."

"What?" he spluttered. "Listen, I... I... I don't really know what to say. I'm worried that if I say anything much I'll lose it, or something."

"Please don't. It's never much fun. For what it's worth, by the way, you're coping pretty well, all things considered. I've seen much, much worse."

Simmonds headed towards the restaurant to get some water, coffee and cigarettes.

When they were alone she said: "Well, now. Mr Atkins, my name is Veronica Brewer. I am a government servant.

Let's just say that I am involved in security matters at a fairly senior level and I have reason to believe – as now, should you – that your life is in serious danger."

He put his throbbing head in his hands. "If you say so."

"You'll just have to take my word for it. The fact is, that car was pursuing you, not us. My assumption is that if we'd not been there when we picked you up you would now probably be in its boot heading for God knows where. I'm glad we arrived on time."

"Have you been following me?"

"Not in the way that you probably have in mind – but yes, we have been keeping an eye on you."

"For how long?"

She removed her gloves and put them into her bag. "It doesn't really matter, does it?"

"It does to me, yes." He paused, drawing breath as if struck by an unaccustomed asthma. "I mean, for God's sake. How would you feel – what would you *do* – in my place?" He winced and realized that his cracked lip was now bleeding again.

"Well, I regret that I can't give out more operational information than I have to."

He tried to collect himself. "You know who I am, that's clear. But I don't know whether you're confused. I'm an English teacher, you see. I work at a school in Highgate, I have a wife – estranged, I mean – and a daughter. I lead a pretty unexciting, unremarkable life. I don't have many friends, but I don't have too many enemies either." He sank into the seat, the acid of the beer rising in his stomach. "I don't know who you are. I have no idea why I am here."

"This is not something you could have foreseen or prevented. It's out of your control. But you need to be involved now. You won't survive long if you're not."

"*Survive*? What are you talking about?"

"We're not sure of the whole picture. Not yet. I do know that some extremely unpleasant characters are trying to find you."

"What are you *talking* about?" He reached for the door handle. "I'm going. I'm going."

"Mr Atkins, when did you last heard from Tabatha Bradley?"

He released the door handle. Amid all this chaos and madness, Tab… But the introduction of her name to the proceedings was as apt as it was insane, provoking a fast-choked burst of laughter within him. She had been gone for so many years. The messages had dried up. Now, in this car park on the dull fringes of London, as he nursed his new bruises and wondered if he would survive the night, she had returned to claim her rights over him.

He whispered, "I haven't heard from her in a while."

"The last *California Literary Review* ad was six months ago, and we haven't been able to pick up any traffic of any kind since then."

"How do you know about the *Review*? How…"

"Miss Bradley is not an ordinary person. To an extent I think you may not have grasped. I don't mean that she is a brilliant student of literature, although she appears to be that, too. I mean that she leads a life quite out of the ordinary."

He stared ahead. While he had dithered and sighed

over volumes of poetry and feeble cryptograms, others had watched from the shadows, and wondered at his credulity. He felt violated, stripped naked, and wished not only to escape, but to be alone. He looked out to the road and wondered how far he would have to walk to find a phone or a minicab. Then he remembered the imprint of Simmonds's fist on his tenderized cheek.

"Your question must be about the ads and why we know about them. I have to run you through a few other things first. Please be patient."

He turned to her and rubbed his chin. "Do I have a choice?"

"Not really. But I always find it nice to pretend. Let's get some fresh air."

She got out, and he followed. As he stepped out on the gravel and the cool air struck him, he was violently sick. The convulsions were over in a few seconds, his whole body like a cat's expelling the bones of something vile and putrid. He spat and gasped, his hands on his knees, his arms trembling again. He wiped his face with his handkerchief, quelling the sobs of misery only with the greatest effort. She took his elbow.

"Are you feeling better?" she asked. "Look, let's stretch our legs. You'll get over it faster that way." She breathed in deeply. "That's much better," she said. "I spend too much time inside. So do you, I imagine."

He clutched his knees, hoping that he would not be sick again.

"In my work, it is so easy to analyse too much and act too little."

"Yeah." Nick rubbed his shoulder.

The car park led to a path which stretched down

to a little stream. There was a slide and a swing not far from the edge. The water sparkled in the light from the hotel behind; beyond its clicking current was a stretch of lawn leading to a copse of youthful oak.

"Do the words 'Second Troy' mean anything to you?"

He tried to think, massaging his temples with his thumbs. Of course he knew them. "Yes. Yes. I do recognize them. Yeats. There's that line: 'Was there another Troy for her to burn?'"

"Correct. Your memory is excellent, as everyone says. The poem is called 'No Second Troy' and it comes from a collection published in 1910. It refers to Yeats's thwarted passion for Maud Gonne, whom he compares in the poem to Helen of Troy. Did Tabatha Bradley introduce you to that poem?"

"Yes," he said. "She adored Yeats. Always did. She could quote chunks of his stuff."

"It's an odd phrase, isn't it – 'Second Troy'? Do you know what it means?"

He shrugged. "No – I mean, of course not. Is that what you brought me here to find out? I mean, it's an image of destruction, obviously. But…"

"The reason I ask is that the words have cropped up in our interceptions recently."

"I haven't the slightest idea what you're on about."

She frowned. "Well, let me try to be clear. We believe that a group calling itself 'Second Troy' is now planning a series of violent operations designed to draw attention to its agenda. There is evidence that its activities, though still secret, have already begun, and that lives have been lost."

He absorbed this, or tried to. It defied explanation – it had no relevance to his life. The low hum of London seemed far away now, but the city's glow crept over the fringe of the trees ahead, leaking into the parkland and their conversation. It summoned him back from the perilous wasteland into which he had somehow strayed. He wanted to run, but was still immobilized by fear and lingering pain.

"What do these – these 'Second Troy' people want?" he said.

"They are the nasty end of something perfectly un-objectionable, you might say. The global justice movement, it's called. But more specifically a response to globalization, and America's recent military adventures. Well, mostly all this is a low-priority chore for my department. We have to keep a close eye on these boys and girls, especially when they have a big thing planned in London, which they do from time to time. But the protesters keep their noses clean for the most part. They know that a pretty girl smiling in a T-shirt or an old lady pushing her grandchild in a 'Stop the War' buggy is far more effective than an ugly great punk with a bolt through his neck."

"And now?"

"A mutation has occurred in the past couple of years. It caught us off guard. You see, the truth is that the rallies have diminished in effectiveness. The WTO and G8 take such thorough measures nowadays to keep away from the mob when they meet, that it's harder to get a reaction than it once was. Politicians everywhere pay lip service to these people, or at least to their slogans, whether it's on GM food, or organic farming, or animal rights, or even imperialism: you know all that, of course. But it would be nonsense to suggest that the movement has achieved very much. Look at it from their point of view. They have plenty of money, lots of expertise, and amazing penetration at all levels of society. The leaders of the movement, whatever anyone claims to the contrary, are overwhelmingly white, middle class and educated. American and European, in constant contact with each other. And some of them are getting impatient. They see the men with beards in the mountains who flew aeroplanes into the World Trade Centre and say to themselves: well, what have I done? Why have I achieved nothing? Or – much, much worse – *I could do that*."

"What, hijack planes?" said Nick. He felt capable of sarcasm for the first time since his capture. "I don't believe it for a minute. These people just want everyone to be nicer, and hug trees and stop building roads and bombing Third World countries. Not to fight a jihad and slaughter the enemy. There is a difference, you know."

"Yes, there is. Very much so. I'm not talking about imitation. I'm talking about *envy*. Our friends on the rallies see Islamist pimpernels and second-rate dictators getting *exactly* the response they want from the capitalist West, and they're furious. I mean, how often can you march to Hyde Park? How many badges can you wear? How many petitions can you deliver? When does it stop being enough?"

To this question, at least, he knew the answer. "When you grow up. When you settle down. When you lose your ideals."

"Absolutely right, for most people. Today's activist is tomorrow's pillar of the establishment. But for a minority the itch is still there. And within that minority, there is an even smaller group who have recently become convinced, it seems, of two things." She lit a cigarette. The tip winked at him like a morse signal.

"What?"

She exhaled. "First, that they are morally entitled to take any and all necessary measures to achieve their goals. That's a familiar ethical position for all guerrillas and paramilitaries – 'by all means necessary', and so on. Nothing particularly unusual in that. The second conclusion is more alarming. And it is that violence is not only legitimate, but highly effective. There's always been some truth in that, of course. All the stuff about terrorists ending up having tea at the Dorchester by invitation of the government. Well, it's a fact, isn't it? But the war on terror is a whole new context, you see. Both sides claim they are winning. And white radicals – no, let me rephrase that, *some* of them – want in on the act. They want to join in, because they have come to the conclusion – and who can blame them – that that is how to get results."

It was hard to cross the dizzying gulf across which she was beckoning with a cruel smile. To the west he could see a gaggle of buildings, their lights bidding him to leave this madness behind and seek sanctuary.

"I… I'm not sure I'm really taking all this in." He thrust his hands in his pockets. It was chillier than it had been when they got out of the car. "I'm very tired and, to tell the truth, very frightened." The dizziness had returned. He wanted to sit down.

"All right. We'll go soon. This group – calling them-selves 'Second Troy' – appeared on the radar very recently. They have already killed – I'm afraid I can't go into the details – and it is clear that they will kill again unless apprehended very soon."

"Where does all this happen?" he said.

"We have identified cells in London, the Netherlands, Rome and the United States. Fairly fluid, I must say. Strong evidence of a German connection, too. But the group exists in virtual reality, mostly. It morphs constantly on the web. That's its true habitat, and a very thick undergrowth it is too, unless you know what you're looking for, which we often don't. That said, their operational strength is impressive. They have been well-trained. Possibly in the Middle East, some of them, maybe by jihadis. And they have already shown themselves to be capable of appalling strength and clarity. We take them seriously. As, I'm afraid, should you."

He regarded her, wondering how he might most quickly extricate himself from this other-worldly ordeal. "How do I fit into all this? I've no political invol-vement at all. Everything you're saying could be false and I wouldn't know."

"You don't. But Tab Bradley does."

He kicked at the edge of the water. "How? How does a Stanford English graduate fit into your hypothesis?"

"Tab Bradley is the leader of Second Troy, Mr Atkins."

At last, he felt able to laugh. "That's absurd. Now *that* really is crazy. How could she be? She was a girl in an art gallery who liked to surf and hated the Republican Party. That's it. Believe me."

Veronica Brewer shook her head. "Of course, you would think that. But how does *anybody* end up doing something like this? Don't you think the parents of the Baader-Meinhof leaders were confused? Do you suppose that every IRA Army Council member was born with an Armalite in his cot? Miss Bradley's public radicalism is the perfect cover for her secret extremism. It's a curious paradox, isn't it? People who know her, but don't know her properly, find it impossible to think of her as what she truly is. They see her beliefs as a bourgeois hobby, so to speak, rather than the lethal fundamentalist convictions that they have actually become."

"Oh, come on. Tab was an activist. She wasn't a terrorist."

"Not originally, no. How long is it since you saw her?"

"That's not the point. I…" He felt his cheeks flush and his ears throb with indignity. She was trampling through the most sensitive terrain of his soul in her flat shoes without thought or compunction.

"How long?" she asked again.

"Fifteen years. Sixteen. More."

"Correct. Your last time together in Santa Cruz. And then her messages. Well, you weren't to know. She kept you up to date, more or less, with the parts of her life you knew about, the parts of her life that were safe: school, books, rallies, beaches, things like that. The life you shared with her. But the *new* stuff – well, she didn't want to trouble you with that."

Nick rounded on her. He was inexpressibly tired, more scared even than he cared to admit, and giddy with confusion. "*What* has she become? What do *you* really know about Tab, for God's sake?" He kicked a stone, sending it skipping across the grass. "This is a nightmare."

"I know more than you, I'm afraid," she said. "Listen: about the time she met you, Tab's life – what's the exact word? – *bifurcated*. Split in two, you know? On the one hand, she carried on her literary work, studied, did well and seemed to be heading for tenure at a decent university. Is that all?"

"I'm not sure," he conceded. "The messages were never that specific, especially after the first few years. She said that she was still at Stanford for the first five years."

"That was true. She was. And then – well, then she came to London."

Many things that had happened to Nick that day had been intolerable: Emily's broken expression, Polly's plea that he make his peace with her mother, even the words of a forty-year-old song. But there was, he now realized, a qualitative difference between things which were hugely unpleasant – hurtfully, brutally unpleasant – and that which was physically unsustainable. Veronica's latest revelation, delivered through the pursed lips of the seasoned transmitter of bad news, fell into the latter category. He could feel stone crumbling into sand within him.

"Impossible," he said, shaking his head with a sudden vigour that brought his nausea flooding back. "Impossible. Impossible. Not here. She couldn't come here. Not without telling me."

"She lived in the city for... oh, eighteen months.

Taught a bit at the LSE. Heavily involved in the political side of things. Lived in a hostel to start with, and
then with two other students in Bermondsey. Seemed
to enjoy London well enough, made plenty of friends.
Activism, student-newspaper stuff. Nothing exceptional.
Packed up and headed home after a while. I think she
was scouting for the future."

"I don't understand. She was sending me messages
all the time, about life in America."

"That's true. This was the point when her talent for
double living became apparent. Her messages were
all about California, and American politics, and ice
cream. Meanwhile, she was a few miles away from you,
feeling the same rain and reading the same newspapers.
I wonder if she worried about running into you. She
came back to London several times, too."

"It doesn't make sense."

"Out of context, I agree. We'd conclude that she was
simply an unhinged liar, who took sadistic pleasure in
lying to her ex-boyfriend. But although the chronology
is hazy, around this time her group of acquaintances
becomes a bit more… shall we say, game? More inter-
national, certainly. People who are steering, or trying to
steer, the global justice movement towards darker things
and more… well, *focused* action. A caucus emerges
around this time, and the hard core of that caucus is
still with us today."

"But Tab the leader? Surely not," he said. "She was a
scatty egghead. Worked in an art gallery. A loner. Always
a loner."

"Outstanding in every way. A gifted general among
all these hotheads. She gives them a battleplan and fills

in the blanks in their world view. The first years, nobody notices much. The practical changes aren't really apparent to start with. Some divisiveness in the movement over strategy, but nothing that would alarm somebody in my line of work very much. No, it was only three or four years ago that the first signs of *mobilization* begin. First of all, it was dogs failing to bark, really. Certain people went ominously quiet. A lot of them just fall away, of course, as they grow up. But not all. Some, we discovered, had gone to ground. Money starts to be siphoned in their direction, although not always detectably. There is talk of target lists, special operations, justifiable methods: a whole new approach. No longer regular activism. Something else. And Tab is at the heart of it all. Hard to prove, of course, but her name and her associates always crop up."

He looked out to the copse. "Still sending me messages. Still telling me about her glittering academic life."

"Yes. Not entirely untrue. She was still teaching, but only part-time, junior college, in San Luis Obispo. Hardly what she had been bred for, don't you think? Well, it was as good a cover as any, and it barely diverted her energies. She had her hands full getting the new system to work, making sure that she had recruited the right people and getting rid of those whom she could not trust. About eighteen months ago, the thing goes live."

"Live?"

"Yes. I mean truly underground, truly operative. That's when my department really became interested. We kept a very close eye on them. Close enough, we think, to make them abort one or two operations. But one slipped through our nets a few weeks back. And somebody died."

"But you can't tell me about that, right?"

"Come back to the car. We should get going."

They walked towards the light and the waiting vehicle. Simmonds was holding the door open for Nick. Less than an hour ago, Nick thought, this man had assaulted him, and now he was behaving like a chauffeur. Was that the point about Simmonds? That he did whatever he was told to do, right or wrong? A coach sped by the car park, gauche and noisy in this rural enclave, this place of appalling secrets. Simmonds and Nick turned round to inspect the honking interruption. But not Veronica, who was already waiting in the car. Nick joined her.

"Excellent," she said. "We've covered a lot already. Let's go, Simmonds."

Nick, clicking on his seat belt, turned to her once more. "I still don't see how this involves me."

"This is how," she said. "A few days ago, one of Tab's people was lifted in Amsterdam. He had no direct contact with her, it seems, although his handler is… one of her closest associates. Anyway, he was dropping off money for some sort of operation. He didn't have much to say to start with. And then… well, let's just say he became a bit more locquacious. He was telling the truth when he said he didn't know what the money was for. But he knew something about the Second Troy hierarchy, a few of the faces. Not much that we didn't know already, unfortunately. But, at the end, he said something very surprising. Which was that he named you."

"Me? That's absurd. You don't think I…"

"No, I don't. You're clean. We checked you out very thoroughly. No, he was talking about Tab – it wasn't clear that he had ever met her. But what he did say was that one person held the key to Second Troy's future. And that was you."

Nick shook his head with the morbid glee of someone upon whom absurdity has no further tricks to play. "Listen, please. Whoever you really are. I teach Shakespeare and Thomas Hardy to the unpleasant children of unpleasant parents who do not want their offspring contaminated by the unwashed. When all this excitement was going on, I was almost certainly in a classroom in Highgate. The idea that I hold the key to anything's future is flattering, but completely ridiculous. You've rumbled my little secret about the ads. Your gorilla has given me a cracked lip for my pains. But I have had no contact with Tab in the true sense of the word for more than fifteen years. This informant – in Amsterdam or wherever – is confused."

"Do you think whoever was driving that BMW was confused, too?"

"I don't know. I don't know. You and your friend strike me as the kind of people who might attract that sort of attention. I don't think I am, to be honest. I'm not the sort of person this sort of thing happens to. I'm not the sort of person anything happens to, actually. And I think it's time for you to take me home so you can get on with whatever it is you people do."

"I have a proposition to make to you, which I hope you'll think through very carefully."

Once more, he sensed desperation creeping into his voice, the lilt of pleading powerlessness. "Oh, come on.

Just get on with whatever it is that you have to do. Please. Don't waste your time on a bystander like me." He looked down. "Just… just leave me alone."

"Yes, but as I keep trying to make you realize, you're not a bystander, are you? A man, with a very large amount of cash in his case, to be spent on God knows what by God knows who, *named* you in interrogation. He said you – Nick Atkins – would determine the future of Second Troy. He said it was down to Nick Atkins, and only Nick Atkins."

"But you're not proposing just to guard me – are you?"

For the first time, he detected disquiet in her. She shifted a little in her seat, and blinked.

"No," she said. "I am asking you to help us, actually."

"Help you?" His eyes were wide with incredulity. "How could I *help* you? I can barely look after myself. It'll take me a week to recover from all this bloody stuff. Believe me, you don't want to rely on me."

She turned to face him, more squarely than she had yet done. She was not quite beseeching him: Nick doubted that she had ever beseeched anyone. But a subtle transfer of power, however temporary, had taken place. "I will be honest with you. I don't have anyone else to rely on. Mr Atkins: Second Troy is a murderous outfit that intends to kill again, very soon. We know that much. We know a little more, but not much. In you, we have somebody whom Second Troy is *looking* for. Clearly, Tab Bradley is trying to renew contact with you, for reasons that are still obscure. And that means you can lead us to her."

He dwelt on her words for a moment. "You want to use me as bait?"

She clicked her tongue. "Of course. What did you expect?"

"Not this. That's for sure."

"You would be looked after. I would ensure that you were guarded round the clock. We can secure your home and introduce surveillance at an entirely different level with your cooperation. I'd be lying if I said you would be completely safe. But you'd be safer than you are now."

"I doubt that."

"You would, of course, need to absent yourself from work for a while. I am pretty sure that Tab is not in this country, and when they come again, it may well take a while before you get access to her directly. I suspect the path will be circuitous and complicated. We would stay with you at all times. There are other agencies which would offer as much assistance as we need. Then we can make our move."

"What makes you sure that they don't just want to kill me for some insane reason?"

"The fact that you're still alive. No, this isn't an execution mission. They know how to do that well enough. You have something that Tab Bradley wants. You and only you. Did she give you anything – perhaps an object for safe keeping?"

He shook his head. "No. Absolutely nothing. She wasn't a big present-giver. I only have a few photos that I took. Letters from our time together. And a pile of yellowing cuttings from the *Review.*"

"There is obviously something else. But I don't know what it is. Not yet, anyway."

"You seem to assume that I'll help you. Hasn't it occurred to you that I might say no? I might just want to take my chances. The truth is that cars didn't start chasing me until you arrived. Maybe they'll stop when you go away. And as for your Amsterdam man – well, it just sounds like a big mistake to me. Maybe he had heard Tab talk about me. Or, more likely, somebody else had heard her reminisce and got the wrong end of the stick. It sounds like gossip gone mad to me."

She could not conceal her irritation. "So your answer is?"

"My answer is no. Obviously it is. My answer is no, because I am just an ordinary person, and to say yes would be crazy, probably suicidal."

He saw her catch Simmonds's eye in one of the mirrors, as a glacial silence fell in the car. Instead of imploring him, she reached into her briefcase and extracted an orange file. There was an air of wounded regret about her, as if he were forcing her to take action which was beneath her: as if he had spoiled the dance with his shamblings. Without preamble, she opened the file between them, flicking a button to turn on an unusually bright reading light.

"This file," she said, "has many things in it, and I hope I don't have to show you them all. Let me start, though, with the main section that is devoted to the actions of a friend of yours: a Mr George Healey, of 2 Abigail Close, Blackheath, London. Further particulars follow. Wife, financial situation, no kids… Ah, but this is the important stuff. Suspicion of drug-trafficking over the following period… eight years in total… Well, that's not good. Never charged, due to lack of admissible evidence. Curiously indulgent policing I would say, which always makes you think. However, a note on file to say that a full financial investigation would probably do the trick. They never did it. Well, he'd gone straight by then, or so he told people. And his customers had all been middle class, to a man. So he got away with it." She curled her lip, as if such misdemeanours were unutterably low-rent. "Thus far, anyway. That could change. It could change quite quickly, in fact."

Nick recoiled. He felt a hollowness within his limbs.

"In case that hasn't convinced you, which I hope it has, you might like to consider this. For what it's worth, I'm sorry to do this to you." She made sure that she had his undivided attention and turned over a typed piece of paper to reveal a photograph of a young girl in a striped polo neck, her head thrown back in gleeful exclamation, her body untidily atop a bike, mismatched front teeth signalling a moment of deep amusement: Polly. Without thought, Nick reached out to strike Veronica Brewer.

The speed and anger of the attempted blow had not taken her completely off guard. Her right arm had risen with impressive accuracy to intercept the blow, which eased off in any case as he tried to collect himself. "By any means necessary": well, she should know. But the savage impulse was back under control, not least because the sharp voice of Simmonds was now filling the car.

"You all right?" he barked. "Need me to stop?"

"No, no," she said. She and Nick allowed their arms to fall. He was sweating more than she.

"I'm fine." She closed the file and replaced it in her case. "Fine."

"My God. You unbelievable, unbelievable…" These were the last words Nick said to her for several hours.

It had long been clear that Veronica Brewer had no intention of taking him back to Highgate. They were heading north of London, but he did not recognize the nameless lanes down which Simmonds was taking them, or the dormitory villages through which they drove, past gables and rectories and fortresses of expensive respectability. It was nearly eleven o'clock by the time the car stopped. They were parked in front of a large house, enclosed by hedges and ten foot fences. A woman in white blouse and long black skirt was taking the rubbish out. There was a shed behind the house in which three derelict bicycles were parked. But theirs was the only vehicle in the drive.

"This is a safe place, Mr Atkins. Whatever happens, you should stay here tonight. Clearly, your home is dangerous at present. We'll get a fuller picture of where we are in the next few hours. Simmonds will show you your room. It has its own bathroom and there should be all the essentials there. If you're hungry, Alison can help, or with any other requirements."

Nick nodded wearily and followed Simmonds into the house. The wood of the floors and staircase was newly stripped and polished, and the tapestries on the wall of the sort that sell for a ridiculous premium in village antique shops. A few old copies of *Country Life* were stacked on the cabinet, alongside a vase of dried flowers, and what looked like a visitor's book. A grandfather clock dolefully announced the hour as if it were more than ready for bed and could not possibly be expected to perform the same task all night. But there was almost no evidence of continuous habitation: no coats, no discarded clothes, no unopened bills, no newspapers, no lists for the morning. This was not a home. It was a stage-set, a house disguised as a place of warmth and belonging.

Simmonds led him up two flights of stairs to the landing which stretched into a long carpeted corridor. There was a further flight up to what looked like a converted attic.

"It's just here." Simmonds pointed to a door, but did not open it. "I'll be next door. Any problems, give me a shout. Good night."

The room had the subdued splendour of an un-expectedly sumptuous bed-and-breakfast run by an old couple. There were lavender-filled pillows, a four-poster bed and a television with DVD player. Adjoining the bedroom was an august bathroom, resplendent with robes and expensive bottles of bath oil. A shelf of books offered the guest – or inmate? – a wide selection of fiction, biographies and works of history. There was even a bottle of malt, and a decanter of water. The trimmings, though welcome, seemed absurd in the setting. Most surprising was the phone. Bugged, no doubt. But then so were his home line and mobile: she had made that quite clear. He kicked off his shoes and threw his jacket onto the chair. Then he lifted up the receiver and dialled Aisha's number. As he pressed the last key, he realized that he had used the wrong sequence. Shit. It was ringing.

"Hello," said Emily.

"It's me," he said, after too long a pause. He did not want to cry, and wondered if he should put the receiver down immediately.

"Oh. It's gone eleven, Nick. What are you calling for at this time of night?" Her voice was reproachful.

He tried to compose himself. "Oh, nothing. I just wanted to check everything was okay. You know, with Polly and everything."

"Of course it is. She's long asleep. Had a good time, she said."

"Not out then? It's Saturday night."

"Not everyone lives the way you and Topper do, Nick. I'm working, actually. And half-watching a film."

"Any good?" He could hear the sadness in his question, the tone of the man on death row asking about the smell of spring blossom and the taste of fresh strawberries.

"Not really. Nick, are you okay?"

"Yeah, yeah. Just… just calling, really."

"Right. Well…"

He scrambled back to his life before the grotesqueries of the evening. "Listen, Em. You don't have to send the lawyers round to school, you know. I know how angry you are. But I'll agree to whatever you like. No need to do that. Please."

"What are you talking about?" she said. "My lawyer hasn't even drafted the first letter. He's useless, is the truth. Of *course* I haven't sent a bloody lawyer to school. Behave, for God's sake. I keep telling you I'm not interested in scoring points. I've decided something and I promise you it's not for effect. Okay?"

"Sure. Sorry. My misunderstanding."

"Listen, Nick. Whatever has happened between us, whatever got broken along the way, I did marry you. And you are Polly's Dad. So if you're in trouble, please tell me."

Ah, Em: there is no hiding place from you. Maybe, at root, that was the problem. Maybe I need a hiding place. "No, no. There's nothing wrong at all. Look, I'll call you during the week, okay?"

"Okay."

"And, Em…"

"Yes."

He remembered the call was being monitored. "Nothing, nothing. Goodnight."

He called Aisha – pressing each digit in the number with neurotic care this time – and left a message full of cheery generalities. He wondered how long it would be before he saw her – and whether she, of all the people he had treated poorly, might still be within an orbit which was not beyond his grasp. It would be good to spend time with her. It would be good to start afresh. It would be good not to have to say sorry. It would be good, it would be good.

He lay on the bed and closed his eyes. The heady aroma of the pillows reminded him of shops in Covent Garden he had visited with his mother and with his father when they were buying presents for her. There was a relaxed luxury and femininity about the smell that seemed ludicrously incongruous in this most masculine of places: a place where fugitives were protected from violence by men prepared to use violence themselves. And what harsh words were uttered behind the locked doors downstairs? Did the lavender obscure the smell of old dried blood? What screams had Alison heard as she cleaned the kitchen and prepared the supper?

Nick slept. His slumber was uneasy and offered no relief. The colours of an explosion multiplied in his mind's eye till yellow was grafted onto yellow, red onto red, orange onto orange. Tab appeared to him, looking as she had when he had last seen her in Santa Cruz. She was angry with him for betraying him. He wanted to reciprocate her anger, tell her that he had a daughter now, to rage at her game-playing and her disregard for others. Was she pleased with what she had done? She wore a rifle across her breast, and this sight so captured his attention that he forgot to say anything. She shook her head, as she had in the past when confronted with betrayal or compromise, and walked off. As he left, walking towards a grey door framed with blinding light, he heard himself ask her why she always had to bring Yeats into it. Why Second Troy?

He woke up at five, feeling battered and dirty. He splashed water on his face and made his way to what he assumed was Veronica's room. He knocked, and she answered quickly, fully dressed and apparently working.

"All right," he said. "I'll do it. But on my terms. All right?" She smiled and ushered him in.

"You're making the right decision," she said. "And now, I think it's a good moment to introduce you to Khayyam. Khayyam has been keeping an eye on you for us. Looking out for you, too, I should say."

Leaning against the window, in a hooded sweatshirt and jeans, was Aisha.

5

"Doesn't it bother you, Clio?" Munroe Stacy drew deeply on his cigarette and surveyed her impatiently, as if she deserved a more aggressive cross-examination than he could be bothered to conduct. Her flesh crawled with the insect bites of reproach. He persisted: "Well, doesn't it?"

Clio X ran her fingertips around the neck of her sweater, and played with the coil of her blond hair. She was tired and edgy, exhausted by the long journey and the fear of discovery en route. The splendour of the room, with its mighty joists, hunting trophies and tapestries only sharpened her fatigue: rest and recuperation were close at hand if only he would shut up. A cat lurked in the corner by a suit of armour, scandalized by the conversation, its ruff magnificent like the collar of a colicky civic dignitary.

"Does what bother me?" she asked, finally.

"Carlo Giuliani," he replied. His boots were on the desk precariously close to a brimming ashtray. The sprawl of newspapers on the leather surface – alongside the espresso cup and the framed photographs – made Munroe resemble a prosperous paterfamilias enjoying his Sunday morning before a bracing solo hike in the

Tyrolean mountains which enfolded them like an icy necklace. Anyone seeing the two of them for the first time might think that he, the master of the house, was issuing a gentle reprimand to an errant maid while the rest of the family were at church. The group had been in the house for less than a week, and already Munroe had assumed an air of proprietorship.

"What about Carlo Giuliani?"

"Doesn't it bother you that so few people have heard of him?"

The question, she grasped, was in itself a form of punishment: a schoolmasterly reminder of first principles.

"Why should I care if other people know? I know. I know Carlo Giuliani was killed by the State in Genoa. I know he was shot, and run over, and left for dead. That's all that matters. Isn't it?"

Munroe laughed. "Oh, Clio, you're one of a kind, you really are. You know, I've been thinking about him a lot these past few days, up here in the mountains. It bugs me like hell that the police ordered up two hundred body bags before the demo. *Two hundred*. Why? For a G8 meeting? It bugs me that they beat up kids in sleeping bags on the floor of a school. And it bugs me that when Carlo was shot in the face – the face – the papers said he was just a no-good drifter. Do you remember? *Time* magazine said: 'You reap what you sow'. That really bugs me."

She nodded.

"I'll never forget it. That day, I mean. Gives me strength, I suppose. That clear, cloudless sky, you know? All of us in the Black Bloc wearing our ski masks.

Waiting for the tear gas in our goggles. It seems feeble now, such immature methods. But I looked at the crowd and the costumes – 300,000 of us, for God's sake! – and I thought: Christ, this is history. All of us edging towards the steel fences – they looked like medieval fortifications – and the cops and armoured cars. They had shut down the airport and the railway stations, and the centre of the town – the Red Zone – was unreachable. They had divers in the harbour, just in case we did something really daring from the sea. But nobody *was*, not then, not really. You know, for the first time, the very first time, I thought to myself that this was an alliance that could actually work, that besieging these bastards with… with all these *colours* and all that…" Munroe looked to the stuccoed ceiling, searching for his word "…all that *joy*… well, for one moment, I thought it might just work. There was a banner which said: 'You are G8, we are six billion.' You know, it made we weep. Over my black mask, for Christ's sake. Sentimentality, of course. Pure sentimentality."

"And then?" Clio asked. In spite of herself, she was intrigued. He rarely reminisced.

Munroe chuckled wryly. "The moment didn't last long. About a mile from the Red Zone, I saw the first tear-gas canister fly towards us – and that was it, really. That sort of yellow mist, like something out of an opera, snaking around us. Pandemonium. One of the armoured trucks was pushed over, and someone sprayed 'We are winning' on the side. Were we? I wasn't sure. And I looked around for the guy I had been working with and – whoosh – he's gone. And then I knew, Christ, yeah, of course, we'd been infiltrated, like everyone feared, and I saw some of the Bloc boys getting to work with crowbars, and I wondered how many of them were actually pigs. Then it was a hail of cobblestones, flying each way. I got clipped a couple of times, once in the face. I gave a *poliziotto* a good kicking for that, I can tell you. Just some young guy. And then I got close to the station, couldn't see much… I was pretty much on my own by then. But I spotted all these blue helmets clustered round something, and after a while, in all the uproar, I could see the blood. Not red, blood isn't really red, you know. It's black. The gutter was black with Carlo's blood. And that's when I knew."

"Knew what?" Clio asked.

"That it was over, at the very moment that people were saying it had begun. Sure, we'd get on TV that day and we'd be deafened by chatter about, you know, *strategy* and globalization and 'corporate social responsibility': we'll drown in the fucking jargon one day, I swear! But the moment they took us out in Genoa, the old strategy died. Marches, the Black Bloc, the pacifists, the whole damn thing was pointless." He closed his eyes, as if in prayer. "It was time for something new, Clio. We needed to think in a completely different way. We had to take control of the process, and acknowledge the need for leadership. All this – our new movement – was born in the blood of Carlo Giuliani."

She felt herself wilting, nerves getting the better of her. "Look, Munroe. I need to tell you what happened. And then I need to sleep."

He stood up, his smile expansive and indulgent. He had, she reflected, the handsome cheekbones of a much taller man. His dark mane, flecked with grey, added to his presence. "Come on, walk with me," he said. "There's a nice little circuit up to the ridge I do whenever I need to think, or refresh myself."

He did not wait for her assent but walked across the room. The bay windows opened onto a verandah. The ironwork furniture, the girdle of lanterns and the ivy clinging to the window frame – beyond which one could see the indoor swimming pool below – all spoke of untroubled wealth, and an enduring confidence in the stability of things. The people who owned this house, Clio thought, would be startled by the passions which extreme greed and extreme want could stir, and the annihilations that occurred when the two collided. These were people whose wealth was so established that they could no longer see it. Would they begin to understand the use to which one of their houses was now being put? And when they did, what vengeance would they visit upon the young man in their midst – the secret, impassioned sympathizer – who had made the house available to Munroe and his friends? Perhaps they would never know. Perhaps the work – the Great Work – would be accomplished by then, and such grievances would seem trivial, the bric-a-brac of a forgotten age.

Munroe and Clio walked out of the drive and up the steep path towards the pines. Behind them a view of mesmeric purity lined the horizon. The valley, with its clefts and ravines, was vertiginously steep, and yet it radiated no sense of danger, of stones slipping underfoot, rain sending boulders tumbling down the mountainside, crashing into houses and stables. Here and there, a spire or a hayloft broke up the wall of needled green. The river, fed by glacier water, gurgled in the distance, through the rough boulevards of beech, spruce and pine, on its long onward journey to the Adriatic. A road wound its way up and through the scattered farmsteads and the apple blossom of Spring, and then was lost in the forest: no cars disturbed the tableau. It was, in every sense, an enclave: of Germanic life in Italy, of impermeable Nature in an urban world, of safety amid danger. Munroe was right to have chosen this place. It had slipped out of time, out of life, without anybody noticing.

"So, Clio," he said. "I guess you're going to tell me why it went wrong."

"It didn't go wrong – they were unlucky." She stopped, steeling herself. "You see, the curve in the road was so sharp. And the other driver must have been good. They didn't stand a chance."

Munroe turned to her. The sun, not yet filtered by the trees, made him screw his eyes up. "Not good enough. We need to be better than that. For what we're trying to do – for something on this scale – we need to be flawless. They should have thought ahead, planned."

"Like Freddy, you mean?"

He nodded. "Freddy was my fault. I should never have asked him to do that job, and we all paid a heavy price."

"Not as big a price as Freddy."

Munroe began to walk again. "Freddy was more stupid than I thought. I didn't expect him to slip up like that." At a fork in the path, he hesitated for a second, and then headed right. A crow flew across his path with blithe confidence. Its dead eye showed no respect for the intruders. "Most of the deliveries arrived safe and sound."

"Yes. But what did Freddy tell them?"

"Not much they didn't know already, I would imagine. They know about me, and they know about you, and maybe two or three others. That's it. Freddy was never inner circle." He stopped again, peering at some animal tracks leading to what looked like the mouth of a warren. "I was fond enough of him to hope it was quick."

"You can be sure it wasn't," Clio said sharply, affronted by his indifference. She looked down at a cluster of fire lilies.

"Hm," he said, sniffing a little. "Is that a wasps' nest up there? Listen: the buzzing is all you can hear."

He was, in the end – for all of his other, murderous talents – a politician. That was what had drawn Clio X to Munroe three years before at a Paris convention. In those days she had been called Jane Cousins, and her clothes had been more floral, more scatty, less severe. She had gone to Paris for an adventure. She assumed that she would be back in college by Monday morning, regaling her friends with the stories of her Parisian excursion: the late nights, the haloes of smoke, the aroma of absinthe, the alluring men with their dark eyes and heartfelt opinions.

But she never returned. Had she spotted Munroe, or vice versa? They had met in a workshop on 'The Primacy of War in a Neoliberal Economy', and she had been fascinated by his ability to combine intensity with evident indifference to the earnest, prolix papers delivered by the participants. He looked like a man in

a room of children. It was as though he were searching
for something else, something much more fundamental
than the wordy arguments being traded by boys with
beards and snaggled teeth. Munroe was not there for
the politics, but for the people. He was less interested
in theories than in the formation of an irresistible
cohort. Even as the verbiage flew across the room – the
stuffy annex of a down-at-heel college – he was sifting
those present into categories, discarding all but one
as useless for his purposes. And it was the garrulous,
naive Jane whom he had invited for coffee, because,
with the uncanny eye of the born recruiter, he had
detected something behind the gauche convictions and
the nervous laughter. It was something she herself had
not known was within her, an inner purpose whose
slow emergence into growling life, in the months that
followed, at first frightened and then thrilled her. Within
Jane, Munroe had detected the germ of Clio, a quite
different woman who saw beyond the political slogans
of her milieu – her dilettante interest in activism – to
the necessary action which might make those slogans
real.

They slept together on the first night, and inter-
mittently thereafter. Initially, she thought herself in
love with him, but recoiled from the idea as she felt
the mutation within. Munroe was there to be her
teacher, not her lover. She read the books he gave her
and listened to what he had to say. He spoke of the
problem and its scale: the rape of the world, the daily
hurricane of man-made horror, and the dawn of an
age of permanent war. Exploitation of the poor on
a scale never seen before in the history of mankind.

The pillaging of the world's precious resources and the capture of the military by corporations. Above all, the shortage of time. He told her of the pacifist methods that had been tried by well-meaning but misguided radicals. He said that new methods were needed, that this had been clear for some time, but that only now had a generation arisen which was equal to the task. He spoke of training camps thousands of miles away, in north Africa, the sub-continent, south America. White men and women at last learning to use arms alongside those of other races and religions: a global community of struggle arising. The world had allowed itself a decadent decade after the fall of the Berlin Wall, but now the time for serenity had passed. He kissed her on the cheek, this time without a hint of sexual intent, and welcomed her to his clandestine fellowship. One night, in his attic flat near Montmartre, he told her that, if she wished to come with him, she must turn her back on her old life, on everyone she loved, on her plans to grow old in peace and contentment. She wept all night, and in the morning told him that she wished to do as he said, and to change her name. To Clio, because she was the Muse of history, and it was history's call she was answering; and X, because her parents' name was, to her awoken soul, a slave name. Munroe embraced her and answered at last a question she had asked him many times: what the letters "ST", which she had heard whispered and painted on walls, really stood for.

Now, on the mountainside, perched between the Ostler massif to the west and the Central Alpine Ridge to the north, she brought news of a failed mission and waited for her next orders. Munroe was no longer absorbed by the wasps' nest, and was looking out across the valley towards the turrets of a small castle nestling in the springy greenery of the forest.

"He got away," she said. "What do you want to do now?"

"Oh, he'll come back. We have something he wants."

"You're sure?"

"I'm positive. The more I think about it, it might even be better this way. Let him come to us."

"I don't understand. How could it be better?"

"You will soon, Cli." He put his arm round her braced shoulder, and led her back down the path. "You will soon."

* * *

"I always thought there was something not quite right about you," he said to her, stirring his tea. "For a start, you were such a crap teacher."

"Don't even bother, Nick," Aisha said. "Let's just make the best of a bad lot. All right?"

"A bad lot?" He snorted. "First of all I find out that MI5 has been watching me…"

"It's not MI5," she said. The tannoy in the departure area announced the delay of a flight to Miami. A gasp of angst curled through the great space as dozens of families contemplated the tedium, runny noses, and sleeplessness ahead of them.

"Then I discover the reason they've been watching me is because an old girlfriend of mine has supposedly reinvented herself as Ulrike Meinhof, and that her new friends want to kidnap me. And then, as if that isn't bad enough, my new girlfriend is in on the act. What are you laughing about? What's funny all of a sudden?"

"You," said Aisha. "I told them you could handle it. You babble and moan all the time, but you can handle things, more or less. You keep control most of the time."

"I don't have any bloody choice, do I?" he growled. "Khayyam."

"Aisha *is* my real name, by the way," she said. "In case you were wondering. But teaching is definitely not my real job. I won't miss those kids. The worst cover I've ever had."

He looked at the screen above them. Still an hour to kill before their plane to San Francisco would begin to board – probably longer.

"What's it like? Being a honey-trap? I mean, am I your first? Do they have a special academy where they teach you to fuck people and then fuck them over?"

She blinked away the insult. "Well, it all depends what you mean. Let's just say I have had to do worse things in the name of the job."

"Oh, really? How much worse?"

"A lot worse. Believe me." In mild irritation, she pushed her mobile across the table, near to a coagulating pool of sugar and coffee.

"What I can't believe is that you, of all people, have been assigned by them to be my minder." Nick stretched his legs under the table, avoiding contact with her. "I regard that as the biggest insult."

Aisha shrugged. "A man and a woman travelling together attract almost no attention. I know you. I think you're up to it, which is not a view all my colleagues share."

She looked different, and not only because she had swapped her classroom costume for a leather jacket, jeans and trainers. Now that the mask had been lifted, he could see a hardness in her face, an inclemency that did not recede even when she smiled. The strangeness of his predicament – its infraction of every rule – was still conspiring to deaden his nerves – and thus, oddly, to contain his fear. And though he longed to run out of the airport, get a taxi and whisk Emily and Polly away, far away from these people, their unimaginable cruelties, what about Topper? Would he be able to save them all, or any of them?

He had only to look at the set of Aisha's lips, the absence of doubt in her eyes, to know the answer.

At least Veronica Brewer had agreed, however reluctantly, to his terms. He wanted to tell his wife and Topper that he was going away for a while. The "legend" she had devised for him was simple, and appropriately flattering to St Benedict's: he was to be seconded with immediate effect to a confidential fact-finding team organized by the Department for Education and Skills. Its work would take him abroad to investigate teaching methods in various countries, and he would be gone for a while. The letter from the Permanent Secretary indicated that St Benedict's would be compensated at rate equivalent to twice Nick's salary.

The deal in place, he called Topper and, with as much enthusiasm and sincerity as he could fake, told him about the imaginary secondment.

"Abroad? Why?"

Nick rallied as best he could: "It's a government programme, and I guess they're looking for someone in my age bracket who teaches English."

"And you're the best they could come up with? Fuck."

"Amazing, I know. So I'll be away for a while. I was wondering…"

"If I'll do you a reference? No way."

"I was wondering if you could look in on Em and Poll once in a while. Or phone them."

Topper still had the fearful antennae of his old profession. "My second sense is telling me something is up, Nicko. Are you all right?"

"Of course I am. Why do you think something is wrong?"

"I don't." Topper paused and qualified this reassurance. "You would tell me if you were in bother, wouldn't you?"

Nick looked around his room, in a location he was still unsure of, speaking down the tapped phone. He felt the chill of absolute loneliness, the isolation that comes with a true secret. "Course I would. I think it might be fun, actually. Better than school, that's for sure."

"Well, that's good. Look, I'm out of town on business tomorrow, but I'll look in on the girls when I get back on Thursday. Sweet?"

"Yeah," Nick said. He wondered if he would ever speak to his friend again. "And Tops…"

"Yes?"

He remembered the picture of his daughter and felt himself buckle under the weight of shabby guilt. "Nothing, mate. Look, thanks. I'll see you around, OK?"

Emily was harder, much harder. He insisted on seeing her face to face, and he knew that she would not swallow his lies for a moment. Aisha, who sat in a car round the corner, warned him not to write anything down, not to tell Emily anything which might remotely threaten the credibility of the legend. To do so would only endanger his wife and child: did he grasp that? He wanted to strangle her with her hair as she spoke.

Emily opened the door. "God, you look shit. Where have you been?" she asked. She was wearing a jacket and skirt, as if she were going to an interview. It was past ten o'clock and Polly was already at school. "Christ, Nick. Have you been in a fight?"

"Oh, this," he said, touching his bruise. "Not exactly. Been a rough day or two. Can I come in, or shall I just stand outside?"

"Yes, come in, come in. I was worried when you called. Just like the other night. You sounded strange. Again."

"Yeah, I'm sorry about that. Bit pissed and sentimental, you know. I shouldn't disturb you, but…"

She swallowed hard. "But it's difficult sometimes. Yes. I do know, Nick." Silence blackened the hallway. "Listen, I'm going to see a client about a halfway decent project, so can we be quick?"

"Of course. Look, it's nothing really. Just some good news about work which means that I won't be around at the weekends for a while."

They sat down in the living room and he delivered his script, more adeptly than he had with Topper. Her laptop was half open on the coffee table beside what looked like Polly's maths homework. A takeaway carton poked out from under one of the chairs, having escaped the early morning tidy-up. The wedding photographs were still on display, as was a picture of Nick and his mother at Polly's christening. But something was different. Yes, that was it: his landscape Ansel Adams print was no longer above the fireplace, replaced by a Paula Rego which, he had to admit, was in much better taste. The still-drawn curtains badly needed to be dry-cleaned, their original cream hue now a washed-out nicotine colour, which the fumbling efforts of the sunlight did little to flatter. The impression was one of turmoil kept at bay, rather than of grief. She was struggling on her own, struggling to keep the pillars of her little world upright without the daily help, punchbag and consolation of a partner.

He finished and raised his eyebrows, inviting her to approve of his fictitious success.

"I see," Emily said. "Well, well done, I suppose. Did you know it was coming?"

"No," he replied. "Not at all. I guess I just fit the profile they're looking for. I must have fallen out of someone's database. God knows where it'll lead, but it's a change of scene at least."

"And you don't know for how long?"

"No." He looked at the fluff on the floor. "A month, I suppose. Maybe a bit more."

"So what about Polly, Nick?" She was right to ask this question, to which there was no answer.

"Well, I'll see her when I get back."

"That's not what I mean. What I'm asking is how she fits into your calculations these days. You've left me. Well, that's your choice. We've decided what to do about that. And now you're off on a big fancy trip to improve your career – or so you say, anyway. And you won't see her for weeks. Weeks and weeks. She's growing up, Nick. You won't have a second chance to enjoy that."

This is the depths to which we have sunk, he thought. We both know that what I have said is a lie, but we can argue about a lie with no less vigour than about the truth. He bristled: "I can't believe you're turning this into a thing about Polly. I thought you'd be pleased. There'll be a bit more money and – well, it'll be good for my prospects. How can that be against Polly's interests? Since when were you so perfect?"

Emily slumped on the sofa. He looked at the hem of her skirt, tight against her stockinged legs, and felt, for a moment, the shock of lust surge within the turgid swamp of his emotions. It subsided as quickly as it arose, flattened by his self-righteousness.

She said: "I'm not perfect, never was. We don't need to wage war, Nick: our war is over. I'm just reminding you that you're not at war with your daughter, and never should be. She loves you very much. She misses you very much. Don't forget that in all the chaos. Whatever it is that is happening to you – no, I know enough, no more, please – don't forget about Polly."

The torpor of guilt – the purest form of wretchedness – descended upon him, and when he spoke, it was quietly. "I don't forget her, Em. I never do. Whatever I do, I don't do that."

She sat up and rested her head on her hands. "I'll tell you something, Nick, about kids, which I only realized very recently. Well, I've thought about things a lot since

you left. Obviously, I suppose. The thing is, you see…
well, how to put it? Children save us, I think."

"What do you mean?"

"What I mean is – I don't know. Well, just that it
doesn't matter what we do wrong, and how bad we
are. All the fuck-ups which come out of nowhere. All
the stuff we promised ourselves we would never do.
Somehow we make good through our kids. Or we
don't. And then we die and are forgotten. And that's it."

He wondered what had drawn her to this insight,
what suffering had dragged her towards this intimation
of redemption. Then he thought, once more, of the
danger he had brought to her door, and the door of his
daughter, the creatures who scuffed and snarled outside
because of his failures. "I don't know, Em. I think I
might be beyond saving."

She was fierce again, though in a whisper. "Don't
you dare think that. Don't you *dare*. You owe her that
much. You have to keep going, and believe in her. You
have to believe that, whatever has happened between
you and me, whatever it is you are up to now – God
alone knows – there is a little girl who can make all that
count for nothing. Okay?"

Those two syllables of supplication unstoppered
the years within him. He felt the chaotic richness of
everything they had done together melting through his
bones, the vividness of it all. For an instant, the death
mask of love twitched into life, then fell still and pale
once more.

She wilted a little, as she reached her conclusion.
"Listen, I want you to know that I'm thinking about
changing the locks. Don't go ballistic. It's not to keep

you out. It's just I need to do things which make me… which make me feel that this house is just for me and Poll now. It's not an aggressive thing. So don't be surprised if your key doesn't fit when you get back."

He nodded, and thanked her for what she had said, promised to let her know when he would be returning, and left without ceremony.

That awkward parting had taken place the day before; now he was back with his keeper, about to embark on what might, he imagined, be a journey towards death.

"But do you really believe her parents will help?" Aisha asked him, as he returned from a café with a cup of tea and some mineral water.

"I have no idea," Nick replied. "Do you have a better plan?"

"It wasn't what Veronica wanted. At all."

"If you really want Tab, you're going to have to get under her skin. I need to see her family and ask them what they know."

"It's risky. What if they are in touch with her and warn her of your approach? Perfectly possible. Then she might disappear for good."

"She already has disappeared. I'm only doing what you told me to do: try to lead you to her. And admit it, you don't have a lead."

Aisha frowned. "Well, we're exposed like this. You and me. It makes my job harder."

"Good."

"You know what I think. I think that there's a part of you that loves this. That has *longed* for this."

"You're insane," he said.

"Am I? One of my tasks was to go through your things and, goodness, what a lot of clippings you have, Nick. This girl really had you on a leash, didn't she?" She smiled. "Doesn't she?"

The violence of Aisha's sentiments and the relish with which she switched tense shocked him.

"She mattered to me a lot once, yes. Now… I just need to end all this. It's my fault, in a way. Not what she's doing, but the way it's spread to my life. I have to sort it out. I have no choice."

"No," Aisha said, nodding with dark finality. "No, you most certainly don't."

Nick looked around. At each of the three tables next to them was a solitary figure, engrossed in reading or silent reflection. A young man with close cropped hair and a hooded sweatshirt fidgeted with the keys on his mobile phone, and avoided Nick's eye. He was athletic and lonely in bearing. His face twitched a little, with a frequency just shy of a fully fledged tic. At the table beside him was a middle-aged man, evidently a businessman in a well-cut suit: he was unremarkable but for his striking blue eyes. His laptop sat on the table in its bag: he was completely absorbed by a paperback whose title Nick strained and failed to see. At the third table was a blonde woman in a sweater: of the three, she seemed much the most nervous, her eyes darting back and forth, from the suspended screen above their heads announcing departures, to her fellow passengers, to the luminous shopfronts that lined the lounge. She was ill at ease, as if somehow thwarted. She looked as though she wanted to merge with her surroundings, to camouflage her silent panic. He wondered which of the three had been watching him, what they might have thought, whether they would have scented the rank sweat of a life turned upside down. A young man, a suit and a neurotic woman: three stories he would never hear, drowned in the crush of a stale-aired airport.

Booming overhead, the mangled voice declared the San Francisco flight open for boarding. He and Aisha stood up and collected their belongings. When he looked up at the tables around, all three had already gone.

PART TWO

COAST TO COAST

I

The mountain road was steeper now, a sudden world away from the angry concrete circuitry of the freeways. From the airport they had headed towards Santa Cruz, taken the turning to Monterey, down Bay Avenue, Porter Street and then, as if roused from a dream – as if returning from a long, painful journey – he was back in Soquel with its modest homes and schools and bars. Not a homecoming: that was not what it felt like at all. The indifference of the place to him was total.

Restless from the flight and barely speaking to Aisha, he could feel the mild palsy of anticipation, the shaking of a body restored to a habitat where it had grown and prospered. It was as though his cells remembered the place, the night air, the breath of the redwoods that stretched languorously to the sky, the years of his absence scarcely a sap-filled twitch in their centuries-old story. He was too tired to sleep, too frightened to talk. Beneath it all, too, Aisha had been right: there was a guilty pulse of exhilaration in his exhausted frame. The warm air that flooded through the sunroof of the hire car was narcotic – the pagan aroma of the woodland. The trauma of return – under duress, chaperoned by a lover unmasked as a vicious traitor – was dulled by the primal beauty through which the road snaked. Cloaked in darkness, the forest whispered that its magic was undimmed.

"It's one of these," he told Aisha, whose eyes were dark-rimmed and intense. "Yes, definitely one of these."

There were three mailboxes at the corner of a turning up a rough road, at the peak of which lights flickered between the awesome trunks. The corroded metal of a trailer-home could be seen, and blue sacks of garbage discarded at the roadside.

She slowed down to walking pace. "What makes you so sure she won't just blast us with a shotgun?"

"Susan Bradley? Hardly. She was always a tough old girl. Texan. But she wouldn't have a gun in the house."

Aisha shook her head. "She's had more than fifteen years on her own with nothing but raccoons and coyotes for company. We could find somewhere to stay tonight and pay her a visit first thing."

Nick considered her suggestion. He remembered what it was like to stay in an American motel, the chicken wire on the walkway, the rippling, illuminated pool a floor below. Neon signs and flashing arrows pointing to reception. The plastic loungers and the cheap wicker tables. Cheating couples fumbling with their room keys. The noise of teenagers parking in the lot, partying, turning up the hip hop until the manager complained, cursing comically in his bathrobe and threatening eviction. The thump of the Coke machine in the middle of the night and the sirens at the fringes of his consciousness, as he slept on a king-size bed with cable TV flickering in the dark, and a pay-per-view guide resting against the last beer of the night. The phone flashing with a message that you didn't answer yet, because you didn't really want to be found. Dawn breaking, breakfast in a diner, another day on the road ahead of you. Would he ever enjoy such freedom again, as he had so many years before?

"I think I should just go in," he said. "I can get more out of her if I catch her off guard. I need to trade on the shock of her seeing me after all these years."

Aisha engaged the car and began the crackling climb up the hill. A startled dog barked in rage and fear, the borders of the copse breached by intruders. To hear the noise of the hound, one would think that strangers never ventured off the road to this huddle of rudimentary homes. The trailer-home – a rusty blue – revealed itself on the left, the dog tethered to a post by its door. All the windows were blacked out. An ancient pick-up stood sentinel in the grassy forecourt, its windshield reflecting the beam from the car which crept on nervously. Nick could smell the hickory chips of a recent cook-out. But there was no sign of human stirring in response to the convulsions of the dog.

"That's it," he said, as the road curved again to the left.

The frame house fifty yards ahead was as he remembered it, a little smaller perhaps. It had been painted an unflattering pink which had flaked badly to reveal patches of the old white beneath. In the porch was a rocking chair with a book and what looked like – in the light of the hanging storm lantern – some knitting or tapestry work. There was a chicken coop carved into the steep hillock on which the house was built, and a decrepit Cadillac parked on the other side. Upstairs, a bedroom light was on, and the clink of washing-up issued from a window downstairs. He felt his heart pounding mercilessly, and wondered for the first time since they had begun their ascent of the mountain whether he was remotely equal to the task he had set himself. He felt old and scared and ridiculous, an impostor on the stage of his youth.

"Are you getting out or not?"

"Yes. Just… just give me a minute." He closed his eyes, tried to collect himself. He opened them and turned to her. "I want you to tell me one thing."

"What is it?"

"If I get you and your people to Tab, is that it? Am I free then?"

Aisha rested her chin on the steering wheel. A creature whinnied somewhere beyond the little settlement, a howl of lamentation in the cooling night. "Listen, get on with it, okay?"

He stepped out of the car and stood just out of the pool of light cast by the lantern, losing track of time as he pondered the house and the dangers that lay within. This is what terror does to you, he thought, and then he realized that it was not terror that was driving him on at all. It was greed – greed for what was lost and should be forgotten – that had brought him to this mountainside. The coercions of Veronica Brewer had been a pretext for the consummation of this terrible desire. Even as he cursed her name, a shameful part of him blessed her for giving him the chance to retrieve the past and its possibilities. The truth was: he had not returned. He had always been there, all these years, a loveless wraith brooding on its loss, waiting for its moment. God help me, he thought. He knocked on the door.

The clinking from within halted for a moment, then quickly resumed. No, Nick thought, she really is not expecting visitors at this time of night. She thinks it's one of the thousand noises that interrupt and pass through a lonely life. He knocked again.

"I'm coming," she yelled.

The voice was less robust than he remembered, but it was undoubtedly Susan Bradley's. Its tone and pitch were Texan, but the sound of the South had been mellowed, attenuated, by decades of Californian exile. He heard the traipsing of her approach, the shuffling steps of someone who does not bother to lift her feet, but slides across worn boards in beloved slippers. The door opened.

"What do you want?" She was smaller than he recalled, and more handsome. The years had turned her hair grey – it was like a silver bonnet now, straight and modestly cut – and she no longer wore it long. But her face was the same: benign crow's-feet at the edges of cheekbones crafted in porcelain, a strong chin, the brow of a discreet intellectual. Her white T-shirt and khaki shorts were clean and pressed. And the dark eyes of her daughter – the unmistakable chromosomal cord that joined Susan and Tab, an affinity as unsettling now as it had been the first time he had met her, in a café in Palo Alto.

"Wait, you're here to fix the shower, right? Two goddam days I've been taking cold showers. Well, get your stuff and do your thing. I'm not staying up for ever. What sort of company are you, anyway, sending people out at this time of night? You're only in Capitola, for God's sake."

He allowed her a little longer to see if recognition

would come. But it did not. He was not the man
paraded before her as an unexpected catch all those
years ago; whom Tab had kept as her prisoner on the
end of a twitching thread; he was just some guy come
to fix the shower.

"I am very sorry to bother you, Mrs Bradley. I know
it's late."

"You're English. Sweet Jesus – an *English* repairman?"
She laughed. "That I surely did not expect."

"You don't recognize me, do you?" He took a deep
breath. "It's Nick, Mrs Bradley. Nick Atkins. Tab's friend."
He paused, reluctant to consign himself officially to the
realm of the forgettable. "From way back."

With apparent warmth, but no more, Susan smiled.
"Well, now. Well, now. Nick Atkins. Tabatha's little Nicky
come back after all these years. Well, well." She paused,
smiled again. "Ain't that just a kick in the head?"

He returned her smile warily. "I guess so. Is this a bad
moment?"

"Always a bad moment when you reach my age,
young man. Irritation is what keeps me going. That,
and garlic pills. How long has it been?"

"Seventeen years, I think. Something like that."

"Well, you ain't missed much. Come on in. Have a
beer." She peered over him at the car and the vigilant
figure of Aisha. "Who's that? Your wife?"

"Oh, no, just a friend."

"Uh-huh." Susan eyed him suspiciously. "She coming in?"

"Oh, no. She thought she'd let us get – well, re-
acquainted. I think she'd feel awkward just now. Please
don't be offended."

"Oh, don't worry. I could care less. If the lady wants to stay in the car, she can stay in the car. Come on in."

She led him into the cavern of the house, flicking light switches as she went. Susan's den was straight across the hall, a room crowded with superfluous couches and beanbags, leaving almost no empty floor space. One wall was covered with books – Whitman, Bellow, Melville, some volumes of poetry – another with poster art. On a side table was a well-thumbed copy of the *Bhagavad-gita* and a hardback edition of *The Mabinogion*. That much he remembered: like Tab, she had always relished mythology, feasted on its symbols and signs promiscuously, like magic fruit. There were no family pictures or graduation certificates. A tray of cactuses on the deep window ledge and a hookah in the corner added to the impression of gentle, solitary eccentricity. What was missing were the photographs of parents, weddings, grandchildren: the tributes to time and its passing, the lineage that would survive her when she was swept away. For all its homeliness and bohemian tease, the room spoke of an atomized existence, the hollowness of disconnection. On the floor, an answerphone blinked with neglected messages.

She returned carrying two open bottles of beer. "Hope you like this. It's all I got."

He took the bottle. "It's fine. Beer is fine. Cheers."

She sat down, and he followed suit. "Cheers. So. Explain yourself, young man. There you were, courting Tabatha, lovestruck and tongue-tied all those years ago. I remember it well now. You were a nice guy to have around. Quite the gentleman. Oh, don't blush. It was a fine thing. We must love one another or die, that's what

Wystan said. True enough, too. I guess you and Tabatha got done loving and moved on, though. Well, there we are. She was crazy for you for a while, though. Crazy. Never seen her like it."

Nick did his best to sound light and easy, to share in the affable reminiscence, as though the feelings she described were long fossilized. "Well, I was pretty smitten myself. But I guess I had to go back to school, and she had to stay here." He took a deep slug of beer. "It was for the best, I think, although we were both sad at the time."

"Yeah, well. She got on with her life after that. In her own way." Awkwardness descended on the room. "So. What brings you up the mountain after all these years? Other than the pleasure of my company?"

He shifted uneasily on a large paisley cushion. "Well, I'm tempted to say I was just passing through. But I don't want to lie to you. I seem to remember you always saw through BS pretty quickly."

This characterization pleased Susan. "Well, I had plenty of practice with Tabatha and her father. Crazy liars, both of them, in their different ways. And these days – well, these days he chases young women as if they'll stop him from ageing. It's his elixir. Always young, and getting younger all the time from what I can gather. Work, and chasing tail. Ugly that he should stoop to that. *Ugly*." She added dismissively: "We don't see one another is the truth."

"And Tab? Tabatha?"

Susan Bradley ran her hands up and down her legs, as if he had asked her the most difficult question in the world.

"So," she said uneasily, "are you on vacation or what?"

Nick retreated, desperate not to unsettle her further. "More like business. I just arrived, actually. It's my first time in California for a very long time."

"You were going to be a lawyer. Right? Like Alan."

He laughed. "Wrong. I… it didn't work out. I worked in television for a while, and now I teach."

"God help you! Just like me. What age?"

"Teenagers. English and stuff. It pays the bills."

"Teenagers? My Christ, I couldn't. The kids I teach – well, they're still innocent, even if they are noisy as a pack of prairie dogs. But once they turn thirteen, it's like the gates of Hell have opened."

"They're okay," said Nick. "The kids, I mean. It's not too bad."

"But not too good either, huh? So you never married."

"I did. I did. That didn't work out, either."

"Kids?"

"One," he said. "Just one. A daughter."

"Just like me, again. Another beer?"

"Please."

While she was in kitchen, he reflected wearily upon the failure of his tactic. He would have to be more direct, more straightforward with her. She needed to know that her daughter was in terrible danger – matched, and probably surpassed, by the danger in which she was putting other people.

"There," she said. He could smell newly applied scent. "Enjoy."

"Thanks. I will."

She stretched out, not seductively, but with a hint of broken charm: the reflex of a woman who once relished her effect upon men. "You know, it's funny you dropping by. I always figured you'd be back."

"In what way?" he said.

"Well, Tabatha mentioned you sometimes. Said you used to send her the strangest messages – in code and stuff."

"Me?" Anger twitched in his belly. "No, no. She was the one who sent messages. All the time. In the *California Literary Review* classified, would you believe?"

This amused Susan Bradley greatly. "The *Review* classified! Jesus. For how long?"

"Till six months ago."

She fell silent, drained her first beer. "My God. She stayed in contact with you that long? All those years? I had no idea."

"Just thoughts, really: news and ideas about what was happening. I was a fool to keep looking for the ads. Being married, I mean. But I did. I did. I think she knew I would, too."

Susan laughed, conspiratorially this time. "Yes. I think she *would* have thought that."

"The thing is – what I need to talk to you about – is that I think Tab is in trouble. That's why I'm here, really. Something has gone wrong, Mrs Bradley. The sudden break in the messages, I mean. I wonder if you know where she is, or where I might find her?"

Susan was curled up on her couch now, a rejected mother suddenly foetal, as if remembering and mimicking the child who grew within her, and was now lost. Her face could no longer disguise her grief:

a hardened grief, he thought, long-suffered, long-moulded into her life, not the stabbing, gut-tearing sensation of failure when first recognized.

"Well, no, I guess I don't," she said quietly. "There's a lot I could say about Tabatha, but I'm not entirely sure I should. Even to you, if you don't mind me saying so."

"She's mixed up in something really bad, I think. I mean, I wouldn't be bothering you otherwise. I think she may have made some bad decisions along the way, some bad friends. I want to try to help her."

Her face twisted with derision. "She is beyond help. That is what defines her. I tried, for so many years, to reach her, to soothe whatever it was that was troubling her. But she loves *secrecy* too much. That's the fun for her. This sort of conversation – two people who care about her, agonizing about her – well, that's what she craves more than anything in the world. I mean, the fact that we are talking like this at all, after all this time. She would love to listen into this. Oh boy."

"What about her politics? Did she ever talk to you about that much?"

"Politics. Oh, sure. I knew she was *involved*. Her father hated it all, of course. He's very conservative now. And I think that only encouraged it in her. All the posturing and the declamations."

"But how involved do you think she got? I mean, she was just an ordinary activist when we were together. Rallies, and slogans, and stuff."

Susan considered this. "More and more, I guess. She became evasive about it. I could see it was getting more central to her life. Well, the poet says as much doesn't he? Too long a sacrifice can make a stone of the heart. And it surely does. It did. I think, at some point, somewhere down the line, Tabatha's heart turned to stone."

Something began to drain his bones of what little energy he had left. It was as though a succubus had taken hold of him, ravenous and angry. He braced himself. "Have you been in contact with her recently?"

Susan flinched at this sudden bluntness. She wanted to speak, he thought, but he also knew that he must be trampling across her nerve endings by asking her this so directly.

After a while, she said: "When Tabatha was quite young, ten or eleven I guess, we sent her up to camp in Tahoe. She was meant to be gone for a fortnight, and she was looking forward to it. I guess one or two of her friends were going to be there, but that wasn't the main thing. She loved the horses and the swimming and all that stuff. It was good for her, and even then things weren't great between me and Alan. I wanted her to have a break from the two of us. The rows, you know? We dropped her off and things were fine. She called me after three days and said what a fantastic time they were all having, how much she enjoyed her cabin, and what a great counsellor they had looking after them. I breathed easier, I really did. Then, not long after, the camp director called me at school and said he was very sorry but I would have to come and collect Tabatha straight away, as she had been having 'serious discipline problems'. That's all he would say. So off I drove, half furious, half panicked. I didn't know what to think, and he clearly didn't want to talk about it on the phone. Well, I got there, flustered, of course, and got to the camp office to find out what was so awful that I had to come right away."

"What had she done?" asked Nick.

"The camp director's name was Hidalgo, Mr Hidalgo, I remember that. He took me into his inner office and shut the door. He said that Tabatha had been in the craft shed with this other, younger kid called Robin. They were on their own for a few minutes, whittling away making wooden animals or something. And the boy – Robin – had said something about her, something rude, and she had pinned his arm down and, very slowly, very deliberately, sliced open his thumb. Just like that. And the first thing they knew of it was Robin screaming – and they rushed in and he was hysterical, of course: blood everywhere, and Tabatha standing there, apparently, like a mute. No reaction at all. Of course, the boy went mad, but more than that, he was frightened, really frightened. When he got back from hospital, he called his parents and begged them to take him home. They turned up, and got all righteous: insisted that he stay, and Tabatha leave."

"Christ. I never had Tab down as somebody who could do that. She was very young, I guess."

"Well, she came into Mr Hidalgo's and I saw all her stuff was outside in a trunk, ready to be thrown in the car and taken away. I mean, they couldn't *wait* to get rid of her. She had really spooked them, somehow. And she didn't say anything for a while, and then, suddenly, she started weeping. I had never seen her like that. Never. Real *affliction* in her voice. And she swore – *swore* – on everything that is holy, that she was innocent, and that the kid hated her, and had cut himself, and then blamed her. For nothing. Just to get her kicked out."

"What did you think?"

Susan shook her head. "I didn't know *what* to think. But I listened to her, so angry and so hurt, and what could I do? What could any mother do? She sounded so *real*. I couldn't just take sides against her. Not with her looking at me like that, pleading with me. So I said to the director that there'd surely been a mistake, and that there was no question of me taking her away because she obviously hadn't done anything wrong. And at that moment – at *that* moment – I believed it. She hugged me all the while, and in the end, after a lot of negotiation, he bought it, too, and relented. He was concerned, I think, but I guess he was impressed by the performance, by how deeply she felt that she had been wronged. So he asked to shake hands with Tab, and they did and we all agreed to say no more about it."

"So did you leave?"

"Yes. Yes, I did. A bit shaken, but with a clear conscience, I have to say. And then… then, as I was driving down the track, past the stables, I saw this boy, younger than her, with his hand bandaged. Standing alone by the paddock. And I realized that it must be him. And I slowed a little and saw his face. And his eyes… the look in his eyes. And then I knew… I *knew* as if… as if I had been slapped hard, sitting there in the driver's seat – that it was true. That she had done it. And that I could just about handle, just about, as horrible as it was. Children hurt each other, don't they? What I couldn't handle was that she had persuaded me of her innocence. That I had been so readily manipulated, so helpless before this young girl, my own daughter. I knew I could teach my child not to hurt people, but I wasn't so sure I could teach her not to lie. I couldn't. That's the truth."

"Did you ever confront her again?"

"Hell, no. I was too ashamed. I had been well and truly beaten. Tabatha loves to win. And she had won."

He cleared his throat. He was getting nowhere. "Well, I guess she won with me, too. But I still need to find her."

Susan stood up. Her proud features were distraught now. "Listen to me, Nick. Listen well. You were always a good boy, and you've become something like a good man, I think. I can see you mean well, and I'm sure you're right about Tabatha. But you don't want to be chasing her. Not now, not any more. She's gone too far. Wherever she is, I don't know. But I do know you won't be helping yourself or anyone else if you try to track her down. She'll always be ahead of you, and she'll hurt you along the way." He was surprised by her resolve, by how businesslike she was. "So you give me a big hug, get back in the car with your friend and head back where you came from. And don't come back."

Nick sighed, and stuttered as he spoke. "I wish that was open to me, but it isn't. It really isn't. I'm not the only one looking for Tab. It's got beyond that." He caught her eye, detected the ferocity of her will. Was she protecting him, or her daughter, or herself?

"What about Alan?" he said. "Could he…"

"*No*," she said in a new tone that surprised him. "*Not* Alan. Keep away from him."

"It's just that Tab always stayed in touch with him. If only for money. He might be able to help."

"He won't help you. Take it from me. I should know."

"Yes, but…" He broke off, wondering if he was deceived. Had he imagined the sound of breaking glass? "Did you hear that?"

"What?" she said, eyes wide with sudden apprehension.

He put his fingers to his lips, and she started. "Wait," he whispered.

"It's probably just a dog," she whispered back. "Wild on the mountain. They come and dig in the garbage."

He smiled. "Sorry. I haven't slept in more than twenty-four hours. I'm a little wired. Look, I'll just go outside and check on everything and then come back to say goodbye, okay?"

She nodded assent, and he left the room.

As soon as he reached the porch – before even the door had swung shut behind him – he realized something was wrong. The car was there, but he could not see Aisha. There was a scuffling, and then he thought he saw a figure in the woods opposite, a hunched creature lurking beside a tree, melting into its bark. There was a flurry as the creature took flight, off into the forest, or so it seemed. Nick cried out and ran down the path, through the dilapidated gate and onto the road. He stopped, looked into the tangle of branches, but could see nothing. Breathless, he scrambled up the hill, over twigs and poison ivy and rocks. Below him the road curved round, and a car, its shape hard to detect in the darkness, roared into life, its eyes blazing ahead, its tires screaming as they sought purchase on the uneven ground. He shouted again, but it was already gone.

A woman's scream pierced the night like a terrible awakening, like the death of dreams. He turned and tumbled down the hill, half running, half falling, his jacket snagging on branches, his ankle turning painfully as he struggled to get back to the road. He was too frightened and preoccupied to hear the sound of a second figure creeping away. Nick did not see this other ghost at all.

The car door was open. He could see Susan Bradley slumped over the driver's seat.

"Susan!"

She did not turn. He ran towards her and reached out to pull her back. Her whole body was heaving, each sob a spasm of uncontrollable shock. She was, he realized, covered in blood, the front of her white T-shirt a sudden crimson, her face and hands flecked with red, too. There was blood everywhere.

But not her own. Beneath her, beyond revival, beyond any help, fallen in a flailing half-turn onto the passenger seat, was Aisha. Her throat had been cut from ear to ear.

2

When they had staggered back into the house, Susan withdrew upstairs, driven by a deep instinct to cleanse herself. Nick heard the shower being turned on, the pipes groaning with effort. Remembering that it was broken, he wondered how long she would take to scrub herself clean. He heard stifled sobs, the whimpering of the deepest fear. And yet she had not phoned the sheriff, had she? Something within her had grasped that this was her problem, too, that her daughter – her twisted flesh and blood – had brought this violence to her door. Parchment-pale and suddenly aged, Susan had sensed with the instinct of a desperate parent that the normal procedures would not work in the inverted world where she had now joined him. He had not been forced to shake his head and say with weary menace: no cops.

How long might it take for news to reach Veronica Brewer through the diplomatic channels? She would realize soon enough that all was not well with Aisha; she would send somebody to look for them both. But he could not stay still, wait for help to arrive. That much was clear. Whoever had slaughtered Aisha – this demon of the forest – was still at large.

When Susan returned, she was wearing a Stanford sweatshirt and fresh shorts. Her eyes were bloodshot and pitiful, and she staggered a little, drunk with shock. She sat down at the table and asked him – as if he must know what the proper procedure in such cases was – what they should do now. He told her that the people around Tab were looking for him, that this was the second time they had narrowly missed their prey. Perhaps they were still outside, waiting in the thicket. He could not understand why they had not continued their advance into the house, past Aisha's dying body, towards him. Something – God knows what – had forced them to abort the operation. But they would be back.

He looked down as he spoke, and saw the violent tremor of his hands. As he observed this spasm, it occurred to him that he was truly on his own now. He had no means of contacting Veronica Brewer. He would have to keep moving, find some way of getting to Tab, wherever she was.

He told Susan that he would drive the car to a more secluded place in the mountains, deep into the forest, and dump it. Someone would see it, investigate, open the trunk, and find the horror within. But that did not matter. By the time Aisha was discovered, Veronica would surely have made contact with him, somehow, through some channel. Her people would clean up the mess before anyone found it.

He did not tell Susan much, but he told her enough. She nodded in abject resignation, sensing that he was right, that his reassurances, though born of a senseless world, were probably the best chance she had: not of protecting herself, but of giving her lost child a chance.

He looked at her and thought: you still think there is a part of Tab worth saving. You are still in the camp director's office, believing her lies. Something within your shattered soul knows that I am your best, your only chance. You and I are in the limbo that separates Tab from absolute punishment.

He reached out and grabbed her hand. He heard his voice quaking. "If it had been me in the car… please help me, Susan. You've seen how badly these friends of Tab want me. And the people Aisha worked for… if I don't help them, they'll hurt the only people I love. Believe me."

She squeezed his hand and spoke softly. "I will help you, Nick. But I need to know. What is it that Tabatha has? What is so terrible that this could happen?" Tears wrenched through her as she cried out. "For God's sake… what has my baby done?"

He withdrew his hand and said nothing. He could not tell her that. All he could do was implore her with his eyes.

"I'll call Alan," she said.

"Why?" he asked.

"Because you were right. Much as they can't stand each other, I think she still contacts him from time to time. Usually for cash. He doesn't talk to her, doesn't discuss things. Just an email and instructions on how to wire money to her. She knows that he won't cut her off. And no, before you ask, I don't know when they were last in touch. I haven't even spoken to him in eighteen months."

"Will he help me?"

"Maybe. Maybe not."

* * *

He called Alan Bradley from the airport, after a few
hours' sleep at a Holiday Inn, and a catnap in the taxi.
His head throbbed murderously, and his feet ached
from the long walk back to the highway after he had
dumped the car, obscured by heavy foliage and as far
from the roadside as he could force it.

Alan answered almost instantly and with pre-emptive
aggression. But when Nick announced himself, the
voice dissolved into pleasantries. *Sure*, Alan remembered
Nick well. The nicest guy Tab ever dated, in his opinion,
and the one she should never have let get away. How
could he help?

Nick asked if he could meet him in New York,
explaining that he was arriving on the last morning
flight to Newark and would need only a little of
Alan's time. But Alan had a better idea. He was meant
to be dining at his club, with fellow members of the
Fountainhead Circle – a sort of club within a club, he
explained. Would Nick join him for dinner? He would
arrange a rental tux and accommodation. Nick could
think of few things he would rather do less, not least
because the dinner would force him out into the open.
But Alan left him with the firm impression that this
was the offer and it really wasn't up for negotiation:
take it or leave it.

Less than twenty-four hours later, he stood, clean
and dressed for the occasion, in the atrium of an Upper
East Side club, drinking his second glass of Chablis,
wondering whether he was in some strange antecham-
ber to death, a final celestial concession granted to the

doomed before the end. How different to the first
time he had been in New York, when he had worn
a T-shirt and sandals, stayed in a hostel and crossed
Times Square mesmerized by the discovery that such
a place should have come to exist. The sensory attack
of Manhattan – rank, stickily hot, exquisite – had been
overwhelming. Each day, he had walked further, seen
more. To visit this place was, he thought, as the night
air clung to him and the sonic fog of cabs, sidewalk
altercation and round-the-clock business enveloped
him, to feel for the first time the sensual abrasions of
all human possibility.

And on one of those evenings, as he waited for
the traffic, gridlocked back up Broadway, a blue 1960
Cadillac convertible – an amiable shark of a car, its fins
gliding through the limpid air – pulled up by the island
where Nick was standing. It was packed with kids a
few years older than him, laughing and smoking. Even
now, across the years, he remembered the music that
was blasting from the lush white leather of the car's
interior: Bowie's *Young Americans*, a slice of Philadelphia
soul he had always loved, but which only then, with
heart-stopping synchronicity, seemed to provide that
moment – that *very* moment – with its own ineffable
soundtrack.

So much optimism, so much bitterness, thought
Nick. How is it possible that the two can be contained
in the same voice, the same car, the same city, the same
world? One of the girls in the back seat saw Nick was
singing to himself and smiled, half in mockery, half
in conspiracy with him. And as he saw her smile, he
thought he understood for the first time the paradox

of America: the pioneer nation, turned sour with anger and resentment and self-doubt, still unable to embrace irony entirely, still unable to forfeit the dream that had propelled it into existence. And this was the city that had become the factory of the world's ideas: of subversives and capitalists alike, of those who would build empires and tear them down, of the movie house and the machine gun.

Now, years later, he awaited his host in one of the city's cathedrals to plutocracy, a costumed fugitive. The tux was a poor fit, marking him out as an interloper. Much worse, he was the first to arrive, standing in the vast atrium of the club, playing nervous hopscotch on the black-and-white Roman tiles.

Two men in dinner jackets, corpulent and bursting, marched past him towards the bar. They did not acknowledge or show the slightest interest in him. One, his hair a shock of grey-tinged ginger, expressed frustration in his every gesture, even as he drank his first Martini, even as he popped an olive in his mouth.

"I don't want another airline, Harry," he said. "I don't care what Mitchell says. He can't con me this time. He must think I've forgotten that Venezuelan piece of shit he sold me."

His companion was more relaxed, struggling to contain his amusement. He ran his hand over his balding head, across which grey hairs crept in a losing battle.

"He only wants to impress you, George," he said. "He thinks you'll introduce him to the President."

"Nick," a voice said. He was awoken from his reverie by a handshake that was hearty and dominant. Alan Bradley smiled with the protracted grin of somebody who assumes his authority will be acknowledged, his prosperity admired. His voice, a rich basso, was unmistakable, but almost everything else about him had changed. The well-preserved quarterback Nick remembered had allowed the laces of his physique to come undone. Alan had put on four or five stone, and moved much more slowly, with the lateral heave of a bartender carrying a keg. The focus of his frame was no longer his impressive shoulders, but his low-slung belly. Perched on his head was a thatch of hair that might, conceivably, have been a surgical transplant, but was certainly not of native origin.

"Hello, Mr Bradley," Nick said, cradling his glass to disguise his unrelieved tremor.

"Oh, come on, call me Alan," he said, beaming again, no less gratuitously. "You really are a trouper to come out and see me here tonight. Straight off the flight and all. Is the hotel okay? I hope the tux was ready-hung in the closet for you, like I asked. They know me there, see. It's the little things."

"Oh, yes," Nick said. "Everything was perfect. Really, many thanks. You didn't have to go to such trouble."

Alan took Nick aside theatrically, as if imparting a sensational confidence.

"Don't suppose you've heard of the Fountainhead Circle, have you?"

"Well, no. I've heard of this club before – the building, I mean – but not the Circle itself."

"Glad to hear it. Most folks in this city haven't heard of it either, and I hope it stays that way. In theory, it's supposed to be a society dedicated to the ideals of Ayn Rand, and 'enlightened self-interest', and all that conservative philosophy, but that's a crock of shit. Really, it's a network of businessmen and the occasional biddable politician who – shall we say – shares our interests. I call it the Bagel Bilderberg."

Nick nodded. The bailiffs of deep exhaustion were now claiming their due, pounding furiously on the door of his soul, and he knew that only the drink and the adrenalin were preventing his physical collapse. The atrium swam a little before him, the chessboard of the floor fracturing like a Cubist painting before he recovered his composure. He downed his third glass of wine. His collar itched. "So. Do you spend much time in New York?"

"Uh-huh," said Alan. "That's where most of my business is. But I don't keep an apartment. I have a sentimental love of the Algonquin. My literary side, I guess, which is maybe what drew me and Susan together in the first place. She thinks I am the most appalling philistine, which in some ways I am. But I like to read. I read more now I'm getting older and sleep less. You?"

"Me? Well, yes. I teach English, so it's part of the job."

"*Teach*? My God, no wonder you look so *underfed*. You haven't put much weight on in fifteen years or whatever it is, which is more than I can say. But how do you pay the bills?"

"With difficulty. I have a sympathetic landlord." He registered Alan's glazed expression, the bourbon doing its work. "Listen, I hate to do this to you, but is there somewhere private we can go for a moment, so…"

"Hey, look," Alan interrupted. "We're going up."

The Fountainhead Brotherhood, paired, in most cases, with guests, began their ascent of the stairs to the banquet. They shared a particular sort of amble, which was meant to suggest, Nick realized, the grace and authority of off-duty power. And yet, as he watched the nodding heads in penguin suits make their way up the broad flight of stairs, with its lush red carpet, it struck him that they resembled nothing so much as a gang of sniggering, uniformed schoolboys, playing a game, whispering behind their hands, calling each other names, and conspiring against one another.

The banqueting room was a Regency palace decorated by a jewel thief, its chandeliers multi-tiered and ostentatious, shedding gentle light on the rococo ceiling paintings of *putti* bearing scrolls, heroic demigods at war and voluptuous, laurelled maidens personifying the Virtues. There were twenty or so tables, each with a dozen settings indicating a daunting number of courses. Each had its own magnificent floral arrangement, and the top table – next to which was a discreet speaker's podium – boasted a bronze sculpture of Atlas that was the Society's mascot. Copperplate cards bore the names of each member and guest. The napkins were folded perfectly, the water bottles chilled, even the salt in each cellar sculpted into a pyramid. Alan Bradley was at home here.

After grace was said, the Provost of the Society read what he reminded the company was an extract from Howard Roark's great speech at the end of Ayn Rand's *The Fountainhead*. He cleared his throat: "The first right on earth is the right of the ego. Man's first duty is to himself… The 'common good' of a collective – a race, a class, a state – was the claim and justification of every tyranny ever established over men." Yes, nodded the members of the Brotherhood, that's right. "Has any act of selfishness ever equalled the carnage perpetrated by disciples of altruism?" No, they muttered, never. The Provost's voice rose with righteous anger. "The only good which men can do to one another and the only statement of their proper relationship is – 'Hands off!' " The last two words were roared by two hundred men who treasured their bleak heroism. "This country was not based on selfless service, sacrifice, renunciation or any precept of altruism. It was based on a man's right to the pursuit of happiness. His own happiness. Not anyone else's. A private, personal, selfish motive. Look at the results." The Provost paused gravely, setting down the book, with the certainty of a preacher who has given much to his flock, and asked no less. "Look into your own conscience."

Nick guessed that it was just what they wanted to hear, these well-upholstered sultans of the city.

"Good stuff, isn't it?" said Alan as they sat down. "Touches the spot, every time."

"I never did finish that novel," said the man on Nick's left, who was barely five years his senior. He was still slender, with angular, hawkish features. "Never mind. My name is Haze, by the way. Haze McCann."

"Nick Atkins. I'm Alan's guest."

"You a client of this ambulance chaser? I pity you. And your pocketbook."

"No. More a friend of the family, I suppose."

"I didn't think Alan had a family. More of a… an *entourage*. And quite a fluid one at that."

Nick was flustered by Haze's bonhomous presumption. It seemed only minutes since he had dragged Aisha's haemorrhaging body from the front of the car to the trunk, the hum and chirruping of the forest deafening to his sensitized ears. At that moment, all the hate he had stored up for her in the past days had given way to a stab of helpless pity – pity for the woman whose body he had caressed even as she lied and lied to him. At that moment, beneath the mournful stars in a Californian forest, the deception seemed a small thing. Their past intimacy and the coldness of her skin was all he could think of. His unresolved passion for one lover had ushered another towards a savage death.

Now, in pursuit of some sort of truth, at the very edge of his endurance, and much further than he had ever thought himself capable of travelling, he found himself surrounded by the very people Tab hated most. At their heart was her conniving, shining, fattened father. And with him were men like Haze McCann, another smiling lawyer ready to push Alan aside as he grew old and eventually crumbled, the younger man salivating at the thought of crushing his mentors and supplanting them. This Society of theirs was not a society in any meaningful sense. It was more like a truce between predators, a collective ceasefire which could be broken at any moment, for any reason. Every table was a little Cold War, every *placement* a celebration of Mutually Assured Destruction.

"Don't you just love this?" said Haze, as they ate a first course of quail's eggs nestling in a perfectly crisp and dressed salad of chicory.

Nick picked at his food, unable to muster an appetite.

"What?"

"The whole thing. I mean, what would people think?" Haze rolled the question round his mouth like a pearl dipped in Beluga. "They'd hate us, wouldn't they? If they could see us all in here, I mean. People hate us. They always do."

"Yes. I suppose you're right."

"They'd say that this was the military-industrial complex having its chow. And you know, they're wrong." Haze touched the back of Nick's hand as if to signal that an insight was imminent. "There's nothing *complex* about it at all. It's the simplest thing in the world. Simple. The oldest thing, too." He took a sip of wine, savoured it.

"I suppose that doesn't make it good in a lot of people's eyes," said Nick.

Haze scrutinized him: maybe Alan really had brought an outsider, this Brit in his shitty rental tux, without a proper shave. Hell: he probably shaved *himself.* "True. True enough. But all we do in here is talk about what we do, which is to accumulate wealth and, in some cases, political power. We accumulate and we organize, and the world more or less holds together. As a result of our work, people have jobs, society doesn't fall to pieces, and the people who want to tear the whole thing down are destroyed. I mean, show me a better way."

The courses came and went, and with them wines of such magnificence that it was hard to know which was more inspiring to the palate, more carefully judged. Not for the Fountainhead Circle the nursery food of London clubs: this was cuisine for men who insisted on the best, always, in every circumstance. But to remark upon the quality of the food and wine would have been as gauche as to say how *nice* it was to have one's own private jet, or to buy a house in the Hamptons for your daughter, or to keep a couple of senators on your payroll: it would tell the brethren that you were not really in the circle at all.

For a dazed, drink-befuddled instant Nick felt a pang of guilty jealousy. These men believed themselves to be free, which was enviable. In their own way, they had reached the end of history and found the last man: a pig, gorging itself at a stolen trough.

As the later courses arrived and the plates were taken away, his attempts to steer his host towards the subject of Tab met with evasion and then a whisper of irritation. Though he postured as a New York Falstaff – expansive, bluff, open to the charge of buffoonery – Alan Bradley was fully in control of their evening together, enjoying the choreography, the spectacle and the spent features of his guest. I could be anyone, thought Nick. It is the game he enjoys, the unsolicited opportunity to watch another human being squirm. For him, my awkward, English questions are merely part of the revels.

The dinner ended sooner than he expected: the members of the Fountainhead Circle were early risers. Haze McCann told Nick that he set his alarm for 4.30 a.m. and ran for an hour on a treadmill before breakfast and the morning's first meeting at his practice, which usually commenced at 6.30 a.m. He did not have to start so early, he said, but it made him feel good to know that, as the human race slept, he and those like him were already up, earning money, fixing the match so that they always, always won.

Alan and Nick filed down the stairs, across the atrium, where clusters of men concluded their business, and out into the warm night air. By the entrance to the club, a group of passers-by was dispersing, having gathered to watch a very eminent politician leave in his waiting limousine. They chattered and nudged one another: they had seen the man-who-would-be-President; they could tell their workmates in the morning, over coffee in open-plan offices, of this brush with aspirant greatness. One of them, a tall man in a crisp suit, looked a little familiar to Nick, but was gone before he could see if his over-tested mind was playing tricks on him.

Here he was in another forest, a forest of steel and concrete with its own rhythms, its own nocturnal music: the sirens and the yelling and the seething horns of quarrelling drivers. For a few seconds, the members of the Fountainhead Circle had a taste of what it was they worked so hard to avoid, the terror of a life lived without the security of wealth. A few seconds was enough. Nick watched them fleeing to their gleaming black limos. Alan beckoned Nick to his waiting car, the chauffeur closing the doors behind them and then whisking them away.

The lounge of the Algonquin was darker than the club: its Edwardian opulence seemed forced to Nick – the colonnade of pillars, the stuffed burgundy chairs, and the subdued lighting. But it made Alan Bradley happy, as happy as his membership of the Circle. He lectured Nick briefly on the meetings of the Round Table that had started in 1919 and made the hotel famous, on Dorothy Parker, George S. Kaufman, Robert Sherwood and Edna Ferber, as if Nick were a favoured nephew just out of High School, making his first trip to the city without his parents. His noisy affection for the hotel and its literary aura was evidently a treasured affectation, crude ballast for his professional barbarism.

They made their way up to Alan's three-room suite. "Home at last," he said, as he swiped his card into the door. Inside, on the sofa, oblivious to the two men's arrival, lay a blonde girl, her hair in a pony tail, watching television with complete absorption. She wore white denim shorts and a pink top that revealed her tanned midriff and smooth shoulders. There was a hint of tobacco in the air, although Nick could not be sure. He felt a wave of revulsion as he looked first at the girl and then at Alan. She was no more than sixteen, perhaps younger.

"Kelly!" he said. "You said you wouldn't be back. What are you doing here?"

She looked up, eyes candid and guiltless. "What?"

"How come you're back, honey?"

She flounced back on the sofa. "I decided not to go to Marina's. I hate her. Lydia is out. So…"

Alan's wrath – was it wrath? – began to subside. "Did you eat?"

"Yeah. Some."

"Yeah. Some," he imitated. "Hey, honey. This is Nick, a… um… friend of mine. From London. He came to the dinner."

"Uh-huh," she said, glancing back and then returning to the television, stretching one tanned leg towards the ceiling in a gesture of aristocratic tedium.

There was a troubled silence. For the first time, Alan Bradley seemed unnerved. Nick could think of nothing to say that would not draw further attention to the raw, uninhibited ugliness of his relationship with the girl.

"Hey, look, honey," Alan said after a while. "Could you maybe watch the movie in another room? I need to talk to Nick a little."

The girl exploded, leaping from the sofa, her arms spreading suddenly and wildly. "Jesus!" She fixed him with eyes that remained winsome even as they blazed with fury. Nick saw that her hair was naturally dark, that the blonde was as artificial as Alan Bradley's smile. She picked up her soda and stormed from the room. Seconds later, they heard the dialogue of the movie resume, louder this time.

"Sorry about that," said Alan, wiping his brow on his sleeve. "The spirit of youth, right? Let me buy you a drink."

"That's all right," said Nick. "No, really, thank you. I've had enough. I need to sleep quite soon. Thank you, again, for putting me up here."

The other man chuckled as he poured himself a generous measure of bourbon on ice. "I remember Tab saying that about you. You know, the constant humility nonsense and apologies. So *English*. Charming, in its way. Certainly charming to her."

"I imagine it grates sometimes."

"Not with me, no." Alan gestured for him to sit down, as he installed himself in a cream armchair. "I rather like it. But then I have a weakness for gentility." He stroked his knee. "Something my wife – my ex-wife – could never fully appreciate about me. Like so much else."

"Well, I am grateful."

Alan's eyes narrowed. "Yeah. But you're desperate, too. Aren't you?"

"What do you mean?"

"I don't know what Susan knows and doesn't know. But she calls me last night and says that a guy Tab hasn't seen for more than fifteen years has turned up on her doorstep in the hills, and thinks our daughter is in some sort of trouble. More to the point that he's in a whole lot of trouble, too. I do sympathize. But I am unclear where this is heading. Frankly, I'm only seeing you as a favour to her."

Nick felt relief that at last the matter was being broached. "I wish I knew myself. What I know is that Tab is mixed up in something political, dangerously so. Radical stuff. The people she works with are capable of great violence. I can't find her, and I need to."

Alan scrutinized him, his lawyer's talons digging into the arms of the chair.

"Why?"

"Because for some reason I can't fathom, Tab has involved me. She seems to have talked about me to the other people in her group. They are looking for me. I can't imagine why, but it's clear that I am in danger." He paused. "People have died already."

"Is that right?" said Alan. "Well, well. I must say I didn't expect to see you again. Nice Oxbridge boy. Off to make your fortune at the bar... well that didn't happen, did it? But all this? Well, pardon me, but it's not really the sort of thing I associate you with."

"Susan says that you may have been in contact with Tab from time to time. She says you help her financially."

Alan looked above Nick's head with empty eyes. "Susan said that, did she? Yeah, well. She's still my daughter. I have sent her money occasionally. When she has asked. A fair amount of money sometimes."

"Do you see her?"

He looked at his lap. "Not for a very long time. She disappeared years ago. I get emails from her, not very communicative, asking for help. Never the same address."

"How do you know it's her?"

"Oh, you know the way your daughter talks, trust me. Especially this one. She speaks in her own way, her own private language. Inimitable."

"When was the last message?"

Alan Bradley stood up and went to the bureau by the window. There was a large evidence case by its side, which he opened, removing a plastic folder. He handed it to Nick, who inspected it.

"It's an email?"

"Yeah. The account was already dead by the time I tried to reply. I don't know what the hell it means either."

The message consisted of two words: "WILLIAM'S MELANCHOLY". It was vintage Tab – brief, beguiling and insanely allusive. Nick wondered whether she had smiled as she sat in an Internet café somewhere on the other side of the world, or perhaps round the corner, sending her father a communication that was barely worthy of the name. William? That could only mean Yeats: that was easy, deliberately so. But "melancholy"? What was that? Then, from somewhere in the depths of himself, he remembered the line, or rather the phrase, which, more to himself than Alan, he spoke out loud.

"'This melancholy London' – then something about imagining the souls of the lost. I can't remember it all."

"What are you talking about?" said Alan.

"It's Yeats. It's a passage from Yeats she's referring to. She must have been in London when she sent the message. That's what she was hinting at, I think… That's what she was trying to tell you. That's all."

"But how in hell would I have guessed that? Christ – why can't she just tell me in plain English, like a normal daughter. What possesses that girl?" He punched his fist into his palm. "I do not understand. I just do not understand."

"Neither do I. When did she send this?"

"Six months ago. Since then, nothing."

Nick stood up. He had come all this way to find out that she had sent her last message from the place he had left. Tab, damn her for ever, would love the joke. She had pulled him across the ocean, her laughter echoing down the years, and now she would drag him back for the next act in her terrible drama.

"Thank you," he said. He could think of nothing else to offer.

Alan was facing the mirror above the fireplace. He turned with unexpected speed, confronting Nick fully for the first time. "Listen to me. I don't know you, and I don't trust you. She always said you had what it took, behind all the nauseating Englishness. Maybe she was right. But when you find her – if you find her – you better take good care of her. You better get her out of whatever trouble she's in. That seems to be what she expects of you. Well, do it. Do it. Or I'll come after you with a thousand nightmares in my pocket. So help me God, I will."

The meeting was over: Nick left at once, shaken by his host's outburst. The silence as he left was broken only by the noise of the movie from the bedroom to which Kelly had withdrawn, awaiting the blandishments and apologies that would surely be forthcoming from the older man, after he had recovered his composure and poured himself another, larger drink. Nick's own room was a floor down, and he took the stairs, reluctant to submit to the claustrophobia of the lift even for a few seconds. He wanted to get to safety, to double-lock the door behind him and push an armchair up against it. It would be all right for now, all right until morning. He had no energy to think of what he must do next, what task lay ahead of him.

He opened his door, imagining already the softness of the bed linen on his tired, scratchy skin. Before he could reach round and turn on the light, a hand slammed into his mouth and a fist punched his kidneys. He felt himself retch, spluttering against the bodiless palm in the dark, and his knees buckle as he absorbed the force of the blow. He heard the switch being flicked on and the lock applied. Not for a second did the commanding hand loosen its grip on his mouth. He feared that he would soon be unable to breath.

He looked up to see a monstrous half-man towering over him, deformed and incomplete. The creature's head was almost bald, and scorched with pink scars. Tufts of blond hair fell by his cauterized ears, which bore the marks of blows. The man had no eyebrows, and one of his eyes was sealed shut, as if with glue. A rasping noise emerged from what was left of his nose. His hands – visible now – had the strange texture of melted plastic. Barely human, he heaved with rage and pent-up power. Nick tried to cry out, but the thing lifted a claw to his split lips, his hand tightening on his captive's chin. When he spoke, it was with great difficulty, a wheezing rattle from the depths of his chest.

"If you want to live, do as I say," he hissed. "My name is Freddy."

3

Helpless on the floor of his room at the Algonquin, gasping for air, he asked Freddy only one question: "How soon will you kill me?" He said the words almost inaudibly, and without the slightest expectation of an answer. But it was the right question, delivered in the correct tone of surrender. Having established unchallenged control more quickly than he thought might be necessary, Freddy was able to prop his captive up against the bed, fetch him a glass of water.

"Just relax," he said to Nick. "Here, take a drink."

"Who are you?"

"I'm someone who needs your help. And you need mine, believe me."

"Christ," Nick said, ripping off his bow tie and undoing two buttons to help the flow of air. He breathed deeply. "So what did she tell you?"

Freddy squatted down, his deformed face close to Nick's. "Who?"

"Tab, of course. Tab Bradley."

Freddy snorted. "Oh, I've never met her. Never."

"What do you mean?"

"Only a few people ever did. Munroe, of course. Well, it was all their creation, really. The two of them.

There was an inner circle, some of whom I *have* met. Clio. Rosa. Andreas. But I dealt with Munroe, and Munroe only. That's why he sent me to Amsterdam, I think. Because in the end, I knew so little." He wiped a gluey secretion from his open eye. "Which is why they took their time with me, you see. They had to ask me every *conceivable* question before they could finish." He looked up at the window. "And they did. They did."

"But you are a member of Second Troy?"

Freddy stood up again, as if his melted skin would not allow his body to hold a single posture for very long. "Nobody is a *member* of Second Troy. It's not just another splinter group. We have plenty of those already… God knows." He lit a cigarette and drew on it, wincing. He spoke loudly, with demented garrulousness and the urgency of a man trying to drown out the ticking of a clock. "No unity, no discipline. You see, I was permitted to be close to the chosen, the New Weathermen, like Munroe and Tab. Well, I'm sure you've heard all about them… us. The new underground. It was, I now realize, the most brilliant deception in the history of the struggle. It was an underground movement that was a *front*. A secret to keep you from the *real* secret. The New Weathermen – all the messages warning of attacks on federal buildings, corporate headquarters, banks, all the old-fashioned stuff – was just a fantastic *distraction*. Second Troy was the reality. Is the reality. That was Tab's genius. She always said – or so I was told – that the enemy didn't understand that he couldn't win. So you had to create the *illusion* of victory. So that the other side *thought* they had won. The New Weathermen was created for that purpose and that purpose alone: to be *beaten*. It meant that the real work of Second Troy could proceed unhindered."

Nick sat up and gulped down the last of the water. He could hear a couple whispering to one another and laughing in the corridor as they searched in bags and pockets for their key card. He felt a sudden impulse to cry out, to return to the world of stumbling human normality. He wanted to see his daughter's face. But what would he tell them all? He coughed and cleared his throat, still recovering from Freddy's assault.

"What is the work of Second Troy? I still don't understand."

Freddy laughed: a strange guttural sound that seemed to flow from staccato pulses in his belly. "As if I would know that. Everybody who gets close to this thing makes the mistake of thinking that somebody like me would know the answer to that question. They are so used to dealing with anarchist collectives, shambolic groups and structures that are easy to infiltrate and destabilize. But Second Troy doesn't work like that. It is an ethic as much as a group. The pursuit of great objectives by… well, new methods, of course, but more than that. Methods without limit, or constraint. And only one person knows everything."

"Tab?"

Freddy nodded. "She holds the key to everything. Munroe understood that, accepted it even. He had become completely disillusioned with collective decision-making, all the talking shops, the failures. He believed a new phase of command and control was needed, and he was content to do all the work with people like me, let Tab stay in the background. She used code names

– Adeptus, and Magister, and all these things, mystical almost. I don't really know what they meant."

"I think it's Yeats."

"What?"

"The poet Yeats," Nick said. "Her obsession, you know. Those names you said – they're from the Golden Dawn. It was a crazy masonic order he belonged to. The whole point, if I remember, was to prosecute some 'Great Work'. Christ knows. I wonder what 'Great Work' Tab and her friends have in mind."

Freddy shrugged. "They talked of such things. A great task ahead, a great undertaking. But Munroe said that, in the end, we were not really members or agents in the old-fashioned sense – he used the word *tesserae,* the pieces in a mosaic whose design would become clear only when our work was finished. He said that when the world saw the mosaic they would not be able to believe its beauty… that it would be remembered and talked about for centuries. But the point about the mosaic, for now, was that only one person knew the whole of the design."

"Did you know anything about her?"

Freddy turned away. "Enough to end up looking like this."

"Why have you come after me?" Nick asked.

"Because you are the key to all this, or so it seems. I remember Munroe told me – we were in Paris… oh, a while back – that Tab had got a little drunk with him once. It was so unlike her, to drop her guard like that. But she did – or at least Munroe says she did. Anyway, it was at the end of a stressful time when the whole movement was being infiltrated, at war with itself."

Nick grimaced as a spasm of pain coursed through his arm. The noise of the New York night crept into the room. "Were they lovers?"

"I don't know. It wasn't the sort of question you asked, not if you wanted to stay alive."

"What did she tell him?"

"They were holed up at one of our safe houses. The two of them talked about their lives before joining the movement for the first time. You know, he told her about growing up in Scotland, hating it, anti-nuke stuff, left-wing nationalism, then moving to London and becoming immersed in the hardcore green stuff. She told him about California, her academic life, her decision to commit her life to the cause, that there was only one person in all those years who had ever touched her, who understood her fully. And that was you.

"Apparently, she said there was a moment – a particular moment she had in mind – when she realized how remarkable you were, deep inside. She wouldn't go into it, what had happened. The point was that – how did Munroe put it? – only you *got* her. I guess he was a little jealous of that, too."

"But the whole point is that I *didn't* get her. She ended it with me. Years and years ago. I'm not sure I'd even recognize her now." Nick knew this was a lie even as he said it.

Freddy continued: "She said to Munroe that you would play a part in the work of Second Troy one day. A very significant part."

"That's insane. I'm just a teacher. The whole idea is madness. All this is madness." He felt his head begin to loll in exhaustion. "Christ. I am so tired…"

"Munroe seemed to believe her, anyway, odd as the whole thing was. He told me all this with fascination, envy, amazement. I think he felt he'd said too much to me even when he said it. But we were tight, Munroe and I. He occasionally let slip something interesting. Very occasionally."

"Why are you telling me all this?"

Freddy sat down, crossed his legs with effort. "The people who did this to me let me go after two days. I was half-dead by then, delirious. Drugs, you know, they use – as well as everything else. If people had any idea what is done in their name… Well, they tidied me up – more or less – and dumped me at a roadside. Outside the city. I was amazed that I wasn't dead. I saw several faces when I was in there, so it's obvious they're letting me stay alive for a reason. They expect me to lead them to Second Troy. Well, that's fine by me. The struggle is over for me. But I want to find out who betrayed me in Amsterdam. If I have you, I buy myself a return ticket to Munroe, who must assume I'm dead. They need you, and I have you. So I have a suggestion."

Nick sat on the bed and surveyed the pink-canvas atrocity of Freddy's face. He wondered what force on earth could inflict such horror upon a man, and have the cruelty to let him live, to limp forth into a half-life of vengeful misery. "Go on," he said.

"Work with me to find them. This message…" he flourished the piece of paper he had removed from Nick's inside pocket "…might be a start. It must be code: 'William's Melancholy'. Does it mean anything to you?"

As he gathered himself to explain Tab's six-month-old communiqué again, it dawned on Nick that the message was not meant for her father at all. It was meant for him. She had kept many secrets even from her closest comrades: that much was clear. She had toyed with them, made some of those who followed her doubt her very existence. She had laughed in the dark as her puppets cavorted and crashed into one another. And now, in some unfathomable way, she had used her father as an errand boy with a message for him, and him alone.

"London," Nick said.

"What?"

"She's in London, I think. Or she was. That's what I reckon the message means."

"Tell me how." Freddy's claw tightened on the paper. "Immediately."

Nick repeated what he had said to Alan less than an hour before.

"Why not contact you direct?"

"Maybe she did. Maybe she tried. God knows. But she sent this around the time the messages for me in the *California Literary Review* stopped."

Freddy stood up again. Nick could see him grimace as his skin stretched across his hot, tortured body. "London. Well, that's interesting."

"Why?"

"It means that there'll be Second Troy personnel there who know where to find her, or Munroe at least."

"You sound sure."

"I'm not. But it's a lead. I had the feeling in Berlin

– before all this – that the movement was preparing for something big. I mean I was handing over a very, very large sum of money. I wondered if this was the great task Munroe sometimes talked about. I always assumed he was talking theoretical shit – you know, the grand sweep of history, the destruction of global capitalism and militarism – but there were times when I wondered if it was something more specific he had in mind. I had a sense that, maybe even without us knowing it, we were being summoned to a central point. A day of reckoning, if you like."

Nick listened and chose his words with care: "Whoever did this to you – the British authorities found out what you said about me… that you named me. That's why they took me in and why I'm here. They haven't tracked me down yet, but they will. The woman you killed was my minder."

"I didn't kill her."

"What do you mean?"

"It wasn't me. I followed you to Soquel, sure. But I saw a scuffle – couldn't make out what was going on, it was so dark – and headed back to my car. I couldn't be sure that it was safe to make my move then."

"Who, then?"

Freddy shrugged once more. "Does it matter?" He stroked his hand as if cradling a wounded animal. "There are so many people it could be." He smiled faintly. "Let's see if we can find out in London."

* * *

"You're mad," Topper said by a coffee kiosk at the edge of the arrivals area. "Strictly certifiable. And you look like shit. What were you doing in America? Come back with me now. Come on. We'll clean you up and sort you out. Put you in a bubble bath and give you a decent meal."

A few steps behind Topper stood Chris, in bomber jacket and jeans, muscular and disapproving. Chris did not like threats that had not been neutralized, messes that had not been tidied. To see somebody as important to Topper as Nick in distress offended his sense of the way the world should be.

"Can't do it, Tops," Nick said. "Can't. I'm just check-ing in, like I promised. I called because I wanted to do this face to face. It was probably a mistake. I'm sorry." A small child ran past him towards an elderly African in a spectacularly colourful kaftan, who was pushing a trolley and smiling broadly.

"What's going on, Nicko?" said Topper, chewing his gum with consternation. "You're in trouble, big time. Aren't you?"

"Possibly. Probably. Yes. Listen, before you ask, it is her. Or something to do with her. I have to find her. And that's all there is to it. You have to trust me."

"Yeah, right. You have such a good record in that department."

"Come on, Tops. I don't have much time. Certainly no time for games."

Topper turned away in exasperation. "Look, what would you do? My best mate calls me in the middle of the night from New York, says it's urgent. Sounds funny, to say the least. So I come here. As anyone would. And now you're giving me verbals and telling me to back off."

Nick shook his head. "I'm sorry. I'm sorry. I needed to see someone sane." He looked at the weary travellers bustling around. "And I needed to ask you… Keep an eye on the girls for me, if…"

"What are you talking about?"

"Tops, you know what I mean. You, of all people, know that Tab is trouble. Wherever I am headed, it's going to be…" he closed his fist in exasperation "…I don't know. Bloody *trouble*. But I… there are good reasons why I have to do this. I hope I'll be able to explain it all soon, but not now. Okay?" For the first time he could hear the pleading in his own voice.

"Okay," Topper said. His face was etched with alarm and fearfulness. He could see that his friend meant what he said.

"Be quick now," said Nick. "I don't want you to bump into him."

Topper patted him sturdily on the back and shoulder. "Take care, all right?" Topper turned, nodded to Chris, and was gone.

Nick waited outside the Men's room. This time Freddy was taking much longer, hunched in a cubicle, doing his best to suppress his groans as he applied ointments and treatments to his face, soothing the wounds and wiping them clean. Freddy would not say much about what they had done to him, or who, precisely, they were – if indeed he knew – but he was quite clear about what his response was going to be.

And, to his surprise, Nick had quickly concluded that his captor's analysis was right.

* * *

Change Alley rattled with the echo of fleeing boots, followed by the angry footfall of pursuit. The Red Gang had broken up on Cornhill, finally aborting its mission to gather at the statue of Wellington by Bank station, armed with paint pots. The legend – "Warmonger" – agreed after many hours of acrimonious debate in a Southwark squat (fending off such rivals as "Fascist", "Capitalist Pig" and "Duke of Death") was not now to be daubed on the equestrian plinth: not today. Instead, the twenty-strong group dispersed as they heard the whinnying and snorting of the steeds, the mounted police flexing their arms and testing their batons at their side. There were only four of them, cantering over from Queen Victoria Street, but they achieved swift mastery of the proposed battlefield: four visored horsemen of the cancelled apocalypse. Behind them rose the mist of tear gas, the dregs of a canister thrown earlier.

From the glass-lined alley of Gracechurch Street could be heard the clamour of the Green Gang – each wearing a mask of the designated colour – instructed by the same meeting to paint-bomb the buildings around Liverpool Street and smash the windows of as many global chain stores as they could find. The whine of sirens competed with their raucous expletives and the shattering of glass. Two of the green protesters, both in camouflage jackets, were unfurling a banner with the words "LIFE BEFORE PROFIT" painted on it: they succeeded in hanging it loosely from a set of traffic lights, the other end draped over the awning of a coffee shop, inside which a handful of stranded City workers stood open-mouthed and trembling. The banner flapped in the wind, pathetic in the midst of these giant, implacable buildings. The disturbance continued, but the crystal temples of the City seemed only to shudder irritably, as if swatting away an irksome insect at dusk. The four horsemen galloped towards the fracas.

Freddy and Nick stood on the island at the end of Threadneedle Street, breathless and flustered, surveying the disaggregation of the march they had started to follow only a few hours ago. This is the place to be, Freddy had said. This is where we'll find the people who can take us to them. The march – a fairly routine invasion of the City, gazetted on the usual websites as a rally to "Reclaim the Capital" – had become livelier than he expected, more so than anything he had seen in London for four or five years. The tempo of the movement was building, he told Nick. But the days of paint bombs and dreary banners were over: the new order of Munroe Stacy and his allies was at hand.

A television van rumbled into view, but was thwarted by a police barrier, hurriedly erected. A teenaged boy with green punk hair skipped past them. "They've released the Walbrook! The river's free!" he yelled. "Through a fucking hydrant! We're taking the city back." He leapt up onto the stone by the statue and confronted them with crazed eyes. "I am fucking *Wat Tyler*, man." Their silence visibly angered him. "Who the fuck are you?"

Freddy answered: "Grown-ups."

The punk spat in disgust.

"What's with the fucking mask, anyway? You look like the invisible man." He pointed at the thick gauze burns bandages with which Freddy had covered his face.

"Oh, I'm not invisible," Freddy said. He carefully lifted the mask with rough fingers and pressed his face close to the punk's. "Am I?"

The amphetamine shine in the boy's eyes gave way to abject panic. He fled towards the police barrier, and the safer prospect of arrest.

Nick allowed himself a smile. "You shouldn't do that, you know. You'll draw attention to us."

"Listen, there are few consolations for being disfigured for life. That's one of them."

From Bishopsgate, the dregs of the march – hundreds rather than thousands – were making their way towards London Bridge, escorted by police vehicles and more horsemen. Their jubilation was muted now, as dusk settled on the stone and glass of the City – unchanged, unmoved – and they beat a retreat across the river. The chanting continued – "*Ya Basta! Ya Basta!*" – but it was desultory by comparison with the collective fury the crowd had mustered only half an hour before. Whistles blew and banners fluttered in the sky. But the marchers were refugees now, not soldiers in a struggle. The struggle was over for the day.

"Where are they going?" Nick asked.

"Some of them will be going where we're going," Freddy replied. "It's a place called Pedro's off Tooley St. A hang-out for greens and squatters on the first floor of an old warehouse. Sells beer and cigarettes and coffee. Weed, if you want it. A good place for the children to lick their wounds today, I'd guess."

Freddy stepped off the dais by the statue, and led Nick towards the human river which was now edging slowly towards the bridge. The sun, ruddy and iridescent, clambered back towards the West, casting a rouge fuzz upon the skyline of Westminster, the great wheel, the concrete theatres of the South Bank. Beneath the bridge the tour boats ploughed through the water towards Tower Bridge and Greenwich, broad and lumbering, their passengers startled by the marchers, who cried out slogans and obscenities. To the protesters' fury, a group of tourists waved back, raising their wine glasses and lifting their sunglasses to get a better view of the City's eccentric tribes.

Freddy walked more slowly than Nick would have liked, but there was no way to hurry him. He could still move quickly if he had to – as he had, with violent accuracy, in the hotel. But the cost was phenomenal. With every step it seemed as though his skin might tear, as if the pulverized structure of his body needed only one last trauma to disintegrate entirely. But he kept going, hate-filled and hate-driven, his zeal for the movement, Nick realized, now supplanted by his desire for vengeance before his system gave way and closed down for good.

At the station, a meek platoon of teenagers – crusty and exhausted – slouched off to catch trains or call friends. One couple, jeered at by their comrades, climbed into the back of a black cab, which drove off under a final hail of rotten fruit and vegetables. But Freddy had been right about Pedro's. Thirty or so of the remaining marchers filed off down Tooley Street, their collective force diminishing with every pace: by the time they reached the bar, they were nothing more than a rag-tag of kids, excitable and calling for a drink. The angry rioters had shrunk into adolescents on an outing.

The entrance to Pedro's was manned by a Rasta called – Freddy explained – Manila Joe, who wore a fruity yellow T-shirt, cut-off jeans and opaque black sunglasses. His moustache twitched with disapproval as Freddy and Nick approached. He put down his news-paper, sat up on his stool and prepared to obstruct their intrusion.

"Joe!" said Freddy, before the doorman could issue his veto. "It's Wolfgang! Don't you remember me! I guess not – it was before the car crash. Nobody remembers me when they see me now. I was here last year." He lowered his voice. "With Clio and Rosa. Don't you remember?"

"No," Manila Joe replied. "Who's this?"

"This is my friend from the Camden Rejectionists, Olly. We've had a real day, a real day. But it wouldn't be complete without…" he signalled to the first floor "…a bit of relaxation."

The Rasta's hostility was subsiding. "What happened to your face, man?"

"Oh, guy. Like I said – a crash. My brother was driving… he was stoned. I went through the fucking window. Fucked up. Hundreds of stitches."

Barely perceptibly, Manila Joe nodded. "That's fuck-ed up, man." With a gesture of his head no less minute or imperious, he admitted them. The smell of beer and dope was overwhelming as Freddy and Nick made their way up the sticky stairs, flecked with cigarette butts and stained by pint glasses. A huge Zapatista poster covered the wall of the landing – "*Zapata Vive! 1994*". The hum of life from the bar was insistent – the sound of pungent youth at play, kicking against every shin it could find. By the entrance was a framed picture of Marlon Brando in *The Wild One*, on which someone had scrawled with a marker pen: "Q: What are we rebelling against? A: What have you got?".

"Christ," said a girl, edging past them and down the stairs. Her hair was matted and streaked red, the colour of her mini-skirt, and she wore an ancient T-shirt, slashed at the shoulders and the belly. She stumbled and giggled as she continued down the steps. A bearded man looked at her with the mute anger and disapproval of a helpless boyfriend, his fists clenched against his combat trousers as she completed her lurch down the stairwell.

At the far end of the room stood the bar, a row of barrels covered in faded flags and banners. Beer flowed from a gigantic keg, beside which was a table covered with a forest of rum bottles. There was a glass-doored fridge full of soft drinks, and a hissing espresso machine, above which hung a multicoloured banner bearing the slogan: *Carnaval Contre Capitalisme*. The words tore into an image of a shattered skyscraper, its windows a thousand nervous eyes, the pyre beneath the building angry and righteous. Quebec, April 2001: Tab had been at that great gathering of the movement, according to Freddy at least. A few months later a different image of a skyscraper ripped apart from the skies would acquire quite a different significance. But the banner still hung, unrepentantly, behind the bar at Pedro's.

Not a table in the joint was free. At eye level hung a fog of tobacco and ganja smoke, hovering over a crazy arrangement of sofas, old pews, stools, rocking chairs and beanbags. Magazines and papers were scattered on the floor in one corner, where a television had just been switched to the news. A huge roar went up as images of the march appeared on screen, drowning out the monotone voiceover. A girl was hoisted onto the shoulders of her friend, spilling her drink all over him, as the picture of a shattered shop-front flashed on screen. Applause rippled through the crowd: punks, greens, anarchists, rude boys, Rastas, metalheads, deadheads, deadbeats, freaks, kids and couples. As the noise subsided, Nick thought he recognized the music pumping from a battered DJ's desk on the other side of the room: it was Pete Seeger, *Guantanamera*. But the Cuban lyric – *Yo soy un hombre sincero, de donde crecen las palmas* – had been carved up and reset to a pounding rap rhythm, a sonic attack on the gentle poetry, which gave it an unsettling ferocity. In front of one of the speakers, two girls in headscarves rocked to the implacable beat, knocking over the rum glasses at their feet, which shattered quickly under the soles of their boots.

Nick had to raise his voice. "What are we doing here?"

Freddy turned to him, impatience blazing in his open eye. "You'll see, if you shut up." He led the way to the bar, where a young woman was racking glasses.

Freddy leant against the barrels and tapped on the wood. His posture was one of familiar expectation.

The woman, her long hair tied back with a bandana, frowned at him, her expression hard and unresponsive.

"Cherry pie, cherry pie, why do you cry?" he said.

The woman flinched and her eyes narrowed, as if a nerve had been touched.

"Don't you recognize me then, Roz?" he said. "It's only a mask. And you've seen plenty of them today, I imagine. Come on, Roz."

The woman's guard fell, her horror and bewilderment now quite open. "Freddy? But… how?"

Freddy lifted a shaky finger to his mouth. "Don't ask. I'll tell you another time. Let's just say I have seen better days. Listen, Roz…" he drew closer to her, as the woman struggled to control her reflexes, to maintain her composure "…I need your help."

"Freddy, I…" she stuttered. "Christ, Freddy. I heard… Well, you know…"

"Yes, I know. I'll tell you. I promise. But Roz – not now, okay?" The pulse of the music accelerated, the sound suddenly more invasive and primitive. "Right now, I'm looking for Clio – or Rosa."

Roz wiped her forehead. "I haven't seen Rosa for weeks." She looked at Nick. "What's his story?"

"Olly? Oh, he's just someone I picked up along the way. Camden crew: he's a good man, is Olly. And I'm a bit nervous about travelling alone these days. If you know what I mean."

Roz ran one thumb against the other, aware of the threat that underpinned his enquiry. "Well, I haven't seen Rosa. She shipped out a while back. A few of them did."

"I see," said Freddy. "And Clio?"

Roz looked down at the bar and back at Freddy. She tilted her head, almost imperceptibly, towards a wooden door behind the bar area. Then, by way of dismissal, she resumed her work. Freddy nodded and whispered to the woman: "Thank you, cherry pie." He lifted his hand to his mouth, and blew her a ragged kiss, the twist of his lips sacrilegious and empty of love.

Nick had not noticed the door before. A coat was hanging from it, obscuring what appeared to be another gaudy political poster. Above the peg, there was a faded "Staff Only" sticker. They walked past the minor obstruction of three kids squatting on the floor in animated conversation over a spliff. Freddy gestured for him to follow and, without knocking, turned the handle.

The corridor within was dark and airless, its carpet worn. Freddy closed the door behind them, plunging them into blackness. He clicked the light switch and a single light bulb above them revealed a long passageway, lined, incongruously, with flock wallpaper, with a row of old cement bags running down its centre. At the other end was a second door with the words "Staff Lounge: Keep Out" stencilled on one of the upper panels. The sound of a radio being tuned rose from within.

"I wonder who's at home," said Freddy quietly. "Come on."

"Are you sure about this?" said Nick.

"Do you want this to be over, or not?"

He did not wait for an answer but made his way towards the door. Again, he raised his gloved hand to his lip, before entering.

There was a blaze of light as the door opened, and

then Nick felt only the sharpness of something entering his neck, and his body sagging with frightening speed. For the third time in a matter of days, he was being overpowered, and he recognized the inevitability of defeat more quickly than before. He was drifting now, and he could not see Freddy. Was he behind him now? He could not be sure. The colours in the room seemed suddenly lurid, unreal, and the light was blinding. He could see the dark silhouette of a woman with long hair and, as he fell deeper and deeper, he heard her speak into a phone, a distant voice miles above him.

"You were right," she said. "He found us here. No, no. We won't be long now. But listen. He wasn't alone. No. He was with…"

Then a rolling wave of warm blackness overwhelmed Nick, lifting him to its crest and taking him under. Yes, was his last thought, just like the poem, always her poems. Yes, yes: "the darkness drops again".

On the pavement, across the road from Pedro's, a smartly dressed middle-aged man spoke quietly into his mobile. "Yes, they're both inside. Well, I can't be sure. Look, don't mention her again. I told you, it was dark." He paused, recovering his poise. "I think it's time for you to start clearing up your mess, don't you?"

In her office, Veronica Brewer clicked her phone shut. She looked across at Simmonds, who was staring out of the window at the traffic heading into Westminster. She started to speak, and then thought better of it.

Maggie Atkins stood at the table in her kitchen. She clutched her left arm, unnoticed by her granddaughter, who was humming and playing with the pans at her feet.

"Something's wrong," she said, to herself.

PART THREE

SECOND TROY

I

Even after all these weeks, and the demands of his duties, the sunrise made his heart catch and his eyes mist over. Munroe Stacy hated his occasional sentimentality, but he also knew that this was not one such lapse. The purity of the moment was absolute, and that was enough to spur deep emotion within him. All the straining of the soul, mind and muscles that lay behind – and ahead – seemed justified as he watched the Tyrolean mountainside awake through the vast bay window of his room. All the scarring of the self was worth it to see this, and to savour what it meant.

Like golden horses charging across the peaks, the light rolled up and over into the valley, spreading quickly and majestically. It was uncompromising. Every recess of the forest, every surface of the timber buildings, every burst of alpine poppies and heath carnations, was illuminated and revealed. He could see the sheep and cows in paddocks on the other side of the river, and the farmer stretch as he readied himself for an hour at the wheel of an ancient tractor. A lone car rumbled below, heading along the river towards Meran. Far above, he could see the shimmering cataracts of melted ice, so at odds with the subtropical fauna over which they loomed.

Below him, a detachment of five began their morning training. What would they look like, he wondered, to the outside world? Like a group of affluent young people – all under thirty – dedicated to the preservation of health and fitness. They were performing some basic tai-chi moves, inhaling and exhaling, their arms moving in and out like a rippling tide. One of them – a Catalan girl he had recruited in Prague – took the lead with subtle assurance. The other four, two men and two women, followed without missing a beat. He liked that. He was tired of wasting time on arguments about the internal politics of struggle, the supposed poison of power. On this, the Bolsheviks were right, Castro was right, the Sheikh in the mountains was right: struggle was pointless without the clarity of control. For decades, the movement had been ruined by indulgent nonsense, by the longings of fattened middle-class amateurs for a syndicalist hobby. Well, Munroe was all for syndicalism: for a global kibbutz where people lived in brotherhood and power was shared like sweets. But that was the end, not the means. The struggle itself required a dictatorship of the oppressed to be expressed through its leadership. It was the only way. That was what he had grasped, and what the Catalan girl, her auburn hair lustrous in the morning light, had intuited as well. She had taken a lead, and the others had followed. Without rancour, without resentment, a natural happening. It was a scene of peace: an outsider, straying into the compound, would not guess at the infinitely serious purpose which had brought these passionate young men and women to this place. A purpose whose true nature even he did not fully know. Not yet.

From all over the world they had come, having waited so patiently for his call, in the barrios, on campuses, on reservations and in refugee camps. They were the strong, the educated, the well-trained few who had risen from the desperate masses. It had taken him three years to marshal these people on a mountainside, amid the hamlets and the old mining villages, but a lifetime to reach the necessary understanding himself. He had not lied to Clio: as his eyes stung with tear gas in Genoa he had realized that something new was needed if the movement was ever to rise above the ritual game of confrontation and mutual tease with its enemy. Before that moment, he had believed in the power of protest, a power he had first deployed as a child at the nuclear base in Faslane, and then in countless other towns and cities around the world. Genoa had opened his eyes. But it was not until the day, two months later, when he saw the planes plough into the towers that his spirit had lifted and he had realized that, now, yes, anything was possible. For more than ten years, he had signed petitions, mounted rallies, attended seminars and – wearing a black mask – smashed a few windows. But so decadent was the movement that, more often than not, he had first found it necessary to push fellow demonstrators out of the way before he could throw his rock. No, they had said: we must never demean ourselves with violence. We must never degrade ourselves and our ideals by mimicking the atrocities of the corporate oppressor. We must not frighten off our moderate supporters. This, they had said to him, as he wielded a *rock*: as if a rock through the window of a coffee shop was remotely comparable to the death of half a million Iraqi children, or the rape of the rain forest, or the ability of a corporation to take control of Bolivia's water supply, or the enslavement of whole populations by the invisible hand of the market – a hand that had long since clenched into a fist tattooed with a corporate logo.

Munroe had always known they were wrong, these pacifists, but on the great day, as he stood in a Paris bar and watched the second plane plough into the South Tower, he knew that many others would realize the truth, too. It might make you feel good to adopt a macrobiotic diet, or to put up no-smoking signs, or to demand speed bumps in your neighbourhood, or to litigate for cycling paths. But it achieved nothing. At a rally in the same year, he had heard an Inuit academic booed by liberals as he warned the crowd "not to rule out any tactical option available to you". Some walked away in disgust as he told them that a "candle-lit vigil never stopped a gun from being fired or saved a starving child. It just made you all feel a bit better". Even more stormed off when he said that they should hold a workshop on stripping and caring for an M16 semi-automatic: that would be of use to future generations, unlike the planned seminar on "Local litigation, global peace". But Munroe agreed with the gravel-voiced man, who spoke like some shaman transported from an ancient past to hand on difficult truths to a decadent generation. The West could no longer claim exemption from the violent reality of the world beyond its shores. That was the wonderful legacy of the day when a million tons of steel, glass and concrete had exploded in fire from the sky. The scales fell from a billion eyes in a single moment, from Kandahar to Canberra, from Paris to Paraguay. Anything was now possible. Everything was at last connected, welded together by the forge on Manhattan island.

For that reason alone, Munroe knew that all the work of twenty years – all the arguments, plotting, wasted opportunities and fallen comrades – had been heading towards this hour and this moment. The astonishing beauty of the dawn and the land it revealed was equal to that moment. He basked in the stillness of the forest, the steep meadows amid the coniferous woodland, the land's indifference to the houses and barns that dotted the valley. No wonder its people had fought so jealously for their freedom, and even now refused to change their ways or to bow to the decrees of intruders. It was worth it, always worth it. It reminded him of something she used to say: All that we do must come from contact with the soil. She said it was a line of poetry, and that it was the truth. She was right. Here on the edge of a thousand shades of green, swathed in silence, dazzled by the light, here at last was his epiphany, a private reward for his labours and what he knew must lie ahead of him, and the fellowship of Second Troy.

Clio was waiting for him in the corridor and nodded to him. "Is he ready?" Munroe asked. She nodded again and led the way.

* * *

"What did you tell her?" the first man asked his employer.

"Business," he said. "I hate lying to her."

"Better this time, though. She really doesn't need to know about this one."

"I suppose."

"How bad will it be?"

"Not sure. I get the feeling it's a real mess. I couldn't find out that much from him."

"So are you scared?"

"Don't be daft. I bet you are."

"Me?" The man laughed, snapping shut a rifle. "You forget what I used to do before I worked for you. I was in Kosovo, mate."

"Oh, of course. I forgot. Kosovo."

They tried to remain serious about the task ahead, and then cracked up.

* * *

Nick Atkins calculated that it was now a full week since he had first felt the firm grip of Simmonds as he left the Wykehamist. He had travelled across the Atlantic and back, spoken to both of Tab Bradley's parents, dumped the body of his treacherous lover in the pitch-black of a forest and followed a man disfigured by torture to London, where a trap awaited them both. Before that trap had snapped shut, he had been taken against his will twice – first by Veronica Brewer and then by Freddy Hengel – but he knew, even as his body went limp in the backroom of Pedro's, that this time it was different. This time there would be a reckoning.

His quarters were not those of a hostage, although the windows had been blacked out. A servant's rooms, he guessed, from the modest furniture – a sofa, an armchair

and a coffee table – and the little kitchenette and bathroom. There was a smell of hygiene and transience, and
a discarded chauffeur's cap in the wardrobe. From the
footsteps outside – in the corridor, on the gravel below
and on what seemed to be a landing above him – Nick
gathered that there were many other people in the
house. The distant slamming of doors suggested to him
that he was in the outhouse of a larger building. He
would listen to cars come and go, especially in the night,
and sharp, whispered exchanges, none of which he was
able to follow. He heard snatches of English spoken
more than once, and Italian and French. He heard the
voices of men and women, focused and agitated. He
could sense their tension seeping through the pores
of the wallpaper. But none of them appeared to be
interested in him. There was food in the fridge and the
cupboards, and he grazed lazily, feeling like an animal
in a laboratory experiment, observed by technicians
through one-way glass or a close-circuit camera. He
slumbered as best he could in the gloom, desperate to
let his body recover from the pummelling of the last
few days. But he was surprised to find – as Aisha had
predicted – that he did not break. Something deeper,
beyond the weakness, the pain and the fear, urged him
to stay alive.

Every time he heard a voice or footfall, he wondered
if it was Tab. A vicious thread had connected them for
more than a decade and a half – a thread of memory,
codes and the cruel refusal of human beings to let one
another go – and now he had gathered it together in
his hands, and stumbled towards the other end, to find
the person holding it, and to confront her at last. He

tried to imagine what it would be like to see her after all these years, to gaze upon the face he had loved more than any other, and to ask her why she had punished him in this way. How, he wanted to know, could love become so twisted and deformed that it ended in this way. What was the force that seized love, and re-moulded it furiously into something baked hard with malevolence? And then he wondered if he would be able to say anything at all, whether she would simply laugh at him and his pathetic malleability.

And yet, more even than of Tab, he found himself thinking in these lost hours of Emily and Polly, and asking himself if he would ever see them again. It was becoming difficult to remember why he and Emily had stopped talking to each other, and how their intim-acy had crumbled. He could recall the fights, and the moments of decision, and the painful leave-taking; he could remember Polly's eyes when he first explained that he was going to try living somewhere else for a bit – wasn't that exciting? – and that she could come and visit him *whenever she liked*. What he could no longer see, through the fog of the past week, was the road that had taken him to that estrangement. He delved deep into the stew of his resentments, into his treasure trove of pettiness, and came up with nothing. His parting from his wife and daughter seemed causeless: it was like a rupture in the fabric of time and space that was impossible to explain, meaningless except in its terrible consequences.

Above all, he remembered a day when Polly was four and he had found himself pledging eternal fealty to a deity in whom he did not believe. The three of them

were in the park on a cold autumn afternoon, wrapped
in the scarves of the previous Christmas, Polly in mit-
tens, her parents in thick leather gloves. Nick wore a
baseball cap with a smiling face on it that made the girl
laugh. She ran off to play on the slide. He and Emily
sat on a park bench and started making a shopping
list for a supper party, kicking idly in the fallen leaves.
Their discussion of the relative merits of lasagne and
roast chicken quickly degenerated into a light-hearted
but intense argument about the sexual proclivities of
one of the guests. Nick insisted that he was, Emily that
he wasn't, and that since he was her friend, she would
know. Nick waved his hand dismissively and said that
she was too close to see the obvious. She laughed and
grabbed his glove. Nick was about to deliver his next
salvo when he saw Emily's face turn the colour of
lilies. Her lively, rosy features were suddenly waxen, her
mouth a perfect O of speechless horror. He wondered
what he had said to upset her so, and then realized
that she was not looking at him at all, and that her grip
on his hand had loosened completely. Her attention
had been captured by something else, outside the bubble of their marital banter. He turned to see what it
might be.

Beyond the slide – a good twenty yards – Polly was
standing in the middle of the park highway, a vision of
helplessness in her dungarees, parka and yellow bobble
hat, looking at a dog capering on the grass. A gardener's
van, swerving and careering down the tarmac, was
seconds away from her. As Nick launched himself from
the bench, trying to force his body to superhuman
heights, to find the extra inch per second that might

stand between a near-miss and a broken life of mourn-
ing, he found himself saying a prayer. Not quite a prayer,
in truth. For part of what he said to himself took the
form of a command: "*No*. You cannot take her, not like
you took my father, not now, not like this". He begged
whatever power there was, whatever force occasionally
stooped to regulate the chaos: "*Please*. Don't take her
away. You can have whatever you want from me, you can
take all of it. Squeeze what you like from my soul. But
don't take her. Please". Feet pounding, breath running
short, stitch savage in his breast, the van drawing ever
closer to her fragile little body, as she turned to wave at
him… One more whispered imprecation: what harm
could it do, to reverse this catastrophe, to unmake it? Just
one tiny click on the universal dial, which would make
the difference between everything and nothing. *Please.*

The van stopped. There was the length of an adult
body between its radiator grille and Polly. A man
fell out of the driver's door, drunk and crying. Nick
swept Polly up in his arms and, without looking back,
without acknowledging her squawk of surprise – she
had missed the whole thing – raced back to Emily, her
arms outstretched in need, panic and abject gratitude.
Nick put Polly down and watched as Emily hugged her
with greater force and insistence than he had ever seen
a person embrace another. It was as if the small body
now captured in his wife's long, slender arms contained
all that was precious and life-giving in the world, the
solution to all wrongs, and the balm for all fears. It was
as though something dark and terrible had visited them,
and then, capriciously, at the last moment, chosen not
to enact its unspeakable plan.

During all his hours of captivity, Nick had not expected a polite knock at the door. He sat up, ran his
fingers through his hair:

"Come in."

The door opened, and the woman from Pedro's –
the last person he had seen – walked in. He had been
blindfolded throughout his long journey.

"I am Clio," the woman said finally, waiting for the
dark, powerfully built man behind her to step into the
centre of the room. "And this is Munroe."

* * *

The verandah outside the drawing room was still cold,
but the heater made it habitable. Munroe lit up and
offered Nick a smoke. He shook his head, and Munroe
shrugged. "Clio, make us both some tea, will you? I'm
gasping right now. I bet you are too, Nick". Nick nodded and turned his head in vague acknowledgement of
the woman who had masterminded his sedation and
smuggled him to this unexpectedly lovely location.

"Some view, isn't it?" Munroe said. "I'll miss it when
we head out, I really will. I've been on the move too
long. Haven't had a home to speak of for more than
ten years, but…" he drew greedily on his cigarette "…I
could really handle this." He smiled. "One of the few
advantages of the life I lead."

"Where is Tab?" said Nick.

Munroe laughed. "Where, indeed? That is a good
question – though not, unfortunately, the main one."

"It's the only one I want answered."

He spoke with the soft courtesy of the educated, rural

Scot. "I imagine it is. I've looked forward to meeting you, Nick, I really have. For a long time, actually. I think you must be quite something in your own way. I mean, look around you." He gestured at the four-wheel drives parked on the gravel below, the boxes of supplies and his people hurrying about their business. "All this began with her and her ideas. Oh, I've played my part, don't get me wrong. Engels to her Marx, maybe. I've brought in people, trained them, placed them in cells all over the world, made them ready. Called in a few favours from contacts – the jihadis, and so on. But Tab – well, she has that something special. But you knew that."

"No," Nick corrected him. "I knew a young college girl, with a head full of politics and books. She sent me a lot of coded messages over the years, and like an idiot I read them. Whatever it is you're doing, I can't connect the Tab Bradley I knew to any of it."

Munroe sat back in his wicker chair. "I wonder if that is true. I wonder. You know, something drew you together in the first place. But something kept that connection going all these years, too. More than a youthful romance, surely? I envy you, really. She is the strongest person I have ever met. And she acknowledged some sort of strength in you, too. She respected that deeply. You inspired her. Well, I think Freddy mentioned all that to you."

Nick looked up. "Where is Freddy?"

"Ah, Freddy," Munroe sighed. "Look, Freddy didn't make it this time. He got here and – well, what with the drugs and the journey, and everything – he went into shock yesterday and was gone pretty quickly. Massive cardiac, there was nothing we could do. Freddy had just had enough, is the truth. But I was able to do one thing for him before he went. Which is to tell him that he wasn't betrayed. Only two people knew everything about the Amsterdam operation. I didn't tell a soul. And the other person – well, I'll come to that in a minute. Freddy wanted revenge – that's why he followed you, tracked you down in America. He knew that we were looking for you, too, and that if he stuck with you, he'd get to us again. But he got something better than revenge. By bringing you to us, he has made possible the completion of our mission. People will write about him in history books one day."

"You're lying," said Nick. "Why did you back off in California?"

"We weren't in California," Munroe replied. "We lost you after you were taken into official custody, but I knew you would end up looking for us, and finding us, as long as I gave you a helping hand from time to time. I took a risk, but it was a good gamble. Freddy took you straight to Clio, who was ready and waiting at my instruction. Ah, here she is."

Clio X put two mugs of tea on the table in front of them. She looked at Nick with eyes much angrier than Munroe's. "When are we…"

"When *I* say so." Munroe grinned broadly. "Okay, Clio?"

Clio nodded, chastened, and withdrew.

"So. Where was I?" Munroe said, sipping on his tea. "Oh, yes. So we weren't tracking you in America. I could have activated a unit there, but I didn't want to jeopardize the bigger picture. I knew you'd have company. I gather somebody eliminated it."

"Yes. Slashed her throat." Nick paused. "Any idea who might have done that?"

Munroe raised his hands as if in surrender. "It could be any number of people, you see. A great many people are entangled in this, and in the thwarting of Second Troy. But they will fail. Now *you're* here, they will fail."

"I keep hearing that I'm crucial to all this. I wish to Christ you, or someone, would explain what the hell you mean. I am so *tired* of being told that."

"Drink your tea, calm down, and I'll tell you," Munroe said, very quietly. "All right?"

Nick nodded.

"Second Troy was the name Tab gave to this group. Right? The New Weathermen was its public face, but all that was a diversion, a way of keeping the enemy busy. Worked very well, actually. They were very happy chasing imaginary plots to blow up post offices and government buildings and all that – old-fashioned stuff. Conventional struggle, requiring a conventional response. Second Troy was the real thing."

"Named after the poem?"

"Yes. Tab's trademark, right? *No Second Troy.* But she said that, in this case, the poet was wrong. That there *was* another Troy, for her – for us – to burn. It was the whole stinking system, ruining the Earth, murdering the innocent every day, feeding off war and depravity as never before in the history of our species. Her insight was that our response had to be on an appropriate scale. We had to do extraordinary things to get the attention we needed, to shatter confidence in the system, to rock its foundations. You see, Second Troy was a *principle*, before it became the name of a group. It was her way of saying that a revolutionary who believed there were no targets left was simply blind, or morally bankrupt. There were targets everywhere. Everywhere *was* the target."

"So what are you planning to do? Who are you going to kill next to make your point?"

Munroe laughed. "Actually, the funny thing is that I have *absolutely no idea*. Tab's been working in isolation on Second Troy's principal mission for five years: five long, lonely years of planning and research and checking. Can you imagine the rigour of someone capable of that solitariness – the burden of that knowledge?" Munroe shook his head. "I couldn't do it. And we both knew that. So she took it on. I set the scene: money, people, back-up, infrastructure. We did a few ops, one of which worked rather well, two of which were aborted. But it was all preparation for this."

For the first time, in an unexpected moment of revelation, Nick knew what Munroe was going to say next. He felt a wave of relief compete with disgust that he should have been so deluded ever to think that the ending would be simple. "My God," he whispered. "She's left you in the lurch. Hasn't she? She's gone."

Munroe clenched his fists slowly, involuntarily, and then recovered his poise. "Very good. Let's say she isn't here. I think that's enough detail for now." He stubbed out his cigarette. "But the plan is here. It's in her laptop. All of it."

"So what is your problem?"

"The problem, you see, is this." Munroe Stacy stood up and walked around the table. He rested his knuckles on the table and leant over Nick, intimidating, and pulsing with restrained fury. "We can't access the plan. There is an entry protocol which is… unusual."

"Meaning what?"

"Meaning that I have an enormous sum of money in cash…" without warning, he grabbed the edge of the iron table and hurled it over "…but I don't have a fucking mission!"

Clio ran in, reaching for a weapon tucked into the back of her jeans. Nick heard the footsteps of others heading towards the disturbance. Munroe did not turn this time. His voice was suddenly calm once more. "It's all right, Clio. It's all right. We're just having a little conversation." He kicked away the shards of the mug at his feet.

"Now I think we should go over to the barn."

* * *

The gallery of the hayloft, overlooking a huge den, had been converted into an office space. There was a glass table, chairs for a meeting and an elaborate workstation with several screens, printers and a bank of telephones. On the wall was a map of the world dotted with red and green tacks, beside a huge and gaudy *fauve* painting of a family at play in the orchard behind the house. There was a separate workspace on the other side of the room, bare except for a spotlamp and a laptop. The machine had seen better days. It was battered and scored with the lines of many fugitive years. But it hummed into life when Munroe switched it on. He tapped a few keys, and then clicked the mouse on one of the icons.

"Now," he said. "Watch carefully. What follows is my problem, and now yours."

Nick sat awkwardly on a minimalist swivel chair, as the screen flickered from a normal menu of options to black. After several seconds, the single word **ACCESS?** flashed in the centre. Munroe pressed the Return key theatrically and stood back.

"Now," he said. "See what you think."

In larger white lettering, words now scrolled across the screen:

QUESTION ONE: COUNT ALL LACKING FOUND...

"What in God's name does that mean?" Munroe asked. "*What*?"

"What happens when you try to answer?" said Nick.

"We tried to escape the whole game. Mistake. That was taken as a failed attempt: you only get two attempts. And the protocol has been written so that the plan is destroyed if the code-breaker doesn't get it right. For whatever reason, she meant the file to be available to somebody who understood her mind, and her private riddles, and all that poetry rubbish. She created a protocol that, in the whole world, only she and you could use." Munroe paused, savouring the import of what he was telling his captive. "All along you were her back-up system. That's why you're still alive."

Nick did not take his eyes off the screen. "Where is Tab?"

Munroe leant over him again. "I'd advise you to get

to work on this." He sighed. "I've cut enough eyelids off for one lifetime."

Nick inhaled deeply. Sweat curled down his back. The tremor in his hands had returned. "All right. All right. I understand what you're asking me to do. But if I'm to concentrate I can't have you breathing down my neck. It's just not possible. The codes are always odd. Always. So these questions are bound to be demanding – I mean, look at the first one – and if I get even one of them wrong, we lose the whole mission blueprint. Right?"

"Yes," said Munroe.

"In which case, I need some space. So leave me alone."

"You must be joking."

"I'm not. It's in your interests that I don't screw this up. Isn't it?"

"No way. Forget it."

Clio interjected: "We can see what's on screen on the PC downstairs. You can see everything."

"What if he does something stupid?"

Clio had no answer to this, and remained silent. Nick said: "I won't. Now, please. Just let me get on."

"All right. We're downstairs. Don't forget that." He and Clio made their way down the spiral staircase to the floor below. Nick could hear their whispers, and the sound of a second machine booting up. He looked down and saw a third figure, Latin American in appearance, standing in the hallway of the door. He was holding a sniper's rifle, his fingers curling edgily around the barrel. Nick turned back to the screen, his stomach lurching like a trapped beast.

QUESTION ONE: COUNT ALL LACKING FOUND…

"My God," he heard himself whisper. "My God." Count all lacking found. It made no sense, triggered nothing, even in the deepest pit of memory and feeling. He knew the poems, or thought he did. They had been the matrix of his secret life for more than fifteen years. He had learnt to recognize lines and phrases quickly. But this bore no relation to those lines. He stared into an abyss of unknowing.

Count. Wait, perhaps… A number, maybe? This was a favourite trick of Tab's: to use the location of a phrase within a poem – verse 4, line 4 – to indicate a quantity, or a number of years, or a score in a term paper. So – COUNT. But count what? All lacking found. Was it a poetic phrase, an anagram, a cryptic puzzle? He wrote the words down on the pad of paper by the keyboard, his hands still trembling.

ALL LACKING FOUND. Mix up the letters and see what you come up with. He laboured over it, despairing. A CLAD FULL KING ON. FALKLAND ICON LUG. GALA DUCK FULL IN. ALAN FUCK GOLD NIL. Some furious reference to her father, his avarice, his nihilism? No. Christ: just words. Just nonsense.

Then, something was illuminated in the dustiest archive of his mind. A poem. He could see it – just. Letters shimmering across the years, lines forming and then retreating from view. Sweat ran from his forehead.

And then he had the line. It was Yeats's *The Municipal Gallery Revisited*: "But in that woman, in that household

where / Honour had lived so long, all lacking found."
It was Lady Gregory, the poet's great patron at Coole
Park, his scholarly heroine. How did she come into it?
He started to type her name – and then deleted the
letters. The content was irrelevant here. Remember
the word COUNT. It was the location that mattered
– probably. He felt the sting of the sweat in his eyes and
wiped them on the sleeve of his T-shirt. His mouth was
parched, his head throbbing.

If he was right – which verse, which line? Count
"All lacking found".

He closed his eyes, and tried to see the poem in his
mind's eye: its shape, what it looked like on the page.
There was a time when he had known it so well, its
structure, its homage to the poet's circle: "my glory was
I had such friends". He could *see* the line. Yes: it was in
the fourth – no, the *fifth* stanza. Yes, the fifth. And it was
– what? – the second or the third line? The… the third.
The third? Definitely the third. The answer was V, 3.
The answer was 53. At least, that was what he thought
it was. And if it wasn't? Then the screen would fizz into
blankness, and he would die.

He typed the two digits and pressed the Return
key. Nothing happened. Then the screen flashed twice.
From the mezzanine, he could hear Munroe curse and
Clio gasp, in the den below. Was he wrong? Had his
memory deceived him?

QUESTION TWO: REMIT FAMILY YOU'VE MIXED (2, 2)

He slumped over the keyboard for a moment. He felt

perspiration trickle down his back, the material clinging coldly to his skin. Downstairs, Munroe and Clio were silent once more. The Latino marksman had not moved.

REMIT? An anagram of TIMER. Was there something basic here about the hours remaining before the mission, or its precise timing?

That left you with FAMILY YOU'VE MIXED (2, 2). MIXED could signal an anagram of FAMILY YOU'VE. Couldn't it?

FLAME IVY YOU. VALE IF MY YOU. Meaningless. His brain felt dry, sapped of juices.

Suppose that the anagram was TIMER: that dealt with "Remit" and "Mixed". Then 2, 2 would refer to the second letter of the second remaining word. Family You've. That would be "o" – interchangeable with 0 in Tab's code. Timer 0. That made sense – of a sort. It might mean that the mission was about to start.

Or it might not.

He typed in the word and the digit.

INCORRECT> ONE TRY LEFT

He could hear Munroe growl in fury. And now what he felt was not fear, but a loneliness that was much deeper. Perhaps the code was no longer within his power to crack, the connection torn at last by her journey into a dark and terrible place.

One try left. And then what? Death, or yet more questions, yet more torment of the mind.

He screwed up his eyes and looked at the clue again. He took deep breaths and asked what she was trying to say to him: to *him*.

MIXED: well, that surely meant an anagram. Perhaps – perhaps an anagram of *all* the other words: REMIT FAMILY YOU'VE. He stared at the words. His eye was caught by the group of letters "MILY". Was there an "E"?

Yes. Two, in fact.

In Tabatha's code, "EMILY" was always a signpost, an invitation to him to scroll through the writings of her beloved Emily Dickinson. EMILY: that left RMITFAYOUVE. He scribbled furiously. MAY OF VIRTUE. No. A FURY MOTIVE. Not quite. MY FAVOURITE. Yes. MY FAVOURITE EMILY.

Tabatha Bradley's favourite poem by Dickinson had always been 'A great Hope fell'. Of that Nick was sure. Had she changed her mind? Perhaps. But then the code would be unbreakable: and that, he saw, was not the point at all.

> A great Hope fell
> You heard no noise
> The Ruin was within

He remembered that stanza. But the code said 2, 2. The second stanza, the second line. That was what the numbers surely meant. But what were the words?

Something about "The mind was built…" So hard, after so many years to remember an exact line. And yet those lines were there. He was sure of it. They were part of what she had left within him.

> The mind was built for mighty Freight
> For dread occasion planned

There it was, like a stone breaking the surface of an ebbing tide, a solid presence that had been there all along.

He typed in the second line. FOR DREAD OCCASION PLANNED. What was the dread occasion?

The screen flashed and new words appeared.

QUESTION THREE: CONSUMED BY MAUD GONNE'S INFANTS?

Back to Yeats, and Maud, the Helen of Troy of his maddest yearnings, the proud radical to whom he proposed so often and whom he eulogized in verse. Insanity, torment. And her infants? Her children? What could Tab mean? He remembered her talking at night of a daughter and a son – Sean MacBride – and perhaps another. But what could that possibly mean? It would not be so straightforward. Some detail of biography. No. With Tab, everything that looked simple was bound to be just the opposite.

INFANTS, too, was an odd word for her to use.

He wiped his face again and looked down. How many more of these questions could there be?

CONSUMED BY: that could be a "container", as Tab called it when she first explained crosswords to him. The next words, then, might include part of the answer. What words could one draw from MAUD GONNE'S? There were so many: DUNES, GUNMAN, SUN, DUNGEONS, MASON, AMONG.

He threw down the pen and watched the words swim madly. He had nothing left.

AMONG. AMONG what?

AMONG INFANTS. What could that mean? Among children, that… *Among School Children*.

Perhaps the code still worked, after all. But then the question mark. That meant that the clue was odd, awkward. Or perhaps it was directing him to – to a question in the poem?

How can we know the dancer from the dance?

That final line of the poem, so familiar to him, concealed in her crazy verbiage. Was that what she wanted? Was that all, in the end?

He tapped in the words.

QUESTION FOUR: WHICH OF BACH'S CELLO SUITES DID YOUR FATHER LIKE BEST?

At last, he thought, a sliver of honesty. This is not a security protocol at all, is it? It is a conversation between two lovers, a bitter kiss across the years. It is for me, and me alone. But what is left of you, Tab? Do you amount to anything more than your manipulations, your strange presence in this room as a sprite in the electronic mist? Can you truly be distinguished from your games?

How can we know the dancer from the dance?

To this question about Bach, he would never forget the answer – as she knew – for it was something she had asked him on their second day together, entangled on her bed. He had told her about his father, and his gifts, and their frustration, and his passion for Bach, Mozart and Britten. And she had asked him this very question, and he had smiled and told her: the Fifth, in C Minor. So, seventeen years on, he typed in the number 5 and ruefully waited for the response.

LAST QUESTION: YOU DID WHAT I COULD NOT.

It wasn't really a question. But he knew at once what the answer was. And he understood, at last, why it was that she believed him to be strong, and what she had meant when she described a moment of revelation to Munroe, in Paris, all those years ago. It was that moment on an Arizona sliproad, when, exhausted and appalled, she had lacked the strength to put a suffering dog out of its misery. He had done what she could not. He had done the brutal deed. And she had never forgotten that moment when will had deserted her, and he had stepped into the breach. For all these years, she had been atoning for that failure, never once letting go or letting another do her work for her; never, perhaps, forgiving him for seeing her like that, and having the compassion to help her and the pitiful creature. All these years, her purpose, her cunning, her brutal devotion to a gentle cause, haunted by a hot spring night on a roadside when her sinews had gone slack, and she had needed love. She had never forgiven him, for that and all that it meant. He typed: KILLED THE DOG.

And then an image was coalescing on the screen, the coloured squares of a media player setting itself up. A green rectangle formed, and numbers flashed as a file loaded. Nick heard Munroe and Clio rushing up the stairs to claim the prize, to read, copy and memorize

the precise, exquisitely planned nature and detail of
their mission. All the volunteers in the great house, and
the cells in the cities around the world, and the millions
who would hail the genius of their work when it was
done – all would take their cue from the information
that was about to be downloaded, now that the code
had been broken. The raging fire – the purgation in
flames of a world gone bad – that Second Troy existed
to create was about to be lit. And now Munroe and
Clio were approaching, to remove him from the stage
of history, so that they could take delivery, at last, of
their sacred script. The "dread occasion".

"Hi, Nicky."

The words filled the room as he felt the barrel of
Clio's pistol against his head. He turned again to the
laptop – slowly this time – to see what was flickering
on the screen.

2

The image was of poor quality, low resolution and tarnished by abstract electronic strands. But it was clear enough: a portrait of a phantom, edgy and unworldly. A woman in her late thirties, with short, dark hair, a small scar on her left cheek, and unforgettable, unchanged eyes. She wore a crew-neck black sweater and fingerless gloves; she fidgeted with leads and a microphone. The room behind her was impossible to place: white walls, a picture hanging and what looked like a shelf of books. The woman's face was worn and weary, the lines by her eyes unfamiliar, and the lips cracked and imperfect. It was the face of someone in a hurry, fearful and driven, anxious to get something done. It was the face of a fugitive and the face of a leader. It was Tab's face.

"Nick, the fact you're seeing this now means that everything else has failed. If I'm right, Munroe or one of his little helpers will be holding a gun to your head, and my hunch is he'll be pretty pissed with me, and life in general. Hi, Munroe. Sorry about this. You'll understand soon enough, too. My old comrade. But Nicky, I don't have too long, so I'm going to say what I have to say real quick."

"What the hell is this?" said Clio.

"Shut up," said Munroe. His face was pale with fury, yet he was as gripped as Nick by the performance on screen.

Nick wanted to reach out and touch the screen. He felt foolish. But the sight of her, no longer frozen in time on a Santa Cruz beach, but older, as he was older, was unbearably moving to him. She was not a mythic figure, after all; not a sorceress, conjuring up dark forces, or the pimpernel of other people's imaginations. She was his lost love who had changed, who had aged and who – you could tell from her eyes – was less sure of things, and of herself, than she had been all those years ago. She had not lost her beauty – her bones still looked fine, even in the grainy image – but it was the real beauty that matures with the daily frictions of the world, that loses its arrogance and learns to laugh. At last, in this terrible setting, with the scent of death hanging in the air, it seemed that they were once more equals. No codes, no games.

"I knew that you'd keep reading the messages – you *schmuck*! And I knew you'd buy what I was telling you, too. Well, it wasn't all lies. But a lot of it was. Towards the end, anyway. I needed you on the outside, for me. Just in case. And if you know about London – me being there, I mean – if it's any consolation, I never looked you up, never spied on you." She faltered. "Christ, Nicky you must be all grown up now. I wonder what you look like." She ran her palm over her hair.

Munroe was shaking with rage: "This is not fucking happening. Where is the mission?"

Tab gathered herself once more. "I'd better move fast. Listen, Nicky. There's something I need to tell you.

Don't worry about all the stuff going on around you. I'm hoping you'll get the answers to all that pretty soon. But one thing you need to hear from me."

Silence filled the room like a mist; Nick felt that he might reach out and run his fingers through it. Still, the gun did not move from his head.

"Whatever happens to you now – and I hope it isn't bad… God, I do – you deserve to know that I didn't leave you all those years ago for the reasons I said. Not entirely, anyway." Nick could hear Clio breathing; he could hear his own straining heart. "The thing is, you see, Nicky, the thing is… I was pregnant." Her voice faltered. She looked down, abject and defeated for a few seconds, before she recovered her composure. "I was pregnant, Nick, and I was scared." He could detect, even from the tiny speakers on the laptop, the quaver in her voice. "So… so, so. I'm sorry, okay? Maybe I had no right to do that, but I did. I didn't think it was fair to tell you until… well, in the end, I did have the baby. And I knew straight away that there was no way I was up to looking after her. Cute little thing she was – oh my, the most beautiful child. But me? A mother? I couldn't think of what else to do, so I told Alan, of all people, and asked him what to do. Nazi bastard though he is, he sort of understood, and he offered to take her in. I told him he didn't know the father, that it was a one-night stand. I didn't want to involve you at all. And Alan's raised her, all these years, looked after her. And I bet you he did a damn good job, too. Because he had a second chance, you see? He screwed up royally with me and my mum. But with Kelly it was always different."

And now, through the mist of the years, all was clear and sharp – all that mattered anyway. The messages were unimportant – her deceptions were unimportant – for she had at last spoken the truth. There had been a child. The child he had met in the hotel, flouncing from the room because Alan would not let her watch the movie. Tab's child. His child. Kelly.

Tab heard something behind her: "So, now you know – I think my time's up. Oh, one more thing, before I go. And, this *is* for everyone – so pay attention, Munroe. Just in case you were wondering, Yeats *was* right: there is no Second Troy. There is no mission. The whole thing was a fiction, you see. Just one of my stories. Well, I'm good at that. Oh, sounds like they're coming, now. I'll sign off and…"

There was the sound of banging on the door and shouting, then a few seconds of fuzziness, and then the recording ended abruptly, restoring the rotating colour-ed squares to their dance. The number in the right-hand corner of the window said 00:00. The screen exploded as Munroe fired two rounds into it.

"Bitch!" he shouted. "Lying bitch! Where is it? Where are all the plans? Where is the mission?"

"Munroe!" said Clio. "Get a grip. It might still be on the hard disk. You don't know what all that was about. What she's playing at with him." She jammed the pistol into Nick's temple, making him cry out. "I think we should sweat him. He obviously knows more than he's saying."

Munroe aimed his pistol at Nick's feet. "No, no. I'm not going to sweat him, this interloper – this… this *nobody* – I'm going to blow his toes off one by one,

until he decides to tell us what the fuck is going on."
He looked at Nick's terror-stricken face, and then again
at his shoes. "So. Left foot, big toe first. Ready? Good.
Here we go then."

"Munroe! Munroe!" The voice carried enough urgency to make him and Clio look over the balcony to
the barn hallway, where two young Europeans with a
hostage were pushing past the marksman into the main
room. "We found her in the grounds," one of them said.
"She had a piece, and a minder with her. The minder's
dead." They shoved their captive into the room.

Nick strained to get a better look. Their captive was
bound and badly bruised, blood trickling from a wound
above her left eye. But her physique – she was tiny
– was unmistakable. The new arrival at the mountain
headquarters of Second Troy was Veronica Brewer.

* * *

"Simmonds was right about one thing," she said, as she
nursed her bruise with a makeshift ice pack from the
kitchenette. "These people are well-trained. They took
him out very quickly, poor sod, and they made short
work of me. Looks like they've got you nicely tamed,
too."

Nick shrugged. He wondered why Munroe had
bothered to put them back in the servant's quarters
rather than killing them both. Veronica guessed what
he was thinking.

"Don't be fooled, they will shoot us when they're
good and ready. But they want to know more before
they do."

Nick shook his head. He did not want to have a long conversation with Veronica prior to his execution. But there were still things he needed to know.

"You left me high and dry in America. Why? One of your best people was slashed up and you did nothing. What sort of outfit are you running?"

"I tried. I really did. Khayyam – Aisha, that is – didn't check in, so I knew something had gone badly wrong. But, well… it's complicated, but I couldn't track you down until you got to London."

"Why didn't you step in then?"

"I did my best. They whisked you and your friend Hengel away too quickly. But we were able to pick up your traces and we followed you here. We'd been trying to work out where this place is for a long time. Unfortunately, we were apprehended as we got here."

"What happened to your back-up?"

She said nothing.

"Veronica, I asked you a question: where is the back-up? I mean, you and Simmonds in the woods, on your own… Where is your team?"

"There is no team. There's nobody coming in."

"Are you mad? You came here without back-up? Does anybody actually know where you are?"

She stood up, wincing, and walked over to the sink, filling her glass and gulping water greedily. He could see that she was in considerable pain, that she had taken a serious beating. She returned to the sofa and closed her eyes. Then she began, in a barely audible whisper, covering her mouth with her hand.

"You know so little about Tabatha, you see, even now."

"What do you mean?"

"She was the best agent I have ever run."

"What?"

"By a long margin. Superb. A controller's dream. She knew what to disclose and when. How much to hold back. How to maintain her cover. She was amazing. I ran her, but in truth I learnt a great deal from her over the years."

"Over the years? What are you talking about?"

Veronica sat up, holding her head in her hands. She continued in a feeble whisper: "I first heard of her ten or so years ago. She was in London, working with the movement, which was starting to get going properly. One of our informers was a postgraduate at the LSE, and I looked after him. He told me about this remarkable Californian girl who was involved in some of the political groups – radicalism, environmentalism. There wasn't exactly a global justice movement in the sense we mean today. The point about Tabatha was that she had authority. People listened."

Nick shook his head. "I wish there were words for you, Veronica. I really do. How despicable you are. I wish I could comprehend how you could send me to do what I have done without telling me this."

"A few years passed. Things changed. I suppose the Seattle riots in '99 were the turning point. Tab came back to London, and this time, I was told, she was having doubts. The movement, or elements within it, wanted to explore new techniques. My information was that she was troubled by the way things were heading, people like Munroe. It was as though she had waded in too deep and not liked what she found. I put somebody on to her full-time. He worked her, befriended her, reported back. Looking back, knowing what I know now, I think she probably guessed what was happening. She was so much more intelligent than the person I sent. But, in any case, it worked. At a very carefully chosen moment he asked her if she wanted to do something about the people in the movement she was worried about. Whether the best thing she could do to protect what she believed in was to stop the ultras from ruining it. And he told her that there were people who could help her, if she wanted help."

"He was recruiting her?"

"No. I recruited her. About a week later. She understood completely what was happening and why. She never asked me who I worked for exactly, and what I would do with the intelligence she handed me. But she had made an absolutely fireproof moral decision that she was not going to see the thing ruined, even if this meant that she risked being branded a traitor by her people, or even killed. It mattered that much to her."

Nick could not conceal his derision. "Did it never occur to you that she might enjoy the deception? That it was just another one of her games?"

"No. It did not. I believe that she believed in this work. Very much. She risked her life for it."

"Yes. Risked her life. And mine."

"I don't think you realize how remarkable a woman she was. How privileged you are to have been so close to her."

"Was?"

Veronica ignored his question. "We worked together, developed a bond. She trusted me, I think, and I was inspired by her courage and intellect. She rarely needed prompting, and she was always one step ahead of the people around her."

"But if she was working to stop all this, why did she create Second Troy?"

She laughed. "Oh, Tabatha didn't create Second Troy. Oh, no, no."

"Well, who did, then?"

"I did."

"You?"

"Yes. Of course. Well, Tab came up with the name, as I'm sure you've deduced. Poetry was certainly not my forte. But the operation was mine."

"What operation?"

"It was a flypaper operation. The idea was to draw the fanatics in the movement into a trap – the real hard-core, I mean – and then close them down all at once. They were elusive, well-funded. So, just as Munroe was setting up the New Weathermen, Tab and I were building Second Troy. First, through contact on the web, and then by developing a network proper. A *global* underground. The plan was to get them all to the very brink of action, and then move in. I envisaged taking down the key fifty or so people, all at once. It would have destroyed the radical wing for a generation."

"But you said people had already died. That more would die."

For a second, Veronica Brewer came as close to blushing as Nick believed her to be capable. "Yes. Yes. Well, sometimes in my business the fiction becomes real. Second Troy was *too* good an idea in the end. It attracted money, people of high calibre, recruits who were willing to lose their lives. It was much, much worse than I had thought. The level of readiness was higher than I had feared. In a way, Tab had understood better than me how dangerous it all was. We had tapped into such anger, but also such energy and potential for discipline… It was waiting to happen, all this, and – I regret to say – we made it possible."

"My God. And Tab?"

"Dead, I suppose. No, I'm certain, actually. Her communications stopped six months ago, and that could only mean the worst. I don't know what happened, exactly. Nothing Munroe is doing now tells us very much on that score. Certainly, he was expecting to find a real mission on the disk. My guess is that he sensed that she was trying to slow things down, thought she was going soft, having second thoughts, who knows? He was deeply jealous of her, naturally, and wanted all this for himself. I very much doubt he knew she was working for us. But it is only a hunch. And then, after she disappeared, the operations began."

Nick expected to feel grief, but was too numbed by what had happened in the barn and by what she had told him.

"And how did I fit in?"

"You were essential. Her most brilliant creation."

"I'm not a *creation*."

"Oh, but you are. Or, at least, you were. Clay in the hands of a master sculptor. You see, if things went wrong, we had put in place all sorts of systems so that I could find her. And find Second Troy. But they failed, one by one. Elaborate mechanisms, all malfunctioning. For months, I looked for her by conventional means.

Tried to track her down. But she had put in place her own last-ditch tracking device, which was you."

"Me? How?"

"It was genius. She knew that, if something happened to her, they would try to open the mission file on the disk. To do that, they would need to get through the questions, and only you could do that."

"What about Freddy? Didn't he tell you anything you didn't know?"

"Well, the people who interrogated him didn't know about you. But from our point of view the really important news was that the mission was about to be launched. The preparatory work was complete. That meant that they were likely to come after you. We already had Aisha in place, keeping an eye on you. And then it was just a question of them finding you, and you leading us to them. To here."

"Who killed Aisha?"

"I killed her," said a mellow, deep voice. Nick turned and saw that the door had been opened so quietly that neither of them had noticed. The man was familiar – tall, middle-aged, patrician. Nick realized that he was the man in the suit from the airport; the man outside Alan Bradley's club; probably the man who came looking for him at school. Even in his woollen jacket, thick cord trousers and mountain boots, he retained a certain urban elegance, undiminished by the revolver in his right hand. It was as though he were going out of his way to avoid giving the impression that he was anything so uncouth as an assailant.

"Hello, Diether," said Veronica. "I didn't know you were coming."

3

The utility vehicle pulled over at the roadside. The driver turned to his passenger and nodded. The passenger checked the sat-nav system.

"Not far now," he said. "No more than a kilometre. I would say it must be up that track."

The driver patted his jacket, instinctively checking his handgun. "Do you think he's expecting me?"

The other man laughed. "No idea. I mean, he sent the email. But he…"

"By the way – I forgot to say – that supplier in Milan was better than I expected." He pointed to the array of weaponry in the back of the vehicle, concealed by canvas. "This is good kit."

"Friend of a friend," his passenger said. "Very reliable, apparently, which is why I used him." He smiled to himself. "Top gear."

* * *

"Munroe will come," said Nick, after a few moments had passed. He regretted his pathetic tone, even as he spoke. Diether sat in the armchair, legs crossed and his gun trained with chilly nonchalance on Veronica.

"No," the German said. "Not yet, anyway. Your guards are dead."

"Did you have any trouble finding me?" said Veronica.

"Not really," said Diether. "How could I, if it was me who told you where they were and set you in the right direction? I was always a few steps behind you. It's not hard to track one officer and her minder. But that's the trouble with unauthorized operations. Isn't it, Veronica? No back-up. No equipment to speak of. Nerves getting to you. And now, with Simmonds and Khayyam gone, you're completely on your own. Nobody's coming to get you, are they?"

When she spoke, it was brightly. "Anyway, I did as you suggested, Diether. Here I am, cleaning up the mess. Much good it did me."

"Oh, I don't know," said Diether. "I doubt you would have wanted to miss this particular denouement. Your protégée has certainly delivered, or so I gather. To have accrued so much power that she was the *only one* who knew what the mission was. And there was no mission! A remarkable woman, as you always said. Perhaps it would have been helpful if you'd said a bit more."

"So, Diether," Veronica said. "Are you going to help me?"

Diether ignored her enquiry, which bore, for the first time, an edge of panic. Nick saw that her eyes were wide and fearful. The great wall of her officiousness was at last crumbling.

"I imagine she has told you a reasonable amount," Diether said to him. "But, if I know Veronica, it will have been skilfully edited. I have a suspicion that she will not have been completely straight with you."

Nick's voice was as croaky as Diether's was mellifluous. He craved a drink of water, but dared not move. "Who are you?"

"Me? Oh, I'm what Veronica would call a 'private sector partner'. She is gifted in the use of euphemism."

"What does that mean?"

Diether laughed again. "Anything she wants it to mean."

Nick saw how pale Veronica had become. He said: "What does it mean in your case?"

Diether rolled his shoulders: "I work for a corporation whose interests coincide occasionally with hers. That is to say, we acknowledge the same threat in groups such as this one. Her interest is national security, mine is shareholder value. She defends the realm, I defend a market position. Happily, the two things are often much the same. So we cooperate. In Veronica's case, I might add, we cooperate extensively and…" he brushed a speck of fluff off his jacket "…*personally*, so to speak. An unmarried woman needs a nest egg to look forward to, after all – an elderly mother to care for, and no husband to feather the nest. More to the point, this whole operation was far beyond her remit. Completely off the screen. I doubt her superiors know very much about Second Troy. Simmonds and Khayyam did, but who else? She needed outside help because the official machine would never give the green light to something so reckless and – it turns out – so disastrous. Sometimes, I must confess, the cautious instincts of the public servant are admirable. We'd all be better off if she had heeded them in this case."

"Enough," Veronica hissed.

Diether continued to behave as if she were not in the room. "I began to make my own enquiries. We set Freddy loose to take us to the heart of the thing, as I knew he would. It worked well. The only setback was in California. Well, Veronica had evidently failed to brief her own agent about my interest in this matter and, when we came upon one another, young Khayyam acted… unhelpfully. She was jeopardizing my activities and my surveillance of Freddy, who was close by on the mountain. Very regrettable, but I had to do what I did. Then you were on your own, and had to get rid of the body. And it *did* mean that Freddy got to you more quickly in New York. I mean, he didn't have to get past anyone, right? You had lost your guardian. Once you were back in London, I contacted Veronica to let her know that it was time for her to put things straight. Which she has signally failed to do."

"But why did you come here? Why not leave it to her and her people to finish?" asked Nick.

Diether blinked, betraying a flicker of emotion. "I have done this sort of work most of my life, for the State initially, and then for various private interests. But I came to this particular job through a family connection. My sister married the boss. You might have heard of my sister. Her name was… Anna Schmidt. She died quite recently."

"My God. The Schmidt operation. Freddy told…"

"Yes, indeed. Freddy. Poor Freddy… that was an unpleasant business, his little stay with us. And, of course, wholly unnecessary, as it turns out."

"What do you mean?"

"Well, there was no need for all those questions, all those rather *intense* hours in Amsterdam. I ought to have known *everything* he told me already. I mean, a business partner has the right to expect cooperation, transparency and pooling of information. Yes? But the problem with Veronica is that she kept things from me. There I was, monitoring the rise of something called Second Troy. She had fed it with titbits about its enemy. Just to make the high command – Munroe Stacy especially – believe that what they were doing was real. So she made sure that her agent, the great Tabatha, was supplying Second Troy with enough intelligence about the corporations. One in particular, to which she had privileged access. Mine."

"The Schmidt Corporation?"

"Yes. Indeed. How else could Second Troy have known so much about my sister Anna's routine and the protection detail in Munich? I must confess that it baffled me at the time. The kidnap was too perfect. I assumed that there was a mole inside the corporation. And, in a way, there was. It was me. In the sense that my work with Veronica was, ultimately, the reason that this happened. That is, the reason that my sister died."

"Diether, I…"

The bullet entered her forehead. The silencer meant that the sound of Veronica Brewer's tiny body slamming against the back of the chair far outstripped the sly whistle of the gun. As she fell, her eyes already had the glaze of a marionette's, a last breath sighing from her mouth. She slid to the floor, revealing a new sanguinary poppy spreading thickly on the headrest.

"Well," said Diether, standing up. "I'm finished here."

Nick could not speak. He looked at the gory wreckage that was the back of Veronica Brewer's skull, and wondered how many seconds would pass before he joined her, open-mouthed and lifeless on the floor.

"You can go, by the way," Diether said. "I make it a principle only to kill people who directly damage the interests of my employer. I am old-fashioned in this respect." He savoured the scene, then left with the elegance of a courtier retreating from the throne room.

* * *

Topper and Chris were stationed now at the edge of the forest, looking down at the complex of buildings. The taller man had settled his sniper's rifle on its tripod and was looking down the scope. His boss was peering through binoculars.

"How many do you think?"

"There's something going on in the barn. I can see a fair few… ten maybe. At least. Look, there's somebody."

They watched as a grey-haired man stepped briskly across the lawn, his relaxed demeanour at odds with the pistol at his side.

"He's got a piece," said Chris. "But he doesn't look like a guard."

"No, but that one does." Topper pointed up at the verandah, where a man with Nordic features was shouting something. The grey-haired man turned and without a second's hesitation fired a perfectly aimed shot at the guard, who clutched his chest and spun to the ground. As he fell, a second man emerged from the state room and fired back. The grey-haired man emptied two more rounds, then foraged for a clip in his jacket as he began to run towards the woods.

"Fuck," said Topper. "Oh well. Here we go then."

* * *

The sound of the shots from above jolted Nick from a torpor that had become almost catatonic. How long was it since Diether had left the room? Minutes, probably. Perhaps only seconds. But it seemed so much longer, as if helplessness had stretched and pulverized time. His cage door had been opened, but – like an animal whose instincts have been dulled by repeated trauma – he had not dared to flee. He stood instead by the body of Veronica Brewer, struggling to fill the blank canvas that was his mind. Strong enough to kill a dog. Strong enough to survive this far. But what was expected of him now? Outside, Second Troy had begun its great work: not the destruction of the fortresses of global capitalism, but a tragedy of self-immolation. He wondered who was firing at whom, and whether there was a chance that he might slip unnoticed from the compound. He might just... but then again... what would... how...

"For fuck's sake," Topper said. "Why are you just standing there?"

At the door stood his friend, out of breath, his jacket stained with grass and dirt from the wood: he carried a Beretta in his right hand.

"Why am *I* standing here?" Nick said, irritably, as if Topper's arrival was an unforgivable impertinence. "What the hell are *you* doing here?"

"There's gratitude," said Topper. "Why do you think? Because of your bloody message."

"What message?"

"The GPS coordinates for this place. To my private email, two days after I saw you."

"I didn't… "

He was interrupted by the noise of people running towards the servants' quarters.

"Right," said Topper. "I reckon we've got about five minutes before the law arrives. We might just make it out of here alive, if we head up the mountain."

The three men ran down the corridor, stepping over a dead guard, and up a short flight of stairs that led to a terrace. Nick looked down to the barn and saw two men and a woman, running towards them. Chris and Topper opened fire, and then took cover behind the crenellations of the terrace. Stucco chips and shards of plaster showered them as bullets sprayed the walls. Nick, his face flush with the tiles, saw that Topper's leg was bleeding, a lump of shrapnel having caught him. He grimaced as he stood up to resume firing, this time with two weapons. The report from the guns was deafening, filling the valley with a spiteful rattle. "There must be a dozen of them at least," thought Nick. "We don't stand a chance."

"Too exposed!" Chris shouted.

"The state room," Nick called. "It's down those stairs. It gives us a clear shot across the perimeter."

"Okay, you go first, Chris. On three." Topper signalled with his fingers and began to shoot once more at the enraged members of Second Troy.

Moving with practised agility, the reflex of the soldier,

Chris led the way down the steps and, checking the entrance, beckoned the other two men. Topper limped as he ran, but pushed Nick away when he tried to help him. They reached the state room. Chris, his rifle at his shoulder, pointed at an alcove that offered modest cover. Something landed on the verandah, lobbed from below. It hissed and spat, and then began to emit fumes.

"Shit," said Chris. "Tear gas. Out this way." He pointed into the hallway. The room began to fill with the acrid gas. Nick followed him, and looked around for Topper.

He heard a single shot, and turned. A silhouetted figure emerged from the state room, coughing and rubbing his eyes. Nick smiled, and then saw who it was.

"I have had enough of this," said Munroe Stacy. "I really have."

"Right there," said Chris, his rifle trained on him.

Munroe raised his pistol. "Oh, no," he said. "No, no, no. You're not getting out of here. I just executed your friend. And Clio…" he gestured up the stairs to the landing where his lieutenant stood, her gun pointing down at them "…will gladly join me now in executing you both, too." Chris shifted his rifle towards Clio – and then back to Munroe, back and forth.

"It's over, Munroe," said Nick. "It never started."

"You're wrong," said Munroe. "The idea of Second Troy is greater than all this. This is history, not the pathetic little love affairs, funny codes and games that you traded in. Tab weakened… well, that was her loss. The idea survives. The struggle goes on, I promise you. She has destroyed you, but she will never destroy Second Troy." He cocked his weapon. "Never."

Nick remembered Tab's face, the wit that had survived the years of lies and manipulation, the pain to which she had subjected him and so many others, including herself, and he smiled in a flash of wintry knowledge.

"You weren't listening to her, were you, Munroe? There is no Second Troy."

A shot rang out. Then another. Nick heard hurried footsteps, someone rushing from the scene. Munroe fell to his knees and opened his mouth. His eyes were startled, as if what had happened were an outrageous breach of destiny, an intervention at odds with the laws of the universe in which he had come to believe. No words came from him. He swallowed hard, twice, and then crashed to the ground like a felled oak. His leg twitched, and then was still.

The person already at his side, Nick realized, was Chris.

"Jesus. Are you all right?" he said. "I got the girl." He pointed up at the landing, where the slumped body of Clio X lay in a pathetic yogic contortion.

"And Munroe," said Nick.

"No, that wasn't me," he said. "I fired second. I only shot at the girl."

"Then who…"

"Shit. Tops," said Chris, brushing aside the question. Nick felt his stomach turn as he remembered what Munroe had said about Topper. They ran into the state room, shielding their faces as best they could from the fog of tear gas, and found their fallen friend by the entrance to the verandah. He was silent and immobilized, bleeding heavily from his chest.

Chris put a hand on Topper's neck. "He's not dead. Quick, let's get him some air." They dragged him out of the state room, through the hall, and beyond to the shock of cool air in the drive. There, with their weapons already aimed at the door, were three policemen.

"*Polizia!*" one of them shouted, and then in the mixed language of the region said: "*Was ist los? Wie heissen Sie? Englisch?* English?"

Nick nodded. He knelt by his friend. Chris shouted for a doctor, throwing his weapons down, and one of the policemen ran over to assist. Nick could see other officers and police vehicles down the drive: they already had four of the remaining cadres, and would sweep the complex for the rest. Diether – thought Nick – Diether must have sounded the alarm before he faded into the shadows, his vengeance complete.

Topper was still breathing, but he was bleeding into Nick's hands, a bullet having entered his body just under his right arm, at point blank range. His eyes flashed opened, and he retched, the tear gas compounding his affliction. Nick smelt smoke and, turning round, caught a glimpse of the flames that were now engulfing the barn. He wondered if a member of Second Troy had torched the place, or if the police already had instructions to erase whatever they found. Already, the fire was spreading from the upper windows, smoke pouring from every opening, sparks darting across from the beams and threatening to infest the outhouses, perhaps the main building. Soon, the pressure of the flames would burst the walls, and the inferno would swallow all in its path, angry and insatiable. It spat in fury, molten shards sizzling into the air. The pyre was becoming a force unto itself, consuming all before it, erasing the ancient stone building and the madness to which, in its final days, it had played host. The house belched smoke in ever greater and denser blasts towards the glacial mountain peaks, towards the heavens and the pitiless judgement of the wind.

Nick heard sirens, and his mind drifted for a second to the flames of a fire in another forest, and to the moment so long ago when he had realized that his life with Tab was at an end. Colours and light flickered across the years, merging into one strange dance of fire that had perhaps ended, here, at last, with the head of his truest friend in his lap. One grief – fresh and powerful – stood ready to replace another.

Topper stirred. "Jesus," he said, in a voice that was horribly low and distant. "I'm in fucking bits, here, Nicko. He plugged one right in me. Scottish bastard."

"Listen, mate, there's an ambulance on its way," said Nick. "Don't do anything stupid now, okay?"

"Typical, isn't it? Twenty years as a drug dealer, and only the occasional scratch. Try to do a good turn for a friend, and you get one in the bloody chest." He laughed, and then began to cough deeply, flecks of blood bubbling at the edges of his mouth. "Listen," Topper said, when the spasm had passed. "You know what you asked me to do for you? What you said at Heathrow?"

Nick nodded, hoping his friend would not see the tears that filled his eyes.

"Well, do the same for me. Gwen…" His words became indistinct. Nick held on to him. One of the policemen approached him, as the smoke from the fire threatened to overwhelm them all, to sweep them into another time and place from which there would be no escape or salvation, where silence would reign.

* * *

Gwen heard the phone before Alannah. She put down the flowers she was cutting in preparation for her husband's return from his business trip abroad. He would be tired and need cheering up. Sunflowers: yes, sunflowers would do the trick. She took the call by the fridge and answered breezily. Alannah came in with a bag of shopping. She saw how quickly Gwen's smile faded, and wondered why.

* * *

In Whitehall, Veronica Brewer's division put out an all-stations alert. This was a formality when an officer failed to make contact or respond to calls. But there was gossip in the canteen of something far from routine having happened, something career-ending. There was even speculation that ministers were asking difficult questions, and that an emergency meeting had been convened on the ninth floor. At least one journalist telephoned a contact to ask whether the rumours of a rogue operation in southern Europe were true. His contact was happy to tell him that there was no such operation and that, if it proved absolutely necessary, he could quote "diplomatic sources" to that effect.

* * *

Emily picked up the phone, steering Polly into the sitting room to watch television. The girl could hear everything her mother said. "This is Emily Michaels. No, Emily Atkins was my married name... I'm sorry, you... What?" There was a brief silence in the hall, and then Emily spoke much more quietly, as if to herself: "Oh my God..."

EPILOGUE

A YEAR LATER

The run was one of his favourites, a stealthy short cut through the park, up the hill to the borders of the council estate, and then back: a one-hour round trip. He liked the texture of the route, past the chic shops, through the families at play by the pond and across the football pitches, until, after another quarter of an hour, he was at the marchlands of a very different place, where there were no delicatessens, no children in Boden, no arguments about the wickedness of America – a grey zone where shoulders were hunched against windswept subterranean avenues, and his hooded top helped him to blend in. He never had any trouble by the estate. It was a good place to lose oneself, amid the satellite dishes and cider cans and the England flags, hung as a reminder that there were human beings in the hutches twenty storeys up.

His new job suited him well, too. The school was more academic but less traditional than St Benedict's, and the reference which Mr Frobisher had provided was sufficiently glowing to secure him the post. Before starting at the new school, Nick had returned to St Benedict's for a few weeks, but he did not say much to the headmaster or his colleagues about his brief "fact-finding mission" abroad. The government compensation St Benedict's received for his absence – greater even than originally arranged, and now linked to an unusual confidentiality clause – was more than enough to satisfy Mr Frobisher.

Just before Nick left St Benedict's for good, a girl in the fifth year had asked him nervously whether Miss Lewis – Aisha – was coming back to the school. Nick told her that it was very unlikely.

It was a year, almost to the day, since the funeral. That anniversary made him dwell more than usual upon what had happened, and the questions that remained. Aisha's fate was no mystery. But the fate of the Second Troy members who were rounded up was never revealed to him. He expected to read about the police raid in the newspapers, but – apart from a few ill-sourced and mostly inaccurate Internet rumours about a confrontation between the movement and the authorities in northern Italy – none of it was reported.

His own debriefing at the British Consulate in Milan had been a sullen and ill-tempered affair. The official given the task – not the flustered Consul himself, but a diplomat hastily flown out from the Foreign Office in London – did not respond well to his angry questions about Veronica Brewer and the threats she had made to him and his family. Nick had lost his temper and thrown a file off the table. The official, lean and unctuous, had simply raised an eyebrow and asked Nick, with infuriating politeness, not to do anything like that again. He said that he hoped there would be answers to his questions in due course, that the whole "mishap" was already the subject of an internal inquiry, and that his own masters were as anxious as Nick to discover how this had happened and, indeed, what "this" – the diplomat chuckled gently at this point – *was*, exactly. Nick asked what there was to stop him going to the press to tell the whole story of Veronica, the Schmidt kidnap, Diether, Freddy Hengel, Munroe Stacy, Tab Bradley and the phantom beast – the grotesque centaur of terrorism and government folly – that was Second Troy. The official listened to this tirade, and replied that HMG would strenuously deny any such story and would do everything in their considerable power to undermine his credibility. Did he wish to see himself described in every national newspaper as a "Walter Mitty fantasist"? Did he really wish to see his mental health called into question by unnamed Whitehall sources? Nick's were not the only feelings which were raw after the Brewer affair, the official warned. Tempers throughout Whitehall had frayed. Given that Nick was involved, it would be advisable to help, rather than to provoke, the government. There was surely room for cooperation and partnership? Nick remembered what Diether had said about "partnership" and its vagaries. But he believed the official's threats. In a Milanese office, with a borrowed fountain pen and a still-trembling hand, Nick signed the Official Secrets Act, took delivery of his plane ticket and passport, and stepped out into the Via San Paolo, where a car with diplomatic plates was waiting to escort him to the airport.

The official couldn't answer Nick's question about who shot Munroe Stacy. The ballistics report, he said with a shrug, had shown that the bullet was not fired from any weapon carried that day by the policemen or by Chris, or by Clio X. It was assumed that Munroe had been shot by one of his own cadres – a disgruntled member of the group, perhaps? This seemed likely, given the crisis into which this criminal conspiracy had been plunged in the hours before the police arrived.

The anniversary of the funeral made Nick think about the daughter he had met only once, in a hotel suite in New York. She was, now he thought about it, a beautiful girl, her beauty concealed for the time being in the costume of the adolescent, the fancy dress of sexual awakening. But, if his recollection of that waking dream was right, she had the fine bones and hair of her mother. She would have some of his features, too, though he could not guess what they would be. And, he knew with absolute certainty, he would not find out. For this girl – this American girl – was not meant to be a half-sister to Polly. She had found in Alan an unlikely surrogate father, who, against all probability, and in atonement for all that he had done wrong and would do wrong in the future, had treasured her and given to her all that he had denied his own daughter. Nick would not be there to see her become a woman. That was the only true gift – the first and last – he had for this child, whom he had discovered and lost in the same hour.

He ran past the playground and saw a young mother pushing two swings at once, her little son and daughter screaming with delight. The scene unsettled him, scratched at his nerve endings. What is it necessary to see of our children and of their fortunes? How much is enough? This thought, too, occupied Nick as he remembered the funeral.

It had been a magnificent occasion, a worthy one. Gwen – poor Gwen – though naturally distracted, had arranged the flowers beautifully. Emily had helped with the order of service and its production, and Polly sang a song, with the incongruous, indomitable relish of a child that made even the most stoical of the mourners weep for the end of things, and the beginnings which, sometimes accidentally, are revealed at the same time.

At the back, still in a wheelchair, in some pain but more anxious for his friend than for himself, sat Topper. He didn't enjoy being so dependent upon Chris, who pushed him around and helped him into the car. He was not looking forward to months of physiotherapy, and at least one more bout of surgery. He found himself brooding often about the email, giving him the precise coordinates of the Tyrolean hideaway. Nick had not sent it. Who then? Somebody who wanted help to reach Nick, and knew that Topper had the means and the will to make sure it did. Someone who had been watching them both. The two men found it easier not to pursue such questions.

At the very least, Topper was pleasantly surprised to be back home so quickly, having expected many awkward questions to be asked by the Italian authorities about the arsenal which he and Chris had acquired in Milan and put to such vigorous use on the mountainside. The Italians, it became clear, no less than the British Consulate, could not wait to be rid of the two of them, and had put Topper and Chris on a flight as soon as he was able to travel. And on this day, of all days, his suffering seemed trivial in comparison to the grief of his dearest friend – the true brother who had lost a parent.

Maggie Atkins had died of a heart attack as sudden and massive as that which had swept away her husband on a train so many years before. She died in the company of her friend Nora, to whom she had complained of minor chest pains and a twinge in her arm. Neither Maggie or Nora had thought much of it. They enjoyed a long and bibulous lunch at their favourite Mayfair restaurant, discussed Nora's latest liaison with a well-preserved dentist called Philip, neglected, as usual, to go to the Royal Academy, and then returned to Maggie's house. They had plotted their evening, which involved a light supper, a glass of champagne and a DVD of *Roman Holiday*. Nora had made a call to A.J., her husband, in the kitchen, while Maggie did some half-hearted washing up. She was reaching the end of her conversation, signing off with as much affection as she could muster while thinking of Philip's shoulders, when she saw her friend slump to the floor, as if flesh and blood, sinew and marrow, had been replaced by the stuffing of a rag doll. Nora rushed to her side, called an ambulance on the phone that was still in her pale hand, but knew at once, with the respectful recognition that love has for death, that it was too late. She cradled Maggie and, weeping, whispered gentle thanks to her: the valedictory rites which Maggie herself had been denied when her husband died, alone, with only his briefcase and folded newspaper for company.

Nick's grief was almost swamped by guilt that he had not been there, as he had always assumed that he would when his mother's time came. Guilt that he had been engaged in the playing out of a small and vicious tragedy that might have become inconceivably great and terrible, but would now be erased from official records, except from those tablets kept in the deepest, darkest vaults by those who govern us. He felt that he had put his obsession with a ghost – a woman who had at last revealed herself, but only in virtual form, through the portal of a computer screen – before his responsibility to his mother, who had shown him true and unquestioning support for a lifetime. But had he not been trying to protect those he loved most – including Maggie? Yes. But that was not the whole truth, was it? He had marched towards the abyss willingly, horribly fascinated to see what had become of his lost love, to discover whether the hole in his heart meant anything, or was simply a festering wound that others, better than Tab, were doing their best to heal.

His guilt was consuming. But, at the funeral, he realized it was misplaced and disrespectful to Maggie's memory. It did not bear any relation to the world as she had seen it when she died. He had grasped this when he listened to the music his mother had chosen, in the instructions left in her will for her funeral. There was the haunting second movement of Schubert's String Quintet in C, played by musicians who were friends of her late husband and who had stayed close to Maggie in her long widowhood. There was 'Ave Maria', sung by another friend. And then – on a portable CD player – there was the Madness instrumental, 'The Return of the Los Palmas 7'. The last selection, he realized, was his mother's farewell to him. It was chirpy and optimistic, the saxophone and piano laced with a little nostalgia, but not sadness: the mourners laughed and tapped their feet. Above all, it was his music: a track he had played to her as a teenager on an old cassette-player in the kitchen, which she had enjoyed and danced to. She had not chosen Bob Dylan or Pete Seeger, or any of the music which she and her husband had grown up to and loved. And this meant something. The dawn that she and William Atkins had hoped for in the Sixties had not come. But things had turned out all right, hadn't they? A son, and a granddaughter, and their time together, and then Maggie's time alone – alone, but not, by the end, lonely. To each generation a dawn, to each a dusk. And Maggie had relished every moment of her dusk. That was why she chose Nick's music, a record from the beginning of the hated Eighties: she had wanted her son to know that he had enriched her life, that parenthood is a gift as well as a responsibility, that she had listened to the soundtrack of his life, as well as her own.

Nick wondered, as he ran: did my mother see enough of me to die content? Yes, I think so. Shall I say the same of Polly, when my moment comes? He remembered, once more, how he had thought of Emily and Polly on the mountainside, and how thoughts of them had eclipsed the murderous game in which he had become embroiled. And yet, a year on, the three of them had not resolved their future. Having sold Maggie's house and banked the proceeds, he had rented a flat nearer to Emily and Polly, and his daughter had her own room there, with its posters, hair bands and dolls. Emily had reverted to her maiden name on credit cards, in correspondence; she had even visited their solicitor and mortgage broker so that all the documentation associated with the house should bear witness to her decision and its proud symbolism. But, twelve months after his disappearance and return, she had not instructed her divorce lawyers. He did not know if she had changed the locks, as she had promised just before he left for America, and he always rang the doorbell respectfully when he went to see them, or to pick up Polly. The three of them were still suspended in the limbo of separation.

Emily had learnt not to ask Nick about what had happened. But she knew about Tab, it transpired, and had always known. Six months after his return she told him so, over kitchen supper. He was not surprised that she should have uncovered his petty duplicity, but he was horribly intrigued that she had never confronted him about it. She replied with a slight shrug, a gesture of disdain he remembered from their courtship, that – however hurtful it ought to have been – it somehow didn't seem to matter. That it wasn't worth turning into what Emily called, with mildly scornful emphasis, "an issue". His scribblings beside the classified ads, the frenetic efforts to decode the latest message, were sad, she thought. She felt not threatened, but sorry for him, sorry for his incapacity to settle and to enjoy what he had. She said she imagined that his absence had had something to do with the woman, or perhaps with another, and a settling of accounts. She knew that he was an easily distracted man, if not an instinctive adulterer. She also said that, whatever had happened while he was away, she was glad for his sake, and for Polly's, that it appeared to have brought an end to whatever pain the past had caused him. She was gruffly gentle with him, as only she could be. His pale-faced silence – his biting of his lower lip as she spoke – was the closest he

could come to confirming what she had said, and to
thanking her.

He picked up the pace as he ran into the park, trainers
pounding the ground, sweat forming on his back.
And still, his mind was a gyroscope of fears and truant
notions… How do we honour our children? How do
we repair the damage we have done?

There, by the pond, was Jonathan. He recognized
him from afar, his controller's awkward manner and
poorly designed coat conspicuous even at a distance.

Jonathan had yet to acquire Veronica Brewer's talent
for merging with her surroundings. He was a junior
officer, assigned to Nick as a matter of routine rather
than urgency. He had not perfected the act, though
doubtless he would in time. He still lacked the confident
menace of his predecessor.

Nick had seen Jonathan only a few times: the first on
his arrival from Milan, when he was spirited through
immigration and taken briefly into a gabardine-grey
private suite. Jonathan, who was three or four years
younger than Nick, appeared with a file, shook his
hand and explained that he was the "liaison officer" who
would handle Nick's case from now on. He said that he
was pleased to hear that Nick had already had a "profit-
able discussion" with a representative of the Foreign
Office in Milan, had signed the Official Secrets Act and
was willing to assist HMG in any "matters arising". Nick
said he bloody well hoped that there would be no such
matters, and Jonathan, with a smile that was meant to be
winning, said that he hoped so, too. Thereafter, Jonathan's
calls upon Nick – though never prearranged – were
indeed of a routine character. He asked Nick if there

was anything that had happened to him or his family that gave him cause for concern. Nick was able to say, quite truthfully, that nothing of the kind had happened. He had resumed his existence as a modestly successful teacher, struggling to bring up a daughter in the context of a broken-backed marriage. He explained to Jonathan that the events on the mountainside now seemed a very long time ago. He did not ask his controller awkward questions. He did not ask, for example, about the bullet that shot Munroe Stacy.

On this occasion, unusually, Jonathan was standing, waiting edgily for Nick. Nick slowed down as he approached, and put his hands on his hips as he caught his breath.

"Hello, Jonathan," he said. "You're disrupting my run, you know?"

"I know. Sorry about that. This couldn't wait, I'm afraid."

Nick registered mild surprise, as he drank from his water bottle. He wiped his mouth. "Really? Well, I'm here."

"Let's sit down. It's not too cold, I think."

"Okay." They sat awkwardly together on the bench. "All right then," said Nick. "What's happened?"

"Nothing, probably," said Jonathan. "You know. Standard check-up.

"Has anything unusual happened to you recently?"

"Well, my car passed its MOT. That was unusual."

"I'm serious, Nick."

"No, of course not. Nothing since last year. Exactly the same life situation and prospects since when we last spoke. And you?"

Jonathan frowned. "It's probably nothing. Almost certainly. But… well… this appeared in today's *California Literary Review.* Have you been checking the personals?"

"No, funnily enough, I haven't. Sort of lost its appeal, after I started getting kidnapped outside pubs."

"Look," said Jonathan. He delved into his briefcase and took out a copy of the *Review,* open at the relevant page. He pointed to the ad:

> I have walked and prayed for this young child an hour
> May she be granted beauty and yet not
> In courtesy I'd have her chiefly learned

Nick felt his stomach fill with icy bile. He wanted to say: "No, no more. Whatever sin was mine, I have now paid the price in full."

"Do you recognize it?" asked Jonathan.

"Yes," said Nick. "Yes. It's him. Yeats. I think it's from 'A Prayer for My Daughter'." How wickedly appropriate, he thought. No book left unclosed, no healing wound unprobed. Was this fresh depravity or a hideous coincidence? The blast of a bullet, or just a car backfiring?

"It is," said Jonathan, agitated. "But it's all jumbled up. Lines from all over the place."

"Who placed it?"

"The credit card number is registered at a now va- cant address in the name of a 'Ms M. Gonne'."

The bile bit at his innards once more. "You're jok- ing."

"I'm afraid not," said Jonathan.

Nick could feel himself yield to the first phase of panic, his nerves sounding a prickly alarm. "Somebody is fucking with you… with me. Aren't they?" He inhaled deeply. The air filled his lungs and calmed him. His muscles were still warm, animated and tested by the run. He was in better shape than a year ago, the wounds of the trauma hardened into callouses. "Do you have a *Collected Poems*?" he asked.

"Yes, of course," he said, reaching into his briefcase. He handed Nick the book. The breeze from the pond made the pages flutter as he opened it.

Nick looked up the poem in the index, turned to the page and read aloud: "Once more the storm is howling…" He felt impatience bubbling away within him. He turned to Jonathan: "Look, I saw all those members of Second Troy arrested that day. Surely they're the people who would know? Shouldn't you, or someone, be asking them?"

"You know I can't discuss that with you. But look, Nick… ask yourself whether I'd be here unless I had to be. I assure you that my superiors are not anxious to involve you again, in anything. They have bad memories, too, you know. You are not their favourite person."

"I'll bet," said Nick. He paused, waiting for his irritation to subside. "All right. Let me look again." He pored over the first stanzas, and then turned the page. There was no obvious pattern, no verbal symmetry that he could detect. It conformed to no matrix or template he could recall: just three lines from the poem, arbitrarily chosen and reproduced for reasons of… of what? Vanity? Madness? Crippling loneliness? As he handed the book back, a final thought occurred to him, a knuckle of doubt poking into his ribs. "The only thing is… well, I suppose they are all first lines of different stanzas. For what it's worth."

"What would that suggest… I mean, in all the old messages, what would that have meant?" Jonathan gave him back the book, as if it carried a curse.

Nick opened and closed his fists, fidgeting in exasperation. "I guess… well, *perhaps* a number."

"How so?"

"Well, look. They're all first lines, okay?"

Jonathan nodded.

"So that's probably the key. So, for instance, the lines are the beginnings of the second, third and fifth stanzas. Not the fourth. The first line of the fourth verse has been omitted. Odd. Doesn't get us very far on its own, does it?" He put the book down. "I mean, I'm not sure about this. It could be… you know, but…"

"Second, third and fifth?"

"Yes… two, three, five. That's one possibility, I guess."

He saw Jonathan's face change from its habitual expression of fretful concentration to something quite different: the childlike countenance of sudden fear.

"What did you say? Two, three, five?"

"Yes," said Nick, shrugging. "Meaningless. Sorry, I'm just guessing here. You can find a pattern in anything, I suppose…"

"Two, three, five," said Jonathan, more slowly this time. He closed his eyes. "As in uranium-235."

"I hardly think…" began Nick.

Jonathan was talking to himself. "Do you know what that is, Nick? The only one of the three uranium isotopes that can be used in weapon construction — that's what. Christ. It's the fissile material you need… that, or plutonium."

"Look, it's a poetic game, Jonathan. I'm not even sure I'm right. I'm really not sure at all."

His controller turned to face him squarely. "I know, I know. You keep saying that. But you could be. You could be right. Couldn't you?"

Nick looked away, across the pond to the island where the ducks took sanctuary and built their intricate, baroque nests. He watched as the wings of a bird disrupted the surface of the water, thrashing in ugly confusion until the disorder gave way to the sudden perfection of flight. Like the poet's swans, like the wild swans at Coole. I have looked upon those brilliant creatures, and now my heart is sore… Finally, he said: "Yes, I could be."

"The jihadis have been trying to get it for years. So did Saddam… came close, too. There's enough of it about. Christ knows. All those Russian republics, stuff floating around. More than anyone knows." He shook his head. "Did you know, Nick, that exactly a month after September 11, a CIA agent called Dragonfire reported that a ten-kiloton nuclear bomb sold to Islamic terrorists on the Russian market was on US soil in New York City? Did you know that? Not a *day* goes by when this prospect doesn't exercise us, my people. And now this… *Who* could she be working with? If there's even a *chance*…" The breezy controller had become an incoherent novice, out of his depth, out of control.

Nick shook his head, did his best to smile. "But you know what happened, Jonathan. You know how it ended. The whole thing collapsed that day. The place was burned to the ground. Veronica is dead. Munroe is dead. Clio is dead. There was no mission. You know what she said on the recording: there *was* no Second Troy."

"Yes, Nick, I know all that. I read your debriefing notes, the file. But what if there *was* a mission after all? What then?"

What then? How could anyone possibly know? How can we know the dancer from the dance?

"Is it her?" asked Jonathan. "*Is it?*"

Nick stayed silent. To this, there was no answer. Neither Tab nor her body had ever been found. The location and timing of her video recording was unknown. No official statement about her fate or whereabouts had been made: her parents were visited separately by federal agents, who fed them a story devised in London and fine-tuned in Langley, Virginia, to the effect that their daughter, after many years in the radical underworld, had become involved with the European drug trade and was missing, presumed dead. Nick had heard from neither of them, and made no attempt to get in touch: he wondered if Susan, in her mountain hermitage, and Alan in his $1,000-a-night hotel room, believed a word of it, whether they slept more easily for the consoling lies they had been told by square-jawed men in charcoal suits.

Was it her? How could he tell? Who, lurking in the shadows, fired the bullet that stopped Munroe Stacy from killing him?

Jonathan muttered to himself, pulling out his mobile phone and fidgeting with it. "It's *possible*. I suppose…

I suppose. It's just possible. That she kept going. All that money she had. I mean, let's just say that there *was* a mission, after all, and Second Troy was just another diversion, just another bloody game. Why should she keep going? How many masks can one woman wear? I mean, when is this going to end?"

"It has ended," said Nick. "If we want it to end, it ends."

"Was she operating solo all along? Or for someone else we don't even know about?" Jonathan shook his head. "I mean, was she never really working for us at all? I... I need to map this out. I need to build a model. But... if so... why tell you? Why tip you off? Why now?"

Nick edged towards him. "You're not listening to me, Jonathan. Do we chase Tabatha Bradley for ever? How many more years does she keep us running after her?"

Jonathan adopted a tone Nick had not heard him use before. "As long as it takes. As long as it takes. The stakes are too high. Two-three-five? My God... the slightest chance... The answer is: until we're sure. Until we're *absolutely* sure."

"I am sure. Sure that this is over for me."

Jonathan shook his head. "We still need you. More than ever. You're the only one who can do this."

"Wrong. Your computers will already have drawn the same conclusion, and probably a hundred others more ingenious than mine. Give your analysts the poetry and the old messages."

"We already have. We can do all that, of course. But you know her mind, Nick. That's the difference. Don't forget: that's why you got involved in all this in the first place. You know her."

Nick felt cramp in his leg and stretched himself. "Do I? I doubt it, you know. After all these years. I really do. I don't understand the mind that does this, if it is the same mind. I can't fathom it." He looked out across the pond. "I can't help you any more."

"You have no choice," said Jonathan. "If this is real, you have no choice. You can't let this go. Even if you don't care about your own well-being. You have a child. You can't just walk away from this, Nick."

Nick crouched and stretched once more. "No," he said. "But I can run. Take care, Jonathan. I hope you find what you're looking for. I really do."

"You know that's not a decision you or I can take," said Jonathan. "I will see you again. Soon."

"Don't take this personally," said Nick, "but I truly hope not."

You have a child. That's right, thought Nick, as he picked up the pace again. I have a daughter and I have a wife, and that is all I have, all I ever had of worth. Jonathan would have to take care of the rest, for there was no more now that he could do. That burden had been lifted from him on the mountain. From now on, it was for others to sift through the cryptograms and the riddles, to try to gain a purchase on the sand that fell through their fingers to the sound of a woman's laughter. If it was her, only one thing was certain: which was that she wanted him to react, to step off the crooked path of his own life once more, and to resume his search for her, for the old reflexes to do their work, for the falcon to hear the falconer. That – more than anything that might trouble Jonathan and his superiors – was what the message meant. It was an invitation to the dance.

He would not do it. She demanded complicity, and that he would not offer again. It was not for him to say whether her threats were real this time, or the ravings of a lost soul. But if he joined in the dance once more, he would breathe life into it. He would ensure the perpetuation of the torment, the virulence of the disease. It would continue its implacable contamination. Of one thing he was sure: if she were alive, if she had indeed revived her games, then she needed him to play his part in the revels. That was the hideous contract, signed in the sun so many years ago. Without him, they could not continue. She had spoken of his strength, and expected him to live up to her expectation. But, now, the true act of strength required of him was not – as it had been a year ago – to survive a week in her netherworld of abduction, secret societies and death, but to resist the summons to go back there. The gate yawned open once more. But this time he would not walk through.

He decided, on what seemed like a whim, to change the route of his run. Yes, if he took the left, instead of the right turning at the road, he would be within five minutes of his old home – the place where Emily and Polly lived – his home. A small diversion. Maybe they would be in. Maybe he could say he had been passing, and offer to take Polly out for a walk. Maybe they would laugh at the sight of him, and invite him in for a cup of tea. Maybe.

He crossed the road and headed past The Unicorn

and Swan, down a crescent of plush terraced houses and through the churchyard. An old woman sat on a bench by the tall stone cross, whispering lovingly to a terrier on her lap. She did not notice Nick as he pounded by, nor the drone of a plane overhead.

He waited for a bus to pass and then sprinted across towards Polly's school. Mumbling breathless apologies, he wove his way through a group of teenagers. On the other side of the street, an Asian boy in a wheelchair was being helped into a black cab by the driver. He followed the road up into a second crescent – a necklace of colourful signs declaring the houses "Sold" – and then took advantage of a gap in the traffic to cross the main road. Left, right, left and left again: he was in their street. The street he and Emily had chosen so many years ago.

"Be secret and exult" – those were the words of the poet Tab had repeated to him so many times, so many years ago. But that was no way to live a life. No way at all.

He slowed down to walking pace and recovered his breath, looked down at the broken patterns in the pavement and the chaos in the gutter. Somewhere behind him, there was music, soft and soulful. He could not hear the words of the song, but the lilting melody helped to clear his mind. He walked and, as he did, imagined for a moment the sight of a girl walking up a sun-beaten beach, her hair wild from the water, her smile impossible to decode, her stumbling so beguiling. It was an old dream now, a hazy, tattered image from another time. And just as he was struggling to tidy its creases, to fill in the gaps, to restore it to clarity, he noticed that the lights in the house were on, that there was a silhouette in the window, and – as he crossed the road – the sound of a child's laughter.

He opened the gate and walked towards the door. He realized that, for the first time in a while, he had instinctively pulled his keys out of his pocket. There was a fresh burst of laughter from within. He picked the right key, and took the last steps towards the porch to see if it would fit.

ACKNOWLEDGEMENTS

I would like to thank Alessandro Gallenzi and Elisabetta Minervini for their faith in this book, generous advice and unfailing support. Mike Stocks was a fantastic editor, to whom I am greatly indebted.

Thanks also to my brilliant agent, Peter Robinson, for his friendship and wisdom, and to the Warden and Fellows of All Souls College, Oxford, for their hospitality while I was completing the novel.

Many books, films and websites proved invaluable in researching the background to the novel. Particular mention should be made of Jeremy Varon's *Bringing the War Home: The Weather Underground, the Red Army Faction, and Revolutionary Violence in the Sixties and Seventies* (Berkeley, 2004), Ward Churchill's *Pacifism as Pathology: Reflections on the Role of Armed Struggle in North America* (Winnipeg, 2003) and Sam Green and Bill Siegel's documentary *The Weather Underground* (2002).

As ever, my debt to my family is inexpressible. My wife, Sarah, and younger son, Teddy, provided me with the love and good humour that make all else possible.

This book is for my elder son, Zac: the "writing book" for which he waited so long.